Ashes

CHRISTOPHER DE VINCK

INSP:RE

About the Author

Christopher de Vinck is the author of twelve books and numerous articles and essays. His writing has been featured in The New York Times, the *Wall Street Journal* and *USA Today*. He delivers speeches on faith, disability, fatherhood, and writing, and he has been invited to speak at the Vatican. He is the father of three and lives in New Jersey with his wife.

Dedication

To *Catherine de Vinck*

Author's Note

All unattributed epigraphs are either excerpts or memories as recorded and shared in the war journal of Major General Joseph Henri Kestens, the author's grandfather. Major General Kestens was awarded the Croix de Guerre for bravery, and served in the Belgian Army during the Second World War as part of the Belgian Resistance, before being captured and imprisoned in Spain. Following his liberation, he spent the rest of the war in London. After the War, he returned to Brussels. His family, including the author's mother, emigrated to New Jersey, USA, via London, in 1948.

"Who would ever think that so much went on in the soul of a young girl?"
—Anne Frank

PROLOGUE

Terror. Pandemonium. Panic. Children wailed. People shouted, 'Get down! Get down!'

Brussels: a city consumed by fear. People rushed out of their homes, spilling onto the narrow streets, crashing into each other with suitcases and rumours about tanks crushing women, Nazis with bayonets, Antwerp to the north in flames. My father had said the invasion would happen. Where was my father now?

Like so many frightened people, I ran too. A man carrying a typewriter pushed me aside. I fell against a woman who asked if I had seen her daughter.

'Julie, she was just here, holding my hand. She was sucked up into the crowd. Do you know where my daughter is?'

I was swallowed into the mosaic of red shirts, blue trousers, cotton skirts. Clothes seeming to move in terror, not filled with people, but with ghosts floating inside the sleeves and coats. Ghosts with grey features, slackened jaws and hollow eyes.

I looked up and did not see clouds and spring leaves, but something much darker that seemed to shroud the entire city. Outstretched wings soared high above my head, and what looked like the belly of a dragon.

I broke away from the mob, pushing my way between men in

clogs and woman carrying crying children and baskets of bread, forcing my way towards Hava's house. I needed to get to Hava. Then I heard a low sound, a growl. The belly of the dragon dropped closer until it finally became a plane swooping down towards the street. Closer. Closer. Then, a burst of blinding light flashed from under the wings, spraying bullets all around me.

People called out and cried again and again, 'Get down! Get down!'

Bullets shredded the back of a man who managed to throw himself over a small boy who shrieked, 'Daddy!' A woman's jaw was severed from her mouth. Blood splashed onto my blouse. I fell to the ground, holding my arms. I wanted my father. I wanted Hava. I didn't know what to do.

Seconds later, the bullets stopped. The plane disappeared. All was silent for a moment, a brief moment, as if the world took a deep breath. And then there was a scream. It was almost as if the wheels of a train had locked and strained against the railway tracks, a high-pitched sound like the wail of metal against metal. Tragedy embodied that scream: horror, conveyed in a single, anguished cry.

A woman held a small girl in her arms. She wailed, 'Julie! Julie!' The little girl's arms dangled at her sides like winter vines. Her head lolled back, her legs were limp. The side of the girl's face and the cobblestones beneath my feet were streaked with blood. She was dead.

'Julie! Julie!' The woman moaned and rocked the child in her arms. She looked at me, as if to ask if I might save her daughter. 'Julie?' she pleaded. I looked at the small curls on the girl's shattered skull, turned, stumbled and skinned my knees. Blood dripped down my legs.

'Julie! Julie!'

I stood up. I ran. More people shouted. I ran on. The silence had been replaced with howls of grief and pain. Trams ground their way through the thick crowd. More planes flew overhead.

'Julie! Julie!'

The sound of the girl's name rose above the calls and cries of other people. I felt that the little girl was chasing me, blood rushing down her face.

I pushed my way forward, squeezing between shoulders, arms, legs, and bundles of clothing.

When I reached the other side of the square, I stopped and leaned against a building and looked back. Like ants whose nest had been disturbed, people stumbled over each other, desperate to save what they could. They carried photo albums, bags of sugar, money, anything to help them out of the city, out of the path of the monster; to help them carry out with them what they knew and who they were.

The Nazis were coming. Belgium was under siege.

Run! I thought. *Run! Run! They must not get me. They must not shoot off my arms!*

I knew Hava would be in her house. I knew that is where she would be.

I ran down a familiar side street. I could see the windows of Hava's home. They were dark.

CHAPTER 1

This is a war to end all wars.
Woodrow Wilson, President of the United States, 1917

My father was a general, a major general, in the Belgian army. He didn't start that way. He had been a private during the First World War, an ordinary engineering student, who volunteered to fight for his country.

Everyone in Belgium knew about my father after the war. An ordinary student who became a private and who, it seemed, fought off the German invasion into central Belgium single-handedly.

In 1915, during the Second Battle of Ypres, the German army advanced towards France, but was stopped by Belgian troops at the Yser River, helped by intentional flooding, which temporarily stopped the battle. When the brutal fighting began again, under heavy fire from across the river, my father ran to an army supply truck, grabbed a shovel and began digging a trench. His commanding officer yelled at him to get down, but my father refused. 'The flood waters will soon go down! We can build a trench and keep the Germans on the other side of the river! We can save Belgium! *Vive la Belgique!*' And he kept digging.

Inspired by my father's courage, his commander ordered hundreds of soldiers to start digging too. Moments later, my father was shot by a sniper across the river and fell face-down into the trench. A bullet ripped through his left arm above his elbow, shattered the bone, tore out the other side and disappeared into the darkness. My father fell unconscious into the mud as blood drained quickly from the three-inch hole in his broken arm.

Thirteen hours later he woke up surrounded by white sheets, the smell of blood and urine, and the voice of a doctor saying to his nurse, 'Do you think I should cut it off from the elbow or from the shoulder?'

Assessing the size of the wound and the damage in the bone, the nurse replied, 'Just cut it all off.'

In the midst of the pain, and before the morphine, my father rolled his head slowly back and forth on the operating table and pleaded, 'Please, don't cut off my arm. Please ...' And then he lost consciousness again.

In modern times, if my father had suffered a gunshot wound, doctors with their microscopes and microsurgical techniques could have repaired his arm. In 1915, the best they could do was respect his wishes, stitch him up, and save the arm, which became just a prop, a dangling appendage, for the rest of his life. I spent much of my life as a child terrified that one day I too would lose an arm and look like him.

Sixteen hours later, in a field hospital in Belgium, my father stirred, licked his lips, and asked for water. As he listened to the water gurgling from the jug to a glass, he reached across with his right hand and patted his left shoulder. Then he slowly began to run his hand downward, against the gauze and bandages, down to his elbow, down slowly inch by inch, until he touched the tips of his cold fingers on his left hand. His arm was still attached.

When my father asked the nurses about the battle, they told him that, because of him, a half-mile trench, in places only 45 metres from Germans bunkers, had been built. He later learned that this section of Belgium sustained some of the bloodiest fighting in the war: 76,000 German casualties; 20,000 Belgian deaths. But because of the 'Trench of Death', as it became known, that had begun with my father's shovel, that one small section of Belgium never fell to the Germans and inspired all of Belgium to hold on and resist the German invasion.

At the end of the First World War, my father was awarded the Croix de Guerre, the highest military medal for service to his country. The king himself pinned it onto his uniform, and the newspapers announced his heroics on their front pages: NATIONAL HERO: SAVED BELGIUM WITH A SHOVEL. His name was engraved on the reverse side of the medal: Joseph Lyon – my father.

PART I. NEUTRALITY 1939

CHAPTER 2

As Belgium struggled to recuperate after the devastation of the First World War, the country reminded all of Europe that Belgium was declared a neutral territory in 1831, and would continue to be a buffer between France and Germany.

I was 18 years old in 1939. My hair was brown. I had read *Gone with the Wind* in French, and my friend Hava Daniels found an advertisement for the film in an American magazine, and thought Clark Gable, the lead actor, looked like Otto the baker. I spent the autumn going to the opera with Hava.

We were Flemish, but of course everyone in Belgium had to speak both Flemish and French. At one time all the officers in the army spoke French, and all the soldiers spoke Flemish. Poor Belgium: half-Dutch, half-French.

I wasn't interested in politics. My father was afraid I spent too much time reading novels. He worried that my legs would be weak because I didn't walk enough. He thought I would go blind because I read so often beside the dim parlour light. He was also disturbed when I said 'Damn it!', imitating an American seamstress in a book I was reading.

My mother had died when I was born. I cooked, mended my father's uniforms, kept the washerwoman busy, and said the rosary three times every night, on my knees before a statue of Mary that I kept illuminated with penny candles.

My father was destined for a military career. He had wanted to be an artist, painting miniature scenes of Belgian farmland onto porcelain plates, but his father had felt that this was nonsense and had sent him to military school where he excelled in mathematics. After his fame in the First World War, he completed a Communication degree at the University of Ghent, was appointed the Military Commissioner of Communications for the entire Belgian army, and was given the rank of major general.

To me, he was just my father.

Our typical days began at the breakfast table where, each morning, he would ask me questions about life. 'What would you do in a panic?' he asked once as he buttered his toast. I could hear the scraping of the knife on the hard bread.

'Run?' I teased.

He did not laugh. A major general in the Belgian army did not run.

'Simone,' he said as he raised the butter knife in the air, 'you will need to know this someday. Think of life as a sailboat.' He lowered the knife and looked at me as I sat in my seat with a cup of tea in my hand, anxious to run off to school.

'Pretend you're on a small sailboat on a lake. You are guiding the ropes to control the shape and direction of the sails, when suddenly a strong wind blows down from the mountain and begins tipping the boat over sideways and rocking you violently. What do you do?'

I was tempted to say that I would jump in the water and swim away, but that was the same as running in fear. So I said, knowing he expected more of me, 'Push the sailboat into the wind?'

'Just let go of the ropes, Simone. Just let go and let the sails flap helplessly. The wind will no longer fill the sails, and the boat will quickly right itself so you can ride out the storm. Remember, in a panic, just let go of the ropes.'

We would spend our evenings together too. One night, after supper, my father sat beside the fireplace with his military documents on his lap. I liked seeing him with a blanket on his knees, writing notes on the pages as I read in my chair beside him. After an hour, he stopped, looked up from his work and asked, 'What have you discovered in your book tonight?'

If I said something vague like, 'Something sad,' he'd ask me to be more specific.

So, I replied, 'Sister Bernadette has assigned us an English novel – *A Tale of Two Cities* by Charles Dickens'. I'm at the part where Sydney Carton pretends he's Charles Darnay so that Charles is freed from prison, escapes the guillotine and is united with his love, Lucie.'

My father closed his papers. 'I remember a line from that book: *A wonderful fact to reflect upon, that every human creature is constituted to be that profound secret and mystery to every other.*'

That is how my father and I got along. He asked serious questions, or shared something that he read or remembered.

On another summer evening, while we were sitting before the flames in the fireplace, he handed me the newspaper and said, 'Simone, you need to know what is happening outside your books. Here, read this.'

My father flattened the newspaper on my lap and pointed to

an article about Albert Forster. I stared at him blankly. He sighed.

'Albert Forster is in charge in Poland. He's a Nazi and calls Jews dirty and slippery. He's a monster, Simone. Look here at what he says: *Poland will only be a dream.*'

I looked up from the newspaper. Being an officer in the army, my father knew much about political and military events.

'That man wants to invade Poland,' my father said, as he lifted the paper from my lap and tossed it into the fire. He and I watched the paper smoke, turn black, and then flare up into orange flames.

I did not know then that the first torch of the war was soon to be lit, but my father knew. I did not know then that the monster of war was on its way to get me.

Many years later I would learn that two to three million Polish Jews and two to three million non-Jewish ethnic Poles would be victims of the Nazi genocide.

CHAPTER 3

Adolf Hitler, Chancellor of Germany, convinced his nation that its Aryan heritage was a superior branch of humanity and that they needed to expand for 'Lebensraum' (living space). On 11 April 1939 he issued the directive 'Fall Weiss' – the strategic, planned invasion of Poland.

The war crept up behind me like poison ivy, a slow progress that I didn't fully recognize or understand at first. The world didn't fully recognize it either. After the First World War, my father had told me that German society had collapsed under the burden of its defeat. When the Nazi Party took control, he told me, Hitler had made promises about the future and reminded people that they were superior beings: white, unique in intelligence, best prepared to rule over the weak ... especially the Jews. And bit by bit, the Nazis began a slow, meticulous rearmament that was done at first in secret.

He told me that the Nazis promised a return of national pride and that Hitler orchestrated the largest industrial improvement the German nation had ever seen. I was mildly interested, but didn't really understand too much of what it meant at the time.

One summer afternoon I was bored. The sun was hot. I felt restless, so I went looking for something to read in my father's study. As I scanned the bookshelf, I found a six-year-old newspaper article tucked inside Thomas Mann's novel, *The Magic Mountain*. It was an article about Nazis burning books. An organization called the German Student Union had decided it was important to burn books in a public ceremony; books that didn't support the pro-Nazi movement.

The newspaper article quoted part of a speech given in May 1933 by Joseph Goebbels, the Reich Minister of Propaganda of Nazi Germany, to more than 40,000 people at a book-burning ceremony in Berlin:

> *The era of extreme Jewish intellectualism is now at an end. The breakthrough of the German revolution has again cleared the way on the German path ... You do well in this midnight hour to commit to the flames the evil spirit of the past.*

According to the article, Thomas Mann's novel was one of the 25,000 books committed to the flames to consume the 'evil spirit of the past'. I was horrified to learn that students my age had burned books, novels, plays, poetry. *How could it be?* I thought. I looked at my father's bookshelf, at all of those beautifully bound pages. I would have to ask my father about this. This could never happen here, in Belgium, could it?

As I refolded the article and placed it back inside the book, I heard a knock on the front door. When I opened the door there stood Nicole, our neighbour's eight-year-old daughter.

'Is Charlotte coming today, Mademoiselle Simone?'

'Yes, *ma petite*,' I said. 'Yes, in a few minutes. I'll get the carrot.'

Every Sunday afternoon, for as long as I could remember, Corporal Anthony De Waden, a soldier in the Belgian army, led a great white horse down the centre of our street, knocked on our front door, and asked, 'Is the general ready?' The army did not name its horses, but I called her Charlotte, and always brought her a treat.

I went back into the house for a carrot and when I returned, Nicole was spinning on the pavement in one of her made-up dances, twirling with excitement as her mother stepped out onto the street.

'*Bonjour*, Simone.'

'*Bonjour*, Madame Johnson.'

'I see you and Nicole are waiting for Charlotte again?'

'Yes, she's a bit late, but Nicole has been entertaining me with her dancing.' The little girl twirled once more and bowed. Madame Johnson picked up her daughter and said, 'When we lived in America, Nicole took dancing lessons.'

'I learned the waltz,' the girl said as Corporal De Waden arrived with Charlotte.

He waved and asked, 'Is the general ready?'

Madame Johnson placed Nicole gently back onto the pavement, waved hello to the corporal and retired to her home just as I heard my father call out, 'Simone!'

'I'll be right back,' I said to Corporal De Waden as I re-entered the house.

I stood in the hallway shadows as my father walked down the stairs in his uniform. His medals hung like cherries. Gold buttons held his jacket tightly against his wide chest. White gloves covered his two hands. In his right hand he held his hat.

When he reached the bottom of the stairs, he extended his right arm and said, 'Mademoiselle Simone may join me outside, if she'd like.'

Major General Joseph Lyon hooked his good right arm under my left arm and escorted me out onto Avenue St Margaret, where Corporal De Waden, Nicole and Charlotte stood waiting. Each Sunday I made sure that I wore a dress, stockings, and my church leather shoes to enhance the spectacle of the general and his daughter walking towards the large, white horse.

As my father placed his black boot into the stirrup and grabbed onto the saddle, Nicole and I fed the carrot to Charlotte. Corporal De Waden made sure the horse was stable, and that my father was comfortable as he adjusted his hat and slipped the reins into his gloved hands.

Every Sunday my father rode Charlotte through Parc de Bruxelles, the largest park in the city. People waved. In response, my father nodded his head, or gave a smart salute – Long live Belgium! – as my father sat erect in his saddle, a living monument in motion, galloping between the tulips, under the great elms, a visible reminder that the reins of victory, order, and law were held in competent hands.

As my father rode down the street, the corporal gave me a jaunty salute and a wink, and then stepped into a waiting car. Nicole thanked me for the carrot and disappeared into her house.

CHAPTER 4

*It must be made clear even to the German milkmaid that Polishness
equals sub-humanity. Poles, Jews and gypsies are on the same inferior
level ... This should be brought home as a leitmotif ... until everyone in
Germany sees every Pole, whether farm worker or intellectual, as vermin.*
Adolf Hitler, October 1939, Directive No.1306 of Nazi
Germany's Propaganda Ministry

A few days later, at the end of August, there was a radio
broadcast announcing that Russia and Germany had signed
a neutrality pact. Hearing people in my neighbourhood speak
about the war, I began to understand that more was happening in
Germany than I had realized.

'Not again,' Madame Johnson said to the postman. 'We've
already had one devastating war.' The priest in church quoted
from the Bible about putting on the armour of God so we could
protect ourselves from the devil.

'Do we have a neutrality pact with Russia and Germany?' I
asked my father that evening.

'Belgium is a peace-loving country,' my father said. 'We are
neutral, yes, in the eyes of the world.' So, I was confident that

Belgium was strong and safe. And I felt stronger and safer because I already knew Hava Daniels.

I had met her at the Red Cross in the middle of July. My local priest had announced at Mass that the Red Cross needed volunteers to pack clothes for people in Poland. My father had told me there was a possibility that Germany would invade Poland, so I had gone to the Red Cross in part because I wanted to make a difference, and in part because I was afraid. I thought that perhaps, in my small, illogical way, I could stop the German army and the threat of invasion if the Polish people were warm, secure, and brave – and had the right clothes. I was properly clothed and secure, but never brave.

When I arrived at the Red Cross, women in white sweaters ushered me into a large room. At one end of the room a pile of used clothes nearly reached the ceiling. At the other end of the room trousers, skirts, blouses, and sweaters had been heaped on rows of long tables. Standing on both sides of the tables women pulled the clothes along, as if on a conveyor belt. They removed trousers that were ripped, or vests that were heavily stained.

A large woman with a carnival smile greeted me. 'We are happy to have the general's daughter,' she said, as she led me to one of the tables. 'This is Simone,' my escort said to no one in particular. 'She has come to volunteer for the day.'

Some of the women smiled; some ignored me. Hava, a girl who seemed to be about my age, turned from her work at the table, and, with a torn sock in her hand, looked at me and said, *'Bonjour,'* and then made room for me beside her.

I squeezed in between Hava and a woman who sneezed often and said, 'Bonjour.' And that was that – Hava and I became immediate friends.

I quickly learned that Hava was also 18 and was in love with the opera singer John Charles Tillman. When Hava and I walked down Rue de Ville after our day at the Red Cross, she, walking in bare feet, slapped her shoes on the railings in cadence with her voice: 'John–Charles–Tillman! John–Charles–Tillman!' She thought he looked like a prince disguised as a famous opera singer. Before he sang at the Royal Opera for the first time, Hava bought two tickets. 'He has come to Belgium to whisk me away with him,' Hava smiled, as she handed me a ticket the second time we met.

She was a girl who possessed enough adrenaline to climb the Eiffel Tower every sixty seconds and who lived with an imagination that spilled into poetic facts – her facts.

'John–Charles–Tillman. John–Charles–Tillman.'

'How do you even know what he looks like?' I asked.

'There are posters all over town announcing his appearance in the opera. He's American, born in Pennsylvania. Can you imagine what a place looks like that has the name *Pennsylvania?*'

I had seen those posters, without paying them much attention. When I looked again properly, I found that John Charles Tillman did, indeed, resemble a handsome prince: black hair; round, boyish face. The opera posters advertised *Salomé*, a story about the Princess Salomé at a time when people believed in prophets, not many years after the death of Christ.

'He dreamt of owning a rowing boat when he was a boy,' Hava said, as she stopped chanting his name. 'I read in a magazine that he loves boats. I love boats.'

'Since when?' I asked.

'Since John Charles Tillman carried me onto his yacht moored at the base of the Statue of Liberty in New York harbour. So ... can you come? The opera house is across town. I'm not sure my father will let me go on my own, but with you there I might have a better chance. What do you think? Next Tuesday, eight o'clock?'

'I think yes.' I smiled. 'What's the opera about?'

'Love and death – the usual story. There's a captain of the guard who's in love with *Salomé*, but Salomé loves someone else. She performs the dance of the seven veils.'

Here is where Hava, right in the middle of Rue de Ville, imitated an exotic princess seducing a lamp-post. The lamp-post wasn't interested but, according to Hava, the captain of the guard would have been.

I was embarrassed that someone might be watching, as Hava unfurled an invisible mask from her face and began to dance seductively around the lamp-post, waving her imaginary veil over her head.

'Hava, stop dancing. The police will be called. My father is a general in the army. It won't look good for me.'

'Salomé slowly strips off one veil at a time,' Hava said with glee, 'and the king promises her that he will grant her any wish if she takes off the final veil.' Hava began a pretend striptease. 'She does so and then demands the head of the prophet.'

I giggled.

'The poor king is so frightened of the prophet's powers that he offers Salomé rings, gold, or wild animals instead, but Salomé is determined to seek revenge upon the man who turned her down. So, the king has no choice but to have the prophet beheaded.'

Hava stopped at the window of a chocolate shop. She turned to me and ran her finger dramatically across her throat. 'When the prophet's head is brought to Salomé on a tray, she feels such remorse that she kisses the prophet's lips. The king is so repulsed – and jealous – that he orders the death of Salomé, too. End of the opera.'

'What part does John Charles Tillman play?'

'I don't know. The prophet I hope. Let's buy some chocolate.'

CHAPTER 5

Europe cannot find peace until the Jewish question has been solved.
In the course of my life I have very often been a prophet and have
usually been ridiculed for it. Today I will once more be a prophet: if the
international Jewish financiers in and outside Europe should succeed in
plunging the nations once more into a world war, then the result will
not be the Bolshevization of the earth, and thus the victory of Jewry, but
the annihilation of the Jewish race in Europe.
Adolf Hitler, 22 August 1939, Obersalzberg, speech to chief
military commanders

Five days later I went to Hava's home for the first time.
When I reached her house on the Marché au Charbon, not
far from the Grand Place, I noticed the door made from heavy
black wood. I had never seen such a door, decorated with brass
hinges and filigree scrolled on each corner. In the middle of the
door was a knocker in the shape of a small brass fist, and below
that was the single word engraved on an iron plaque: DANIELS.

To the right of the door was a small, rectangular decorative
case marked with a single Hebrew letter: ש.

I was about to reach for the brass fist when the black door opened and there was Hava. Her long golden hair, usually neatly combed and braided, was dishevelled. She wore a plain white dress.

My hair was brown, short, and ruled by unmanageable curls that I pinned back.

'You've come after all,' Hava said as she reached out and grabbed my hand. 'I told Mama and Papa all about you.'

'Did you tell them that Clark Gable is my greatest admirer?' We had discussed the actor at our last meeting, after discovering that he had been cast as Rhett Butler in the forthcoming film version of *Gone with the Wind*.

'I decided that they would be much more impressed that you are the daughter of General Lyon. And Simone, I ought to warn you, my parents are from Poland and as serious about God as I am about the opera.'

'Why is it so dark?' I asked Hava as she closed the door behind me and we stepped into the front hall.

Hava whispered, 'Today is the Day of Mourning.' She explained to me that it was also a day of fasting, Tisha B'Av. 'On this day we remember the destruction of the First Temple in our country. King Solomon built it for his kingdom, but in 586 BC the Babylonians tore the temple down.'

I looked at Hava as the dim daylight from the front door seemed to enshroud her in a ghost-like mist.

'The Second Temple built by Ezra was destroyed by the Romans. That's when the people of Judea began the Jewish exile from the Holy Land. Our holy books tell us the Second Temple was destroyed on the Ninth of Av in the Hebrew calendar – or today, 25 July.'

I looked at Hava as the soft light outlined the bones in her cheek, and then I whispered, 'Who cares about old temples!' just as Hava's father stepped into the hall.

'Is this your Red Cross friend?'

Yaakov Yosef Daniels' face looked like a woodcarving: deep wrinkles above a beard of bark. He wore a tangled white and blue shawl draped over his shoulder, the shawl held tightly around his neck with one hand. In the other hand he held an old book.

Yaakov Yosef Daniels looked at me seriously, then said, 'The stones of the old temples are the punctuation marks of history. Have you come to mourn with us?'

Hava explained to her father that I had come to escort her to the opera, as I stood in the hall trying to reverse time and erase my dismissive words from the crumbling temples that began to surround me.

'Opera? For over twenty-five centuries we have celebrated Tisha B'Av, and now my daughter wants to go to the opera?'

Yaakov looked at my wild brown hair and my brightly embroidered dress.

'What is your name?' Yaakov asked.

'Papa, I told you, her name is Simone Lyon. Her father is General Joseph Lyon.'

I extended my hand, but Yaakov raised his book and shook his head. 'It is forbidden to greet each other on this day. Perhaps another day, daughter of the general. We do not eat or drink for a day, in remembrance of those who suffered before us. We do not wash or bathe, but surrender ourselves to the desecrated bodies of our ancestors. We do not use oil or cream on our skin, or wear leather shoes. We atone for the suffering. Follow me.' Yaakov waved his book.

'But, Papa,' Hava said. 'The opera?'

Yaakov stopped, turned, and looked at the two of us standing in the opal light.

'First, you will listen to the song of my world, and then you may go to the song of your world.' Then Yaakov added as he winked at me, 'Different temples; similar form of worship.'

Hava and I entered a room where I was introduced to Hava's mother, Avital, and her 10-year-old brother, Benjamin.

'Welcome, Simone,' Avital said.

As I sat between Madame Daniels and Benjamin, the boy looked at me and said, 'Hi! I can blow a bubble as big as my head.'

'Benjamin,' Yaakov said in a deep voice. The boy lowered his head. Hava giggled.

In the corner of the room was a Sabbath light; a brass, three-branched candelabra. On a side table against the wall a Passover dish waited with its eight indentations for chopped nuts, grated apples, cinnamon, and sweet red wine, parsley, roasted lamb, hard-boiled eggs, and bitter herbs. A wine cup stood next to it. 'This is for when we break our fast,' Hava explained.

Many pictures were displayed on the table: grandparents in their wedding gowns, uncles sitting in canoes, children standing in fountains, plump babies, women under beach umbrellas. And so many books filled the shelves: novels, poetry, history. I even saw a new copy of *Gone with the Wind*.

Hava sat stoically between her mother and father.

'We all suffer,' Yaakov said. 'We witness the sorrow of the flowers, Simone. Although they will blossom, exude aromas, and celebrate themselves with colours of yellow and red, they will perish just the same. But God does not allow the *idea* of the flowers to perish.

'Your father suffered greatly in the war with the Germans,' Yaakov continued. 'He lost the use of his arm, and yet today he is a great general because he remains a good man, and because he understands suffering.' He turned to his daughter.

'Hava, I say to you, go to your opera tonight with your friend, but remember, you are a girl of light. Simone, we live in darkness on this day of lamentation, to remember the light of our souls.'

Yaakov lifted the book he had been holding since he first stepped into the hallway. I noticed the blue veins in his hands, and then I listened as he read:

'Console, O Lord, the mourners of Zion and Jerusalem and the city laid waste, despised and desolate. In mourning for she is childless, her dwellings laid waste, despised in the downfall of her glory and desolate through the loss of her inhabitants. Legions have devoured her, worshippers of strange gods have possessed her. They have put the people of Israel to the sword. Therefore, let Zion weep bitterly and Jerusalem give forth her voice. For You, O Lord, did consume her with fire, and with fire You will in future restore her. Blessed are You, O Lord, Who consoles Zion and builds Jerusalem.'

'Hava,' Yaakov said to his daughter, 'remember what we say to God: *Blessed are You, O Lord, who consoles all men and women and builds every home, for we shall all be restored.*'

Hava looked at me from across the small table and winked.

'Now, go to your opera.'

CHAPTER 6

I have issued the command – and I'll have anybody who utters but one word of criticism executed by a firing squad – that our war aim does not consist in reaching certain lines, but in the physical destruction of the enemy. Accordingly, to send to death mercilessly and without compassion, men, women, and children of Polish derivation and language. Only thus shall we gain the living space (Lebensraum) which we need.
Adolf Hitler, 22 August, 1939, to Reichmarshal Hermann Goering and the commanding generals at Obersalzberg

As Hava and I stepped into the street on our way to La Monnaie, the opera house, she said, 'My father thinks that I'm a sinner.'

'Maybe I can turn you into a saint,' I said as we walked along the warm summer street.

'Maybe I can crawl into one of Benjamin's bubbles and be invisible and enjoy as many sins as I can.'

I laughed. 'You can't hide from God. He's like my father – he keeps an eye on us no matter where we are.'

Hava ran ahead of me, stopped before a lamp-post and saluted.

I laughed. 'Why did you salute the lamp-post?'

'My father always says that I am a girl of light,' Hava answered. 'Maybe God is light. When it gets dark, the lamp-post begins to glow, so I salute the god of the lamp-post. Do you ever notice, Simone, the darker the night, the brighter the stars?

'It's true,' she continued. 'Stars shine brighter on the darkest nights. You probably noticed, Simone, that my family is very Jewish. They say a *lot* of prayers. Van Gogh said something like, *When I have a terrible need of religion, then I go out and paint the stars.* I don't have a terrible need of religion, but I do love stars.'

On that starry night, Hava and I attended the opera, wept for Salomé, and fell in love with John Charles Tillman.

Five short weeks later, Hitler invaded Poland.

CHAPTER 7

On 1 September 1939, Hitler invaded Poland with planes, tanks and soldiers, instigating a quick, fast assault intended to shock the country and smooth the way for his continued invasion, known as 'Blitzkrieg' (lightning war). The Second World War had begun.

I didn't know it at the time, but during the first war with Germany my father had belonged to an underground Resistance group called *La Dame Blanche* – the White Lady. Everyone in Europe had heard of the White Lady, a shadowy ghost who appeared and disappeared just out of the grasp of the enemy. How easy it seemed for the men and women of La Dame Blanche to trick the Germans as they occupied Belgium. The Resistance fighters monitored the enemy's train movements, blew up bridges in the night, cut telegraph lines, and rescued many soldiers who would otherwise have been taken prisoner. La Dame Blanche was the most successful Resistance movement in Belgium

When the Second World War began, my father still had connections with his former Resistance colleagues from the first war: priests, nuns, former officers ... So, when Hitler invaded

Poland, my father knew even before the people at the newspapers or radio were informed.

'Blitzkrieg,' my father said as he sat at the breakfast table, having just ridden Charlotte in the palace gardens. 'I have just received a communication that Hitler has amassed his tanks and planes and invaded Poland.'

I remember my father sitting at the head of the table, his hair neatly trimmed, his tunic unbuttoned. My father never wore his uniform improperly except at breakfast, when his buttons were not clipped together and his brown braces hung loose.

'What does *Blitzkrieg* mean?' I asked.

'Lightning war,' my father explained. 'We have known for many years that Hitler has been building tanks and planes. Germany lost great portions of land during the First World War. Some say he wants it back. He's a madman. Blitzkrieg means attacking with speed, surprise, troops, and light tanks.'

I looked at my father across the table. He was suddenly silent as he stirred his coffee. My father spoke about Prussia, the Treaty of Versailles, and how Hitler hated Poland. Then he placed his fork down and said, 'Not again. We've already had one war. Not again.'

I asked my father where the German army was in Poland. He said that Hitler had invaded from the west, the north, and the south. 'They have planes and fast tanks. Major Roul has relatives in Wlodawa. He says that all communication has ceased from there.'

He stood up from the table, buttoned up his tunic, and said, 'But don't worry, my beautiful Simone. Hitler is far away. Now, I'm off to work.' I saluted, and he leaned over and kissed me on the head. Then I watched him walk down the hall, open the front door, turn, smile, and step out, closing the door gently behind him.

I did not see my father again for four years.

I cleared the table, walked up to my bedroom, and shut the door. We lived in a beautiful, three-storey townhouse. On the second floor we had four bedrooms. One was used as my father's office, another as a library. My father's bedroom faced the front of the house, and my room faced the small courtyard behind the house. Each morning I woke up and measured my day based on the sky and the branches of the apple tree.

If, when I first opened my eyes, the sky was blue and the apple leaves still, I knew that the day would be filled with quiet adventure – reading, or writing a letter to my aunt, a chemist who had never married. She collected my letters in a green trunk she kept in her parlour.

If, when I woke, the sky was blue and the leaves were being pushed back and forth by the invisible wind, I imagined that my day would be filled with agitation: my father expecting me to clean my room, Hava jealous that my father had the use of a horse, my own mood deciding I would be unhappy for the rest of my life because I would be a spinster just like my aunt, and would keep letters from a silly, plain 18-year-old niece.

Wlodawa. Wlodawa. I wanted to know, suddenly, how far from my room Wlodawa, in Poland, was. I was afraid of a war entering my life. My father had warned me about its monstrous effects.

I rummaged inside a cupboard where I kept my drawing supplies, my old dolls, books, and used diaries, and retrieved a coloured map of Europe.

I opened the map like a picnic blanket on the floor before my tall mirror. France was yellow. Belgium was green. Germany was brown. Poland was pink. I placed my index finger on Wlodawa,

Poland, and my thumb on Brussels. Then I compared the space between my fingers to the numbered scale at the top of the map: 1,100 kilometres.

I looked at the girl in the mirror and said aloud, '1,100 kilometres might just as well be as far away as the moon.' The girl in the mirror smiled back. 'No army can hurt you, Simone, if it's 1,100 kilometres away.'

Chapter 8

Our strength consists in our speed and in our brutality. Genghis Khan led millions of women and children to slaughter – with premeditation and a happy heart. History sees in him solely the founder of a state. It's a matter of indifference to me what a weak Western European civilization will say about me.

From Adolf Hitler's Obersalzberg Speech he gave to his commanders at his Obersalzberg home on 22 August 1939

I felt safe and strong. The new war was being fought thousands of miles away. I knew my father would protect me. He had spoken proudly about the Albert Canal fortifications, the modern bunkers and British Hurricane fighter planes that Belgium maintained. The famous fort at Eben-Emael alone had 1,200 troops to protect me, the country, and the Belgian army.

That autumn day in school, Sister Bernadette called me to her desk to tell me that my father had been called away by the Foreign Ministry. 'Your aunt will be staying with you while he's gone. She'll be waiting for you at home.'

At the time, I was not told where my father had gone, but I

learned many years later that he was meeting with other military officials from England, Holland, and France to discuss the war. Sister Bernadette assured me that Belgium had made a pact with Germany and that Belgium would remain neutral territory. Although I would miss my father, I wasn't worried, since I knew that the war was far away.

Sister Bernadette was my literature teacher. We had just finished a discussion in class on lines from William Shakespeare's *Julius Caesar*:

> *And since you know you cannot see yourself,*
> *so well as by reflection, I, your glass,*
> *will modestly discover to yourself,*
> *that of yourself which you yet know not of.*

I was convinced that he had written those lines for Hava and me. I never could see myself, without seeing Hava as my mirror. Whenever she stood before me and sang a song, or teased me, or told a joke, I saw glimpses of myself and I liked how I felt beside Hava: complete.

Aunt Margaret was indeed waiting for me when I returned home from school that afternoon, and that evening, when I could not bear the ticking of the great clock in the hall any longer, and I could not read any more from *Gone with the Wind*, I walked out of my room and found her downstairs in the kitchen making a cup of tea.

'Your father will be away for a while,' she said, as she looked at me. She ran her fingers through my messy hair and added, 'Perhaps it would have been better if you had read more fairy tales when you were a child. There are far more ogres and trolls in this world than you might believe.'

I tried to convince my aunt that, as an 18-year-old girl, I knew plenty about ogres and trolls, as well as more serious matters, but she just shook her head and said that there might be a war, that perhaps we would be in danger. I tried to explain to her that she was just frightened because of the war of 1916.

'No one is unlucky enough to have two wars in their country,' I said confidently.

My aunt looked pale as she reached out and handed me my father's Croix de Guerre. 'He asked me to give this to you.' My father's medal was like his second heart. 'He wants you to have it in case anything happens to him. He said it will protect you against monsters.'

I took the medal, caressed it gently, and kissed it. Then I carried it to my room, placed it under my pillow, and like Scarlet O'Hara, the unstoppable heroine of *Gone with the Wind*, I said aloud, 'I won't think of it now. I can't stand it now. I'll think of it later.'

Although it concerned me that my father was not at home, I held onto the false security that he was somewhere in the Foreign Ministry, tucked away in some important office. I did not know at the time that he was working for the Resistance, that months later he would be on the Nazis' execution list when he would escape across the Pyrenees and into Spain.

The next time Corporal De Waden came to my house he handed me a letter. 'It's from your father.' I opened the envelope and saw my father's neat handwriting.

Dear Simone,

Remember when I told you about Albert Forster and Poland? The monster is growing in strength. Hitler is doing the same. He said this in a recent speech: 'Essentially all depends on me, on my existence, because of my political talents. There will probably never again in the future be a man with more authority than I have. My existence is therefore a factor of great value.'

Simone, nothing depends on one person. This one man has no value. When we all live together as one, goodness survives. I'll be away from home for some time, and my letters might not always be able to reach you. But don't worry about me. I'll be fine.

As for you Simone, don't leave the house if Hitler and his army come. Do not go into the streets. Stay inside and lock the door. It's important for you to remember to stay inside if they come.

Hold onto my Croix de Guerre. You will pin it onto my lapel when we are together again. Listen to your aunt, and rest your eyes between readings. I love you. All will be well.

Papa

I'll think of this later, I thought to myself as I folded the letter and tucked it into my pocket.

CHAPTER 9

On 23 November 1939, a law was passed stating that all Jews over the age of 10 living in Nazi-occupied Poland must wear the Star of David stitched onto their clothes. In the same month, the Soviet Union invaded Finland. The war was slowly approaching Belgium.

As autumn began to fade into winter, I fell into an ordinary routine. My Aunt Margaret stayed with me, mending socks, offering advice on how to comb my hair, and insisting that I read *Etiquette and Manners* by Emily Post every night for an hour.

Corporal De Waden arrived faithfully every Sunday morning with Charlotte. Only now, I rode the horse instead of my father. After one of our rides in the Royal Park, as I was adjusting my scarf before walking back into the house, he tried to kiss me. I had never been kissed by a man before. I thought he was leaning in to help me with my scarf. I leaned away from the corporal, smiled, and went inside the house.

Hava arranged a birthday party for me at her home. She gave me a poster of Clark Gable, and a copy of *Rebecca*, the latest book by Daphne du Maurier. She said, as I looked at the cover, 'Last night I dreamt I went to Manderley again.' When I asked her what that meant, she said I had to read the book. 'It's like Tara, the house in *Gone with the Wind*.'

I had visited Hava's home several times before the war started. That day, Benjamin invited me to his room and said that he was going to paint me a picture for my birthday. I peered over his shoulder as he worked with a little brush and ink and I asked him what he was drawing. 'I'm making you a picture of God.'

'But no one knows what God looks like,' I laughed.

'They will in a minute,' the boy said as he dipped his brush in the inkwell.

When Benjamin had finished with his drawing, he walked up to me with a drawing and chortled, 'See? This is what God looks like.'

'How do you know God wore green shirts?' I asked.

'Well, it must be his favourite colour, don't you think?' he replied. 'Almost everything outside is green.'

'Are those two crosses above his head?' I pointed to the painting.

He rolled his eyes skyward. 'No, those are orange kites, Simone. God has to have fun sometimes.'

Hava and her parents were reading silently in the outer room, when Benjamin and I entered.

'Look what Benjamin drew for me,' I said. 'It's God.'

Yaakov looked at his son and said, 'Benjamin, your God is smiling. Good.'

Benjamin crawled onto his father's lap and said, 'Papa, tell us a story. Tell Simone one of your stories.'

I felt as if I was intruding on the peace of the house. 'Monsieur Daniels, perhaps I should be going home.'

'Sit there, daughter of the general.' He gestured towards a wooden chair next to Hava.

'Tell her the one about the ant. Simone will love the one about the ant.'

Yaakov rubbed his beard against his son's cheek and began, 'There was an ant that lived under the baker's house.'

'The baker lived with his son and wife,' Benjamin said as he sat up on his father's lap.

'Do you want to tell the story, Benjamin?' Yaakov asked as he winked at me.

'No. You tell it, Papa.'

'The baker lived with his son and his wife. Everyone believed the baker to be a man of honour and humour. His only fault was his harsh manner toward his son.'

Benjamin squirmed a bit.

'Whenever a customer entered the shop, the baker wiped his hands, stood behind the counter, and waited for an order.'

'The bigger the order, the better the service,' Benjamin called out.

'Let your father tell the story,' Avital scolded, smiling.

Yaakov continued, 'Yes, Benjamin, the bigger the order the better the service. When asked for ten loaves, the baker would grasp the customer's hand eagerly and shake it vigorously, while shouting at the same time to his son, "Check the oven, fool, and find the most freshly baked loaves for our kind customer!"

'Customers with small orders received older bread, and the son received harsher treatment.'

'Tell about the ant, Papa,' Benjamin said.

'One afternoon an ant entered the bakery. When the baker stepped up to the counter, he wiped his hands, looked around, and saw no one, although he was certain that he had heard the door swing open. "Imbecile!" the baker called out to his son. "Why have you left the door open?"

"I haven't been near the door, Father," the boy answered meekly.

'The father looked around, but did not notice the ant on the floor. "Get back to work!" the father ordered.

'The ant edged around the corner of the counter and whispered to the boy, "Pssst. Do you have some crumbs for sale?" asked the ant.

'The boy looked up at his father, who was busy combing his hair, then he turned to the ant and said, "I don't believe we have a crumb so big that we would have to charge you."

"'Oh, no," said the ant. "A labour made is traded for a payment collected. I will give you a bag of gold for your bread."'

'I like that part,' Benjamin said.

Yaakov smiled and continued. '"But," said the boy, "no crumb is worth that much. Here. Take what you need," and the boy pushed some crumbs from the counter onto his open palm and reached down to the ant.

'The ant said to the boy' – and here is where Benjamin recited the words along with his father – '"Because of your kindness, I will triple my pay for your bread: three bags of gold."

"But," said the boy, "that's a king's fortune for such a small favour. Please. Let me give you a whole loaf of our finest bread. That will last you all winter."

'The ant was about to offer the boy a hundred bags of gold when the father stepped on the ant, twisted his shoe against the floor, and struck the boy on the back of his head. "Fool! Wasting your time fiddling with useless ants. Return to your work!"

'Within a year the colony of hungry ants ate the foundation of the bakery. The building was condemned, the bakery was torn down, the baker died of gout, and the son became a carpenter and prospered.'

Benjamin jumped off his father's lap and ran to me. 'Simone, did you like the story?'

'Yes, I liked it very much.'

Benjamin hopped on my lap and whispered, 'Someday I am going to be a carpenter.'

That night, when I returned home, I taped Benjamin's picture of God above my bed.

PART II. PREMONITION 1940

CHAPTER 10

As Nazi Germany and Adolf Hitler continued their aggressive posturing against the lowland nations, Holland and Belgium began the process of moving their respective armies to a war footing.

One Sunday in January, Corporal De Waden arrived at his usual time with Charlotte. He was just a boy really, in a man's body. I think he was 26. On this day he asked if I would like to ride the horse by myself in the park as he watched from a distance. I had never ridden by myself. Usually, he led me by the reins. I was worried that people would be annoyed to see an ordinary person riding a grand horse in the Royal Park.

'They can't tell a princess from a pauper,' Corporal De Waden said as he adjusted the saddle. As we stood before the house, Charlotte stomped on the cobblestone and little Nicole appeared, waiting for Corporal De Waden to give her a carrot for the horse.

'There's no carrot,' he said sharply to the girl. 'Don't you know there's a war going on?'

Little Nicole stood still, then made her fingers in the shape of a gun and when she aimed and fired at him, Corporal De Waden grabbed her wrist and twisted her around. 'Never shoot a soldier!' Nicole yelped and bit the corporal's hand.

'You little urchin!' the corporal shouted as he pulled out a handkerchief from the pocket of his stiff uniform to wipe away the trickle of blood that dripped from his hand.

Then Nicole looked up as her eyes began to water. 'I just wanted a carrot for Charlotte.'

'Nicole, are you pestering Simone again?' Madame Johnson stepped out of her house, leaned over, lifted the girl roughly and carried her away, *Hopefully taking her to Tara, or to the house of Manderley*, I thought, where Nicole could feed as many carrots to as many horses as she wished.

'She just wanted a carrot,' I said as Corporal De Waden cupped his hands and leaned over. 'What could she know about war? She's only a child.'

'Put your foot in my hands. Use them as a foothold and I'll push you up into the saddle.'

I looked down at the corporal. He had a thick head of black hair combed the way Clark Gable combed his hair in his films. Little girls pointed their fingers at men and shot. Grown men brushed their thick hair against the legs of women as they mounted great horses.

'Now, Simone, you will ride inside the Royal Park with dignity and gladness for being given the privilege to ride such a grand horse.'

The corporal grabbed the reins and led the horse and me to the park, and as we walked among the people, no one waved. No one looked up. There was a gloomy, leaden sheen to the sky that mirrored the grim knowledge that rationing had recently begun in England, and that Finland was enduring a winter of untold hardships following the Russian invasion the previous November.

Irritated by the heaviness of the day, without thinking I gave Charlotte a good kick in the side. She reared. Corporal De Waden jumped back, released the reins, and the horse set off at a quick gallop, down the central promenade.

I felt like an American cowboy. The faster the horse ran, the more the world seemed to rush by in a blur of colour and wind, dissolving the greyness. Then for no reason, I began to shout, 'Vive la Belgique! Vive la Belgique!' A man looked up and waved. A collection of nuns walking under the bare trees turned their heads in unison and stared, as I continued to bellow, 'Vive la Belgique!'

When I reached the end of the park, both Charlotte and I were exhausted. A carousel with many painted horses twirled around with children on each one laughing. The music from the merry-go-round played the famous little song 'School Days'.

With reluctance, Charlotte and I turned around as I guided her back gently through the park the way we had come, the music from the carousel fading in the background.

People rushed to the side of the promenade as if witnessing a parade, but the parade comprised of only one girl riding one white horse. Yet, people continued to smile and wave, repeating my words: 'Vive la Belgique! Vive la Belgique!' So I reached down and shook the hands of the men and woman. Children ran alongside the horse. One man rushed up to me calling out, 'Your father would be proud of you, Mademoiselle Lyon!'

When I saw Corporal De Waden leaning against the gate at the park entrance, I knew that my wild ride was over.

'I could've been in so much trouble! What if you'd hurt someone? Do you know what it means to ride a horse illegally in the Royal Park? Your father gave you permission to ride with *me* in the park, not to rush off like some crazed Joan of Arc.'

That is what he called me – *a crazed Joan of Arc.* I liked that.

When we returned to my house, Corporal De Waden helped me dismount from the horse. He held my waist with his two hands as I slid off the saddle. When my feet touched the ground, the corporal tried to kiss me again, but I turned my head to one side and said cruelly, 'The girl just wanted a carrot for the horse.'

Before stepping into my house, I turned to look at the corporal one more time and said, '*Vive la Belgique!*'

If, like Rhett Butler, the corporal had looked up to me and retorted, 'Frankly, my dear, I don't give a damn', I would have married him on the spot. Instead, he grabbed the reins of the horse and walked away.

Corporal De Waden of the Belgian cavalry did not return the next Sunday, nor the next, nor the next.

Chapter 11

On 10 January 1940, a German pilot, carrying a secret plan of Hitler's attack on Belgium, crashed near Vucht, 108 kilometres from Brussels. This was the closest a German enemy had come to entering the capital. Soon after, those plans were altered to re-establish the secrecy of an impending German invasion.

I was eager to make sure that Belgium stayed neutral, that the war stayed far away from me, and that I was out of harm's way. I had read in the paper that Russia had invaded Finland in November of the previous year. I checked the atlas and thought to myself, *Finland is over 2,000 kilometres from my front door.*

The radio said that Hitler's submarines had sunk a merchant ship off the coast of Portugal. *Portugal is nearly 3,000 kilometres away,* I reassured myself. Up until then, the war had been happening *elsewhere*; but then a small incident happened that frightened me for the first time.

I read in the newspaper that a German pilot had lost his way, and crashed his plane in a wooded area only 100 kilometres from my home. The pilot had been carrying secret documents – Hitler's plan to invade Belgium and to ignore our neutrality. Invade Belgium? Why would anyone want to invade Belgium? I needed to feel safe, so that winter, I spent much of my time at the Daniels' house, my second home, a place where I felt secure.

'Gas masks? What, gas masks again?' Yaakov complained as we sat at the dinner table one night. 'We are not at war. Belgium is neutral. Let Mussolini shake Hitler's hand at the Brenner Pass. Let Italy join with the devil.'

I remember Hava's mother scolding her husband. 'Not tonight, Yaakov. Simone is here with us. Don't bring the war into our home. It's Purim. We have a surprise for you and Simone after we eat.' She looked at Benjamin, who giggled loudly. Hava raised her finger to her lips and shook her head.

I didn't know the meaning of Purim, and when I said so, Yaakov said, 'Simone, you would have been a good Jew for a Christian. And Avital is right. This is not the night to speak of war.'

'Tell the story, Papa,' Benjamin said. 'Tell Simone the story about Esther.'

Yaakov Yosef Daniels cleared his throat and gestured with a small hamantasch pastry in his hand. 'Simone, today is Purim, one of our most joyous holidays.' And so, Yaakov recounted the story of Esther.

'Over two thousand years ago in Persia there lived a beautiful girl, perhaps like yourself, Simone.'

'Stop embarrassing the girl, Yaakov, and tell the story,' Avital said, nudging her husband's arm.

'I'll tell the story. Let me tell the story.'

Hava glanced at me and smiled. *She* was the beautiful girl from Persia. I was the plain girl from Brussels.

Yaakov Josef popped the triangular pastry in his mouth, chewed, swallowed, and continued. 'Esther lived with her cousin Mordecai, a brave, confident woman, who was not afraid to stand up to people. Time passed and Esther was brought to the King of Persia.'

'She became part of the king's harem,' Benjamin interjected, giggling.

'Yes, Benjamin, Esther became a part of the king's harem. You know the story as well as I do. Because she was so beautiful and good, the king loved Esther more than all the other women, so he made her Queen.'

'But the king didn't know Esther was a Jew,' Benjamin called out once again. 'Her cousin said to keep that a secret. I like secrets,' Benjamin said. 'Hava and I have a secret.'

'Benjamin!' Hava said. 'We must wait until the prayers. Let Papa tell the story.'

Yaakov looked at his daughter, then to his son, then smiled and continued.

'The king had an evil adviser, Haman; a man who thought he was better than everyone else. Haman hated Mordecai, Esther's cousin, because she refused to show him respect, so Haman was determined to destroy Mordecai and all the Jewish people. Haman said to the king, "There is a certain people scattered abroad and dispersed among the people in all the provinces of thy kingdom. Their laws are diverse from all people; neither keep they the king's laws. Therefore, it is not for the king's profit to suffer them."

'The king, trusting his adviser, said simply, "We will handle it the way you think best."

'Mordecai learned of Haman's plot to exterminate all the Jews and implored Esther to speak to the king.'

'But she couldn't go and speak to him,' Benjamin said.

'And why, my son, was Esther forbidden to go to the king?' Yaakov asked.

'Because if you didn't have an appointment with the king, and you just showed up, you were killed. It was like going to the doctor and not being unwell. Dr Horowitz gives out lollipops, so one day I went to his office and pretended that I was ill because I wanted a lollipop. He didn't kill me, but he wasn't happy with me.'

I had to laugh. Everyone laughed, except Yaakov Josef. 'Unless there are no more interruptions, I will not be able to finish my story until Chanukah.'

'Go on, Yaakov,' Avital said. 'Go.'

'Even though Esther was afraid for her life, she went to the king just the same and told him about Haman's true intentions. The king was so moved by Esther's courage to protect her people, and so angry with Haman, that the king hanged Haman, as well as his ten sons.'

'So we celebrate the deliverance of the Jews at Purim, Simone,' Hava explained.

'We have a play!' Benjamin shouted as he jumped up from his seat and began to run towards the parlour.

'Benjamin!' Avital scolded. 'Get back to the table. We haven't said the final prayer yet.'

Benjamin quickly ran back to his chair. 'Hurry!'

'We do not hurry our thanks to God, Benjamin,' Yaakov Josef said to his son.

I remember the aromas of that cosy room, the wax candles in the kitchen, Hava's smile when she kicked her brother gently under the table, and I remember the voice of Yaakov Josef Daniels as he recited the prayer of Purim. And then, Benjamin once again leapt up from his seat and called out to his sister to join him in the parlour.

Hava rolled her eyes, and Yaakov announced, 'As Shakespeare wrote, "The play's the thing". Come, Simone. I do not know what it is that my son has created, but it is our custom at Purim that the children dress up as the characters from the story of Esther and act out their interpretation of those historical events.' Just before Yaakov, Avital and I stood up from the table, Benjamin rushed back into the room with three wooden rattles.

'These are called *graggers* – noisemakers,' Yaakov explained to me. 'Each time we hear the name "Haman" we are to make lots of noise with our rattles. It's like hissing at the villain.'

'Count to ten, and then come into the parlour,' Benjamin called out as he raced away. Yaakov, Avital, and I counted aloud.

'And now we come, Benjamin,' Yaakov called back, and as the three of us walked into the parlour, Yaakov leaned over and whispered again, 'Simone, you would have made a good Jew.'

It was clear that Benjamin and Hava were standing behind the curtains ready to begin their play. There was a lot of whispering going on.

As we sat on the worn sofa, Benjamin stepped out from behind the curtain and announced, 'Good evening, ladies and gentleman. To celebrate Purim, we will have a command performance starring Benjamin Daniels as the King of Persia, and Hava Daniels as Esther. Please hold your applause until the end of the performance.'

Yaakov looked at me and shrugged. Benjamin disappeared from view and knocked on the wall.

'Who's there?' A low voice emanated from behind the curtain.

'It is I, Esther. I have come to be the queen.'

Hava stepped out barefoot from behind the curtain, wearing the white dress she had been wearing the first time I had met her at the Red Cross. Across her face she wore a thin veil of cheese muslin.

The curtain was pushed aside in a quick motion and Benjamin walked out onto the stage wearing his mother's silk bathrobe and a crown he had cut from a discarded newspaper. The crown slipped down to Benjamin's nose, but with a quick adjustment, he was the King of Persia.

'I would like you to be my queen,' he proclaimed to his sister. Then he reached behind the curtain and presented Hava with a smaller crown, also cut from newspaper.

'I accept,' Hava said as she placed the paper crown on her head.

There was a sudden pause in the action. Benjamin looked at Hava. Hava looked at her brother.

'Hava … the moustache,' Benjamin whispered.

'Oh yes, of course.'

Hava bent down behind the curtain and returned without her crown, but instead, she wore a small black moustache.

'Welcome, Haman,' Benjamin said in his deep kingly voice.

Yaakov and Avital immediately began rattling their noisemakers. Benjamin looked at me and repeated, 'Welcome, *Haman*,' placing enough emphasis on the name Haman to remind me of my part. I rattled my wooden gragger the loudest.

'I have come,' Haman said, 'to tell you that there is a certain type of people throughout the kingdom who are against your laws. What shall I do with them?'

'Exterminate them,' said the king. 'Burn them all,' said the boy. Then he looked at his sister and said, 'Go back behind the curtain and be Esther again.'

Poor Hava. She stepped back behind the curtain and returned

as a bored sister without her moustache.

'Say your lines, Hava, like we practised,' Benjamin said.

'Your majesty, my husband, I must confess to you that I am a Jew, and Haman (*rattle, rattle*) wants to kill all of my people because my cousin does not bow down to Haman's evil.' (*Rattle, rattle, rattle.*)

'You are brave to come to me without an appointment. You have risked your life to save your family. Because of you, your people will be saved.'

The king disappeared behind the curtain and quickly returned.

'Look here! Haman (*rattle, rattle, rattle*) has been hanged along with his ten sons and here is all that is left of him, this little black moustache. Because of you, Esther, your people will live long and be successful.'

Benjamin turned to face his audience sitting on the fading sofa and whispered, 'Hava, take my hand.'

Hava held her little brother's hand as they both took a bow. That night, Benjamin and Hava Daniels received a standing ovation.

CHAPTER 12

*The German invasion was inevitable. Everyone in Europe knew it
was coming, but they did not know when. After Great Britain and France
had declared war against Nazi Germany on 3 September 1939, there had
been relative calm. As a result, it was called 'the Phoney War' until 10
May 1940, when Hitler attacked Holland, Belgium and France.*

Suddenly it was spring 1940, the first week in May. 'The Germans
are coming,' the baker said as I bought a loaf of bread. 'This is my
last day. I am closing the shop.'

'Simone, where's your father? The Germans are going to invade!'
a neighbour called out as she washed a bucket in the street.

'Invade, invade,' I muttered to myself. 'It's all just talk.' But my
confidence was ebbing with the knowledge that Hitler's army had
invaded Norway and Denmark in early April.

May in Brussels that year polished the boulevards and trees with brassy
sunlight. The street cars seemed to move a bit faster. War was breaking
out all around the borders of my little country, but I still felt secure and
hopeful in our declared neutrality and in my secret belief that my father
would protect me no matter where he was. I had his medal after all.

As it was an early spring, Hava decided that we had to introduce ourselves to nature. 'We have to seduce nature so that the weather stays warm,' she said as she stood at my doorway with two drawing pads, two boxes of coloured pencils, and a false black moustache on her lips. She wore a man's shirt, a pair of men's trousers, boots, a wide, long cape, and a black beret on her head.

'We must be on our way, Mademoiselle Simone. Spring has no patience,' Hava said, as she tipped her hat and bowed before me.

'Hava, who are you supposed to be?'

'Isn't it obvious? I am the ghost of Paul Gauguin, and I died on this day, 8 May, thirty-seven years ago.'

Hava wiggled her moustache and I laughed.

'You mustn't laugh at the great Gauguin,' Hava scolded teasingly. 'We must catch the spring before it escapes.' She handed me one of the drawing pads and a box of coloured pencils. 'We will hunt down spring with our equipment.' Hava held up her drawing pad.

'Hava, what are you talking about?'

'Art, Simone. We are going to create art. We are going to draw spring and, once we do, it will be spring forever. Gauguin left his family and sailed to Tahiti. He wrote in his journal, "All the joys of a free life are mine. I have escaped everything that is artificial, conventional, and customary. I am entering into the truth, into nature." I have a free life, Simone. I have escaped my conventional life and I, Gauguin, am going to escape to Tahiti with my friend Simone. Don't you want to go to Tahiti with me?' Once again, Hava twitched her fake moustache.

Hava didn't have to pretend to be Paul Gauguin, or pretend to be unconventional. She loved to dance because she was the dance. She loved opera because her voice was the opera. She loved to read sprawled out on her couch and become Madame Bovary or Daisy Buchanan. On 8 May 1940, Hava became Paul Gauguin the artist.

After I grabbed a sweater and shut the front door, and Hava placed her beret back on her head, she stepped forward quickly and announced eagerly, 'To Tahiti!'

'Where are we going, Hava?'

'Hava? Hava? Who is this Hava?'

I looked at Hava and giggled, 'Ah, Monsieur Gauguin, where are we going?'

'We are going to Leopold Park to capture the spring season forever,' Hava said, waving her drawing pad above her head.

Leopold Park was located in the European Quarters of Brussels, a beautiful 25-acre park, with a large pond, ducks, swans, and grey herons. When I asked Hava if she knew that the park had Egyptian geese, she turned, rubbed her moustache and said, 'My dear, I am Gauguin, and I know about all exotic things.' Then she took my hand and said, 'Do as I do.'

Hava took one long step and hit the pavement hard with her right foot, and then with the left, and again with the right. I did the same beside her, and with each of our forward footsteps, Hava announced the items on her list of exotic things.

Step. 'John Charles Tillman.' Step. 'Chocolate-covered cherries.' Step. 'Ice cream.' Step. 'Paris.' Step …

Paul Gauguin and I marched down the street sharing our lists of exotic things.

'White wine,' she said.

'Niagara Falls,' I said.

'Kissing,' she said.

'Oh la, la,' I said.

Hava looked at me, smiled, and said, 'Egyptian geese.'

We both giggled as we approached the entrance of Leopold Park that stretched out before us like Eden. Fresh spring leaves spilled from every tree branch. The manicured grass and gentle slopes undulated like emerald waves on the ocean of the gods: men in suits and fedoras; women in spring dresses with braided hair; boys on their knees shooting marbles; girls gathering flowers.

'Follow me,' Hava said, sweeping her drawing pad through the air, as if casting a spell over the entire park.

'Here,' she said as we approached a small stream. 'Here is where we will capture spring for eternity.' She approached a flat stone at the edge of the slow, flowing water. 'For you, mademoiselle.' Hava pointed to another large rock.

She placed her drawing pad and pencils on the grass, unlaced her brown shoes, rolled off her socks and sat on the rock, easing her pearl-white feet and legs into the cold water.

'Oh! This is not like the warm waters of Tahiti,' Paul Gauguin declared, as Hava gave a shiver. 'Brrrrr! Now you, Simone!' she called out.

I didn't think it was a good idea to take off my shoes and socks in public. After all, I was the daughter of General Joseph Lyon, not Cleopatra dipping my bare legs in the Nile, in the company of her slaves and Egyptian geese.

'Simone, you have to dip your legs into the water if you want to be a painter like Gauguin.'

Sighing, I placed my drawing pad and pencils on the grass, stood up straight, and looked around, expecting the eyes of Brussels to set upon my awkward body.

'Simone, it's not like you're taking your clothes off. It's just your shoes and socks!'

I stood like a stork on a single leg, untied my right shoe, pulled off my sock, and dropped it on the grass. I did the same with my left shoe and sock, and there I stood at the edge of the water, feeling skinny and awkward.

'Mademoiselle Simone,' Hava said, as she tipped her beret and pointed, 'your throne.'

I sat on my rock and slipped my feet and legs slowly into the water.

'Very good. Now, Simone,' Hava said as she handed me my pad and pencils, 'look around and stop spring for a second. Draw what you see and it will be captured forever on your paper. We have to remember: art, books, and music are the albums of our memories and feelings.'

I looked at my friend, at her face, the contours of her cheeks, the colour of her gold-polished hair. How did others see my friend? How did they view Hava? Pole? Jew? Esther? Eve ... in Leopold Park?

'The water is delicious,' Hava said, as I picked up a green pencil, placed the sharp tip gently onto my drawing pad, looked up at the trees, and began to take hold of the spring. Hava paddled her legs gently back and forth in the clear water and she too began to draw.

In the end my trees looked like drunken, green squiggles, and my daffodils looked like tired trumpets. But in Hava's drawing, I could see the veins in each leaf, and the grass looked like as it was saying, '*Take off your shoes. Feel the softness under your feet.*' Her daffodils looked exactly how Wordsworth had described the flowers in his most famous poem, '*tossing their heads in sprightly dance*'.

We laughed, Hava and I, as we compared our drawings. 'I don't think you will be an artist, Simone.'

'But that's not fair. You're the great Paul Gauguin. How can I compete?'

We did capture the essence of spring that day in our drawing pads, and Hava taught me that Eden can be found in a single flower.

CHAPTER 13

The Slavs are to work for us. Insofar as we do not need them, they may die ... The fertility of the Slavs is undesirable. They may use contraceptives or practise abortion, the more the better.
Dr. Markull, Ministry for Occupied Eastern Territories, to Reich Minister Rosenberg, 19 August 1940

'You spend too much time with that girl, Hava,' my Aunt Margaret said one evening over dinner. 'How did you meet her?'

'We met last year, at the Red Cross,' I replied, as my aunt cut meticulously into the steak on her plate. 'We have opera tickets for tonight. She likes the opera ... and dancing.'

My aunt's fork and knife clicked on the porcelain dish.

'Who likes dancing?' she asked.

'My friend, Hava. The one I met at the Red Cross.'

'I'm sorry, Simone. I'm a bit distracted.' My aunt looked down, attacking her steak once again.

'Hava's favourite opera singer is John Charles Tillman. He's an American baritone.'

'Stop!' My aunt exclaimed suddenly, as she slammed her fork and knife onto the table. 'Stop, Simone!' She looked at me with a glare I had never seen in her eyes before. It frightened me. 'Don't say another word. I've heard enough about your *friend*.'

My aunt took a deep breath and slowly stroked her left cheek. 'I'm sorry, Simone,' she said in a softer tone. 'I just want to protect you.'

'But, Aunt Margaret, what do you mean? We're home. We're safe. And my father will be back soon.'

My aunt looked into my eyes again, but this time with the eyes of a woman who could see the future. 'There are clouds forming over Europe, Simone. A storm is approaching, a violent storm. I don't want you to be afraid, but please, don't associate with this friend of yours. She's Polish. I won't have you associating with that Hava girl any longer. Have you seen what the paper says today?'

She stood up from the table, entered the parlour, and returned with a wrinkled newspaper in her hand. She opened it at a particular page, handed it to me, and said, 'Read what the Chancellor of Germany said to his chief military commanders in Obersalzberg back in August. It's only being reported now that the war is getting nearer. Read what Adolf Hitler actually said.'

I reached for the paper and, using my finger as a guide under each word, I read carefully:

> ... *send to death mercilessly and without compassion, men, women, and children of Polish derivation and language. Only thus shall we gain the living space which we need. Who, after all, speaks today of the annihilation of the Armenians?*

I placed the paper on the table and tried to wipe away the creases, tried to erase the words, and tried to understand what I had just read. *This cannot be true*, I thought. 'Did he really say these things, Aunt Margaret?'

My aunt nodded.

'Does Hitler actually believe the world has forgotten about the Armenian Genocide? And will he really do the same to anyone Polish?

'The world has forgotten, Simone.'

'But, Aunt Margaret, Hitler won't kill millions of people. Surely the world remembers!'

'Simone, only twenty-five years ago hundreds and thousands of Armenian people were tortured, shot, murdered, and sent into the desert to starve. It was just twenty-five years ago, yet no one remembers. No one cares. Hitler is right: who today speaks of the annihilation of the Armenians? Hitler actually said to his commanders, Let's kill all Polish people and the Jews, because in the long term, no one will remember and we need more space for our country.'

Hava is both Polish and Jewish, I thought, frightened for the first time. But Poland was still 1,100 kilometres away and Hava was here. But where was the German army now?

My aunt picked up the newspaper from the table, crushed it between her hands, and threw it into the fireplace. 'Light a match, Simone.'

I reached into the cabinet and curled my fingers around a small cardboard box of matches. After I lit one and tossed it into the fireplace, the dry paper ignited quickly. The orange glow of the flames illuminated my aunt's face as grey smoke rose up the brick chimney. We both watched as the words disappeared. The paper twisted then shrivelled between the grate and formed a small, insignificant pile of white ashes on the flat stone hearth.

'Your friend is Jewish, as well as Polish, isn't she?'

'Yes,' I almost whispered.

As my aunt was about to leave the room, she turned, looked at me, and said, 'Go to the opera with your friend Hava, but then you must leave her behind. Don't stay by her side. Enjoy the American baritone tonight, but have nothing more to do with that girl. You need to think of yourself and your own safety. I also wanted to tell you that I'm planning to return to Luxembourg soon. I don't like what I'm hearing in the street. You're eighteen now, so it's up to you if you want to stay here or come with me. I'll feel safer in my own home.'

CHAPTER 14

Luxembourg believed that its international pact of neutrality would protect
it from a German invasion, though it was suspicious. Radio Luxembourg,
an English-speaking station, stopped broadcasting and the country began
work installing concrete roadblocks along the eastern border with Germany.
Luxembourgers heard the news about the invasion of Poland and Finland and
worried about the rumours of an impending invasion.

I did attend the opera with Hava that night, and a few mornings later, suitcase in hand, my aunt said her goodbyes.

'There's enough money in the bank,' she said. 'Your father will return soon.'

Aunt Margaret offered again to take me with her to her home, but I refused. I had my school, Hava … 'And besides,' I said to my aunt, 'Papa said that I was to stay in the house, no matter what. I'm safe here. And when he returns from the Foreign Ministry, I want everything to be in order, just as he left it, so that he and I can continue living as we were.' There was no explaining my optimism; that of a young woman pretending that there was no danger lurking in the alley.

'Don't open the door to anyone, and remember to keep away from that Jewish girl and her family.' She handed me the house key. 'I must run. The train leaves in an hour.' She didn't smile.

I kissed Aunt Margaret goodbye, and as I watched her walk down the road with her suitcase, I wanted to call out, '*Vive la Belgique!*' But instead I just sat on the doorstep and cried. Goodbyes under any circumstance are never good.

'Mademoiselle Lyon?'

I wiped my eyes and looked up. There was little Nicole.

'Is the corporal coming back with his horse?'

'*Non, ma petite.*'

The girl sighed, then skipped down the street in the city of Brussels, in the country of Belgium – a place that would soon be changed forever.

CHAPTER 15

The German Panzer tanks were fuelled. Nazi soldiers cleaned their rifles. All of Europe knew that Adolf Hitler was poised to order an attack.

Before the war, life in Brussels was civilized, orderly, and ordinary. People visited the spas, the economy had improved following the Depression that had swept through the United States and Europe. Strawberries were plentiful in the summer. Brussels hosted a World Fair in 1935, celebrating colonization. The Belgian architect, Joseph Van Neck, designed the fair, and Belgian artists were lauded. Over twenty million people visited the exposition.

I liked that Brussels had no suburbs at that time. I could step out of my house in the city, walk for fifteen or twenty minutes, and soon find myself among farms and fields. Hava shared this delight with me.

After Aunt Margaret left, I decided to spend the rest of the day reading my book, *Lost Horizon*. I loved that book about Shangri-La, a magical place hidden somewhere beyond the Himalayas. I read until my heavy eyelids beckoned me to doze, then I slept until awoken by a loud, persistent knocking at the door. My aunt had told me not to open the door, but maybe she had come back.

I jumped up from the couch, looked through the window, and there, standing with a basket, was Hava in a bright yellow blouse, hiking shorts, and boots. I opened the door. 'Let's go for a picnic,' she said, and raised the basket over her head. 'I've got brie, bread, wine, and two apples.'

'But it's late. It'll be dark soon.'

'So?' Hava said. 'We'll be Egyptians and worship the setting sun Ra as he disappears on his ship and sinks over the horizon.'

I looked at Hava and smiled. 'Let's sail to Shangri-La.' I grabbed a light sweater and locked the front door.

As we walked further and further away from the city, the landscape curtsied under a gentle breeze. Farms spread out before us like quilts; fields of wheat, potato farms. Rich tomato plants stood up boldly and greeted us with each advancing step.

The flat landscape bowed before Hava and me as we walked through the Belgian countryside, a paradise of amazing fertility.

For centuries the land of Belgium had been cleared for farming. The fields rested on their backs, waiting for Hava and me to roam their bellies. Distant hills heard us laugh and sing as we looked for the perfect place for a picnic.

Hava pointed to the hidden lichen in the wild grass, small clumps of greyish-blue material like a sponge, with little red caps at the tip of each column. We called them 'wooden soldiers'.

We ate wild raspberries which grew along the edge of a path we followed. I plucked the berries one at a time until my cupped hand was full, and then pressed them into my mouth all at once. Hava ate her berries slowly, one by one. When I made a sour face, after having eaten a small beetle I hadn't seen that was hidden beneath the green leaves, Hava laughed and said, 'Good protein.'

We found the perfect spot for a picnic, on a tuft of wild grass tickling the edge of a shallow stream.

After we ate, Hava and I picked black-eyed Susans and wove them into crowns. We looked for quartz crystals on the path and found a pond. As we walked, we realized we were lost, but we didn't care. A person had to take risks if they sought paradise as their destination.

To the east, through the trees, we discovered what we called 'the secret place'. Branches scratched our faces as we walked through a thick grove of pine trees. The setting sunlight dimmed the deeper we entered into the woods, but then suddenly, we came to a light beyond the trees, a brightness that ought not to have been there.

In the centre of the pine forest was an open circular space, like an empty room. The pine trees formed tall green walls and completely surrounded this hidden place. Hava explained how this secret spot had been created.

'See? A large, flat boulder is embedded just below the surface of the ground so the pine trees' roots can't grow above the large rock, but there's still enough soil for a carpet of wild grass.'

The sunlight poured over the tips of the trees and splashed on the grass like melting butter.

A sudden whistling in the distance startled us, so we stepped quickly between the trees, and away from the path. A moment later, a man in a hunting jacket and red cap approached from the opposite direction, carrying a large gun with a long barrel that extended before him.

'You girls shouldn't be out here by yourselves. There's a lynx nearby. I saw fresh tracks on the side of the pond back there. They love fish and beautiful young women.' The hunter raised his rifle towards us.

I was glad that the man had included me in his reference to beautiful women. No one had ever said that I was beautiful, but I feared his gun, his voice … the fact that Hava and I were alone, and that we were lost.

Hava said, 'Beautiful girls have bigger claws and sharper teeth than any lynx.'

The man smiled and said, 'Follow me. I'll guide you back to the main path, just to make sure you're safe.'

At a small intersection of two dirt paths, the hunter pointed and said, 'The city is that way.'

'Thank you, monsieur,' Hava said.

'*Au revoir*, mesdemoiselles. Don't be afraid of the lynx. You'll be all right.' The hunter smiled again, slung his rifle onto his shoulder, turned, and walked away.

Of course I was afraid of the lynx as we headed back to Brussels. 'Maybe the lynx is sitting in the secret place, eating fish.'

Hava growled at me like a wild cat, and then grinned. 'Let's climb a silo,' she said.

CHAPTER 16

The Führer is deeply religious, though completely anti-Christian. He views Christianity as a symptom of decay. Rightly so. It is a branch of the Jewish race.

Joseph Goebbels' diary, 29 December, 1939

As we made our way back to the city, the sun set. Hava and I ran with the stars above us. 'Look, the buttons of the angels,' Hava called out, as I tried to keep up with her. 'Look at the stars, Simone. There's no easy way to reach them! Come on!' She continued to run ahead of me.

'Hava,' I answered as I ran out of energy and stopped. She stopped and walked back to where I stood.

'We have to catch the yellow stars, Simone.'

I looked at Hava and asked, 'Do you think the stars were made, or did they just happen?'

Hava smiled and said, 'They're made of course, of gold, and they will be above us forever. But you have to touch one first to know for sure.' She pointed to a tall silo in a distant field. 'Follow me.' She set off again at a run. This time I just walked behind.

By the time I reached Hava she was already halfway up the metal rungs embedded on the outside of the silo.

'Come on, Simone. Come on up. I'll meet you at the top!'

Hava was the only person in my life who could entice me to climb a three-storey, cement silo. When I reached the top rim, she was already straddling the edge. I held onto the last metal rung and did not look down.

'Look, Simone. We're high enough to touch a star.' Hava reached up into the darkness, closed her hand into a fist, and then brought down her arm. 'Got one!'

The night sky was splashed with stars scattered above us.

'Open your hand, Simone.'

I opened my hand as Hava placed her closed fist onto my palm. 'Now, be careful. I will release the star slowly so it won't escape.'

I felt Hava's fingers unfurl on the flat of my palm. Something dropped gently on to my skin.

'Close your hand quickly. Now!'

I clenched my hand into a fist. 'Got it,' I said. 'Which star did you catch? Arcturus? Sirius?' I opened my hand.

'The Star of David, Simone. It was my grandmother's. My father gave it to me on my first day of school and I have worn it ever since. Now it's yours.'

It was a small, gold star on a delicate gold chain. 'Hava, I can't accept this.'

'I want you to have it. I've never had a sister, but I feel like I do now. It will protect you from lynx, hunters, and star-crushers, and it will always remind you of me, and of the time we caught a star together.'

I slipped the chain around my neck and felt the warm gold star against my chest. The Star of David – the Star of Hava. No matter what my had aunt had told me to do, I could never abandon my friend.

CHAPTER 17

Luftwaffe was the official name for the Nazi air force founded in 1935. Led by Hermann Göring, it had become the largest and most powerful air force in Europe by the start of the Second World War.

That next morning, a Saturday, there was another loud knocking at the front door. I was in the kitchen boiling clothes. I smile to myself now whenever I think of myself in the kitchen, standing on a chair, leaning over a large, green pot, boiling blouses and socks, stirring the clothes with a broken broomstick.

When I read *Macbeth* for the first time, I laughed aloud in class. Sister Bernadette slapped her book shut and asked me if I had lost my mind. I explained that the witches in the play sounded like me as they worked and spoke: 'Double, double toil and trouble; fire burn, and cauldron bubble'. But I wasn't cooking eyes of newt, or frogs, or even tongue of dog. 'In my kitchen,' I explained innocently to the class, 'I boil underpants, socks, a shirt, and a dress or two.' But I was in double, double toil and trouble with Sister Bernadette because I had said 'underpants' in class. No one said the word 'underpants' in a Catholic school in 1940.

The noisy knocking at the door persisted. I looked up from my boiling pot. The steam from the water surrounded me like ghostly tendrils. By the time I climbed down from the chair and walked into the hall, I must have looked like a spectre, pale and frightened. Through the tinted glass in the door I could see a tall figure in a squared military uniform. I hoped for an instant that it was my father.

I pulled back the large iron bolt, opened the door a crack and called out. 'Yes? What is it?'

'Mademoiselle Lyon. It's Sergeant De Waden.'

I hardly recognized his voice, so changed since the autumn.

'*Bonjour*, Corporal.' I said, surprised, as I opened the door. 'Don't you know that the general isn't home?'

'I've brought the horse.' The young man gestured to his right, and there was Charlotte, nibbling a carrot held up to her mouth by little Nicole.

'Corporal De Waden, it's not Sunday, and as I told you, my father isn't here.

'*Oui, oui*, Simone, I know. I've come to see if *you'd* like to ride the horse in the park again. And look, I'm no longer a corporal. I've been promoted. I've been given this new uniform and a hat with a visor. I even brought a carrot for the little girl.'

I stepped out into the street and looked at the newly formed *Sergeant* De Waden in the bright light of the open air. I glanced down at my dress and worried that there might be a frog or the dead eye of a newt smeared on my lapel.

'I've missed you, Simone.' He extended his right hand. I extended my left hand and, as we shook, I noticed his hand felt surprisingly soft and warm.

'*Bonjour*, Sergeant De Waden.' I tipped my head in a gentle manner.

'*Bonjour* again, Mademoiselle Simone. I've brought the horse.'

'Charlotte.'

'Yes.'

'Do you know *Salomé*?' I asked my old friend.

'*Excuse moi*? Salomé? Is she a classmate?'

I was eager to tell him the story about the prince in the well, the prophet and the dance of the seven veils, but thought better things might be expected of me, the general's daughter. 'No, the opera, *Salomé*. I know opera.'

I know opera. Can you imagine telling a young man that you know opera? As if that mattered, as if that were important. But it was important to me that the sergeant didn't think that I was still a child, now that I was eighteen and living alone. And I knew people were impressed by the opera.

Later that day, when I told Hava that I'd asked a sergeant in the royal army if he knew *Salomé*, Hava said that opera was a secret, and only girls, Clark Gable, and John Charles Tillman understood opera. But I told her it was not Clark Gable, nor John Charles Tillman, who had brought me a horse. She had no response to that.

'Here, take this,' Sergeant De Waden said to me as he proffered a fresh carrot. I curled my fingers around the offering, and my sergeant from the royal Belgian army gave a little nod. 'After you.'

In the street, the sun washed over me as if I were a new bouquet of daffodils, displayed on a market stall. Little Nicole held the reins of the horse.

'I've commissioned her into the army,' Sergeant De Waden said as he stooped down and gave the little girl a penny. She didn't want to give up the reins, but did so willingly when the sergeant coaxed, 'All good horsemen in the king's army must obey orders.'

I handed Nicole my carrot and she touched it to the horse's lips. We all laughed as Charlotte crunched loudly. I was glad to see that even the sergeant laughed as he said to Nicole, 'Off you go now.'

'*Merci*, Monsieur Sergeant,' Nicole replied as she stood at attention and saluted. Then she turned to me, smiled, and skipped off along the pavement.

'You remember that I taught you how to ride a horse properly, I presume?' Sergeant De Waden asked sarcastically.

'Yes, of course.' I looked at the sergeant's chest and noticed for the first time that he wore a number of ribbons and a medal.

He noticed my gaze. 'I wish I could tell you that I earned them for valour.' He loosened a pin from his jacket and placed it in my hand. It felt cold and sharp. 'This one's for horsemanship. We still maintain a cavalry, but it doesn't make much sense any longer with tanks and aeroplanes. It's more for show.'

'What can you do with your horse?'

'I jump, and we train the horses to walk backwards, trot in parades,' Sergeant De Waden said as he pinned the medal to my blouse. I felt as if a frog had jumped out of my skin. 'Your father did us a favour by exercising the horse each Sunday. And people like to see the military in the parks. It gives them a sense that all is well.'

The horse pleased me. It smelled of leather and hay. The thick muscles in its chest and its head were powerful and sleek.

Once, Hava and I had climbed on top of the bronze horse in the park belonging to Godfrey of Bouillon, the leader of the First Crusades. I had been so clumsy, trying to pull myself up onto the back of the weathered horse long after Hava was already clutching onto Godfrey's back yelling, 'Faster! Faster!' as she pretended that she and Godfrey were halfway to Hollywood.

When I called out to Hava for help, she looked down at me. 'How am I ever going to reach Hollywood and kiss Clark Gable if I have to keep dragging you along?'

She released her grip on Godfrey, grabbed my outstretched hand, and pulled me up next to her. I liked standing on top of the bronze horse with Hava. We were surrounded by art museums, the National Library, former palaces, and exclusive shops. I felt as if I were a part of the statue of Godfrey of Bouillon as I stood up straight with my long, awkward arms dangling at my side. I didn't have the figure of Venus de Milo, but I did have my arms.

Hava had dared me to kiss Godfrey's lips. It was difficult to climb over the front of the statue because of the horse's reins and Godfrey's extended, bronze arms, but when I managed to reach Godfrey's face, which was as big as a milk kettle, I asked her, 'Should I kiss him slowly or quickly?'

A man with a husky voice broke the spell. 'I think you two young ladies ought to climb down.'

A policeman reached up his hand and helped us gently back down to the cobblestones of the square.

'Ladies, I do not think that your parents would approve of your horse-riding adventures, particularly yours.' He glared meaningfully at me.

Hava was exasperated that everyone seemed to know who my father was. 'Do you think that if we kissed Clark Gable in Hollywood your father would find out as well, given all his spies?' I shrugged.

For the rest of that afternoon we pretended that no matter what we did, there were Belgian army spies keeping track of the two wild girls trying to escape Belgium on a secret mission to kidnap Clark Gable.

Now, in front of my house, Sergeant De Waden placed his right foot into the silver stirrup that dangled against Charlotte's muscular flank and, in a single motion, lifted himself up into the saddle of the great horse. He leaned down, extended his arm and said, 'I will pull you up behind me. Swing around and hold onto my waist.'

Previously, he had always led Charlotte, while I watched the world go by from her broad back. But circumstances had changed: Seargeant De Waden had been promoted and his confidence and self-assurance had advanced accordingly. His gesture was protective, sure – something comforting in a world that was becoming increasingly unpredictable.

Without a second thought, I extended my hand to him, and again noticed the softness of his.

'Now, when I say *three*, give yourself a little bounce from the cobblestone as I lift you up.'

When Hava had pulled me up onto the bronze horse in the Royal Park, her hair had spilled over her face, and when I was finally at her side, she had brushed the hair out of her eyes. It was the first time I realized that she was beautiful.

'One. Two. Three!'

I pushed with my feet against the cobblestone, giving myself a slight bounce, and then all at once, I was airborne, lifted in a sudden, quick motion. Sergeant De Waden had the strength of ten bronze statues as he pulled me behind him. I felt like a winter shawl flung onto his back.

'Now, hold onto my waist.'

I had never held on to a man before, except for my father on my birthday.

The day I turned sixteen, before I opened my gifts, my father had picked up the music carousel from the parlour shelf. It was a beautiful music box made of porcelain. Three miniature horses, each painted in pastel blue, green, and gold, stood in silence on the carousel, before they rotated in a perpetual chase to the music of Mozart's minuet from Don Juan.

My father had cradled the music box in his arms as he wound up the little gears with the key that was inserted at the base. He placed the music box onto the parlour table, extended his hand to me, and then we danced. I held onto his shoulder with my left hand, and held his damaged arm gently with my right. As the soft music clicked and clacked like icicles and wind chimes, my father spun me round and round the parlour.

Sergeant De Waden guided the horse along the wide boulevard that divided the Royal Park in half and I kept my arms wrapped around his waist. One side of the park was filled with tulips, and the other with azaleas. I remember thinking that there were enough flowers for the entire world in the park that day, or at least enough flowers for my world.

People did not recognize Sergeant De Waden, but they did recognize Charlotte. Old gentlemen stood up and saluted. Children ran alongside and waved. I held onto the sergeant's body; his back was stiff, his stomach muscles taut. At one point, just before he signalled to the horse to move into a quick trot, Sergeant De Waden released one hand from the reins and grasped one of my hands as if I was a part of his belt, or holster. The horse tipped backwards slightly and jumped forward quickly.

Charlotte moved in a sudden rocking motion. The trees seemed to soar above us. People applauded. The clopping sounds of the horseshoes on cobblestones convinced me that with just a simple command we might fly. I held onto the sergeant as the horse entered a full gallop. 'Hold on!' the sergeant called out. 'Hold on!'

I gripped the sides of his body more tightly. The horse clung bravely to the hard surface beneath us, relishing its ability to run. People's faces blurred as we flew past. Vibrant flowerbeds transformed into rainbow-coloured canvasses. Children's laughter caught the breeze, free, alive, joyful.

Without warning, I began to feel as if I were suddenly under water. Sound became muted, drowned out by something louder, close, mechanical. Our bodies seemed to move in slow motion, as time juddered to a halt. The sun dimmed, obscured by an uninvited guest, intruding on one last moment of perfection.

Then, everything exploded in the roar of angry aeroplane engines, growling, spitting petrol fumes. One after another, propellers cut the air above our heads. And still they came. The horse stopped abruptly, as the sergeant pulled on the reins and stared at the spectacle overhead. People stood still. The sky blackened with aeroplanes – German aeroplanes. Shadow after shadow raced over the cobblestones and disappeared into the tulips. A boy asked his father, 'Is it a parade?'

The music of the park's carousel faded and the ride came prematurely to an end. Parents grabbed their children from the painted saddles and ran.

Sergeant De Waden turned to me and said anxiously, 'I must get back to my base.'

PART III. THE INVASION, 10 MAY, 1940

CHAPTER 18

Brutally attacked by Germany which had entered into the most solemn engagements with her, Belgium will defend herself with all of her strength against the invader. In these tragic hours which my country is undergoing, I am addressing myself to Your Excellency, who so often has demonstrated towards Belgium an affectionate interest, in the certainty that you will support with all of your moral authority the efforts which we are now firmly decided to make in order to preserve our independence.

Telegram from Leopold III, King of Belgium, to Franklin D. Roosevelt, President of the United States, 10 May 1940

When I was a little girl my father took me to River Meuse, not far from the city of Namur, to visit my great-aunt, who had spent most of her life smoking cigarettes and playing mah-jong with her housekeeper.

It was summer, but Aunt Dolly refused to install air-conditioning in her house. My father tried to open the window in the room where we sat, and Aunt Dolly scolded him. 'Don't you open that window and let in the germs.' She smacked the table with her open palm with such force that the mah-jong tiles jumped like startled crickets. The game ended, and my father stormed out of the room. He was only a major at the time – a general would have opened the window. My father called to me to follow him. I was only ten. If I had been eleven, I might not have followed him.

He stomped out of the house, cursing the stones under his feet, and I followed. His arms swung back and forth like the arms of an angry wind-up tin soldier. I trailed behind him, swinging *my* arms, stepping into the tracks he made in the earth with his thick-soled shoes. Sometimes I had to take extra steps to keep up with his forceful stride.

When he reached the river on that hot day, my father unbuttoned his shirt, pulled off his shoes and socks, and dived into the river. I remember how white his broad back looked when he popped up from the water and began cutting into the surface with his one good arm.

'Simone,' my father waved, 'come in. It's much cooler in the water.'

I stood on the edge of the river, realizing how little my father knew about me. Perhaps if I had been a boy, he would have known that I could not swim. When I shook my head in refusal, he barked an order that made me jump like the ivory tiles on the mah-jong table. 'Simone! Come here!'

I sat on the grass, unbuttoned my black walking shoes, and from my little white feet I peeled off my pearl socks, as if removing the outer skin of an onion.

'Simone!'

I stood up and slipped my yellow cotton dress above my head, letting it fall to the ground in defeat. I stood beside the rippling water in my thin camisole. I looked at my father – a little girl who did not know how to swim.

'Simone!' he entreated for the fourth time.

I held my nose and jumped into the water. When I sank, bubbles and my father's arms surrounded me in a rush of trapped air and laughter.

'You silly girl!' my father chuckled as I draped my arms around his neck and shivered. 'Don't you know how to swim?'

I looked into his face and shook my head in shame.

'Come here, my brave little swimmer.' My father bent my arms in classic swimmer's positions. He held me up on the water's surface with his wide hand at the small of my back as I learned how to float. I was his tame little seal, eager to please, and delighted to feel the water push against my face as I learned how to kick my legs and feet in a steady churn of water and muscles.

What I remember most were the water lilies. Before we went home, I had gained enough confidence in my new talent that I was able to swim in the river with my eyes open. I liked seeing my father turn into a wiggling form worthy of Picasso's paintings, as I looked at him through the thick lens of the turbulent water. But then I swam out a bit further and dived down into the cool green river. The sun penetrated the surface and illuminated my body like that of a river salmon, and when I looked up, I saw the outline of water lilies: dark shadows surrounded by light. They floated on the surface of the water as I swam beneath them, their shadows rippling over my arms and legs. I felt as if I was in a new world and that things were changing in ways that I didn't yet understand.

As Sergeant De Waden and I rode through the Royal Park, I had been thinking about swimming in that river, the water lilies floating over my head. Until, suddenly, my distant memories of the lilies were viciously transformed into the shadows of large, distant bombers with long wings and churning engines.

The air throbbed and resonated, vibrating with a low-pitched drone that quickly drowned the confused cries of mothers and children. Black dots appeared in the sky, scattered across the far horizon, like gnats on a summer's evening. They pulsed nearer and nearer, their shapes gaining clarity as they advanced, engines straining forward, screaming their arrival.

As the sudden swarm of black bombers thundered overhead, a palpable wave of panic nearly knocked me off the horse. My throat tightened, and my fists clung to Sergeant De Waden so firmly that he almost couldn't pry me from his body as he twisted and shouted above the noise:, 'Simone, I have to go! The Nazis are here and I have to report. Climb down, now! Climb down and go straight home!'

As he guided me from the horse, my throat so tight now that I could barely breathe, I wanted to cry out to him. I wanted to ask him what was happening. I wanted to ask him to take me with him ... if I was going to die ... if he would marry me. But all I could do was stand there in a daze and watch him ride away, his voice becoming fainter, 'Go home, Simone! Go home!'

Hitler had invaded Belgium.

CHAPTER 19

On 10 May 1940, Hitler proclaimed the word Danzig *over the radio – the code word for his troops to begin the invasion of Western Europe – thus sending his forces into Holland and Belgium, en route to France. On the same day, Winston Churchill became Prime Minister of Great Britain.*

Aircraft continued to rumble overhead, unceasingly, one after another. Their shadows rippled across my face and arms. Sun, shadow. Sun, shadow. Menacing, dark, in formation – a monster.

The sun illuminated the heavy iron crosses adorning the aircrafts' wings, the planes' metallic bodies glinted grey against the clouds. The low growl of their engines shattered the peaceful sky, threatening and belligerent.

I could not believe what I was seeing. My father had warned me. My aunt had warned me. People in the street had said it was a certitude. Yet I had refused to believe them. But there it was, the German air force, blotting the Belgian sky, invading my country, invading my soul. Why was this happening? What did these people want with the park, my horse, and with my thumbnail-size country? There was no longer any distance between me and the war, between me and the encroaching monster. Hitler's forces were invading Belgium.

Run! I thought.

At first, in the Royal Park, everyone remained immobile and stared up into the sky as if transfixed by something almost beautiful. Then an old woman lifted her small arm, pointed upward and said, *'Le Boche'*. She repeated the word again, this time with a shrillness to her words: *'Le Boche! Le Boche!'* The sound sent chills through my body.

The people in the park began to run in all directions. I looked for my sergeant and Charlotte, but they were gone. Mothers pushed their baby carriages with force and determination. Girls abandoned their jump ropes. Boys looked up into the sky as their fathers dragged them from the grass.

As the sky swarmed with German planes, a balloon vendor released his yellow, red, and green balloons, which floated upward as if on a mission to chase them away.

Looking up overhead I was reminded of the flying monkeys in the film *The Wizard of Oz*; how they had grabbed Dorothy and Toto at the command of the Wicked Witch of the West. I stood, not understanding, the cobblestones under my feet and the shadows of the planes cutting across my body.

I clutched at my arms and shoulders and whispered, 'My arms! My arms!' My childhood fear of resembling my father crept up on me once again, released from my subconscious by the sinister portent I was witnessing. 'I don't want to look like my father. I don't want my arms to dangle uselessly at my side,' I muttered to myself.

That is when I heard the sergeant's voice echoing in my ears, 'Go home, Simone! Go home!' and I too began to run.

I didn't know then that Hitler's army had invaded Holland, Luxembourg, and Belgium simultaneously. I didn't know that Hitler would soon clear a passage through the Ardennes, a region of thick forest and rough terrain, and surprise the Belgian army. I had no inkling that the SS, Hitler's elite paramilitary force, planned to capture and shoot my father because he had blown up bridges and cut telegraph lines to slow the German advance.

All I knew was the moaning of those horrible planes flying over me as I ran, trying to escape the noise and confusion, trying to get home. I understood that Germany and Russia invaded Poland. I understood that Hitler had invaded Norway and Denmark, but my father had said Belgium was neutral. We were a peace-loving nation. Hitler here, in Brussels, was incomprehensible. All I knew was that I had to escape this monstrous intrusion.

When I reached the street, I saw buses at a standstill and people rushing down alleys. Office workers ran out of the buildings and looked up into the sky. It was as if a mythical and terrible dragon had descended on the city, breathing fire; the harbinger of destruction – the Dragon of the Second World War. Smoke filled the square with a thick, acrid fog and as I ran through the street it squeezed my lungs. I coughed, choked, and saw flames catch hold of buildings and fields – fire so bright it was almost blinding. Brussels was burning.

I remembered my father talking of *Blitzkrieg*. Lightning war. Now it made sense. The planes had come from nowhere, rolling over the horizon like storm clouds on a summer's evening; black, relentless, powerful, unyielding. Tanks rolled over open fields and hedgerows. Elite squads of soldiers with parachutes dropped from the sky, striking the ground like bolts from above.

I must get back to the house, I thought. *Papa said to stay in the house!*

When I reached my front door, I struggled to unlock it. I dug into my pocket for the key. My hand shook. I dropped the key. It bounced on the pavement. People ran back and forth. A woman with a sack of potatoes nearly knocked me over. A man with a cane waved me aside as he rushed through the crowd. I was desperate to find that key. The planes were still coming. Danger was approaching. I imagined I could feel the heat of the engines on my neck. I remember looking down and seeing the high-heeled shoes of well-dressed women, the plain black shoes of a priest. The butcher, the postman, a woman from my church, people I recognized, all hurried away. I felt like a twig caught in a tornado, twirling in the chaos. My hands wouldn't stop shaking.

'Mademoiselle Simone!'

I heard my name as if coming from a tunnel.

'Mademoiselle Simone! Here! Here!'

I turned towards the voice. Standing in the middle of the whirling crowd was little Nicole. She held her hand up in the air, and in her hand was my key.

'I have it here. Your key!' She waved her arm back and forth. My little saviour.

Nicole ran to me, dodging men with suitcases and women with bags of vegetables and bread. 'Here's your key!'

When the girl reached out her hand, I grabbed her arm and pulled her out of the way of a large man pushing a cart filled with furniture. I pressed Nicole's small head against my chest as I held her, trying to protect her, trying to protect myself, trying to protect all of Belgium.

I heard explosions in the distance as planes thundered overhead. Suddenly, as we huddled on the front stoop, a deafening crash like a giant tree falling to the earth erupted from the sky. A bomb struck a nearby apartment building, bursting it open like a nutcracker, sending flaming bricks and shards of glass careening into the streets. The entire front wall toppled over, cries of terror rose from within, and as an air-raid siren wailed, the fire consumed the building. Black smoke rose into the air like a victorious dragon.

Madame Johnson appeared at her door.

'Nicole!' she shouted. 'Come inside! Quick! Come inside now! Simone, are you okay?' I nodded as I released Nicole, who was crying now and desperate to run into her mother's arms.

'*Go home!*' Sergeant De Waden's voice echoed in my head. Then the voice became my father's. 'Stay inside the house, Simone. Stay in the house!'

'I'm okay.' I cleared my throat and waved to Madame Johnson. 'I just need to get into the house.'

Madame Johnson nodded, blew me a kiss, and hurried through her front door.

CHAPTER 20

My Luftwaffe is invincible.
Hermann Göring, German Air Force Minister

One Saturday morning, the year before the Nazi invasion, Hava and I read Edmund Spenser's *Faerie Queene* together. In the afternoon, we walked to the park with jam sandwiches in a cloth bag. We pretended that a large linden tree on the boulevard was the deceitful witch Duessa, who followed us as we walked. Hava liked to pretend she was the Knight of Holiness, peeking under the dress of Duessa. 'Look at the ugly veins on her legs,' she cooed as she stroked the bark of the tree. People looked at us as if we were mad – two schoolgirls laughing under a tree.

Hava insisted that I play Redcrosse, the Knight of Chastity. In the story, when Redcrosse and his girlfriend, Una, were travelling together, they came upon a land that had been burned, stomped on, flattened, and destroyed by a dragon. I still remember the lines that Hava and I memorized: *'That dreadful Dragon they espide,/ Where stretcht he lay upon the sunny side,/Of a great hill …'*

That's what I thought about when the Nazi planes appeared in the sky on 10 May, like hundreds of black dragons ready to destroy everything beneath them with their fiery breath: little Nicole, the park, Hava. I said a quick prayer for Hava and hoped she and her family were safe in their home.

I inserted the key into the keyhole, wishing that when I turned it, the house, like a magic clock, would turn time backwards and I would find my father inside smoking his pipe, reading the paper, greeting me by name: 'Simone!'

As the door opened like the slab from a tomb, there was no resurrection, only silence. The air was still and damp. With each step on the stone floor, the hard heels of my shoes clicked ... clicked ... clicked ...My father's chair was empty. The light from each window was dull. The kitchen tap dripped. Simone. Simone. Simone.

I locked the door behind me, ran to the kitchen and turned on the radio. The news broadcast confirmed the worst:

> ... the complete destruction of the Belgian Air Force. It has also been reported that the bridges over the Albert Canal and the Eben-Emael fortress have been destroyed by bombs. German paratroopers are reported to the north, as are tanks and heavily armed German infantry troops. Hitler's forces are quickly spreading south towards Brussels.'

All I knew about warfare was from reading about the American Civil War in the novel, *Gone with the Wind*. As batteries of infantry had poured shells into Atlanta, killing people in their homes, ripping roofs off buildings, tearing huge craters in the streets, the townsfolk had sheltered as best they could in cellars, in holes in the ground, and in shallow tunnels dug into railway lines. Atlanta had been under siege. Was Brussels my Atlanta?

Nazi troops poured into Belgium like a million ants spreading across the garden on a warm, spring day. I looked at the ceiling and heard the German planes panting and growling. I imagined a giant with a black moustache ripping the roof from my house, reaching in and pulling me away to my death.

I noticed the kitchen had lost its aroma of bread. I heard the wheeze of my own breathing. I had to pretend this was all a mistake, all a dream. I had to make myself believe that I was not involved with the war, that it had nothing to do with me. I had nothing the Germans wanted or needed. I was alone. In my fatigue and fear I staggered from room to room, looking for an exit, a way out, a way to blue sky and the opera, and being eighteen.

After the First World War, the French had built what they called the Maginot Line; long defensive fortifications that stretched along the French and German border. The French nation did not want to be attacked again as it had been during the First World War, so France had constructed bunkers for machine guns, guard posts, anti-tank obstacles, and underground tunnels.

I decided to build my own Maginot Line. I walked around the house and locked all the doors and windows. I reached above the bookshelf in the living room for my father's First World War rifle, and found the bullets in the dresser where he kept pictures of my mother, and where I had finally stored his Croix de Guerre.

I heard more explosions. A floristry shop across the street blazed, flames engulfed the building. Smoke billowed out from the church steeple. The wail of the air-raid signal screamed through the city and shattered the calm I had thought I possessed.

I grabbed the bullets and the rifle and rushed downstairs to begin my Maginot Line. I leaned the rifle against the locked front door, walked through the living room and into the kitchen, where I decided to make some soup. Hava had once shared with me an old Jewish proverb: 'Worries go down better with soup than without.'

As I rummaged under the sink for the soup pot, without warning, the house shook, and more loud explosions rumbled nearby. It sounded like thunder, but when I looked out of the window, the flash of light was not coming from the sky, but from the horizon. Blitzkrieg. Everywhere I looked I saw plumes of smoke rose up above the roof lines of my neighbours' homes. Was my house next? Would my Maginot Line hold? I was shaking, but I persisted with my soup. I needed the distraction of normalcy to keep me from falling apart.

I rubbed my arms, peeled carrots, potatoes, and onions, and as I chopped them on a small board, I wondered if they might be the last vegetables that I would see for some time.

More explosions reverberated in the distance just as I was reaching into the icebox for the chicken broth that I'd been saving. I grabbed a saucepan, dropped a bit of oil into the pot, added the mixed vegetables, and stirred until they softened.

More bombs. I poured the chicken broth into the pot and brought the soup to the boil. I watched the blue flames dance against the underside of the pot as the soup boiled into a frenzy, before I reduced it to a simmer. That's where flames belonged – under pots.

Hitler had not been invited for dinner. Soup did not feed a tank. I would remain a calm, brave Belgian woman and make my soup in defiance of the broiling horror outside my windows.

Chapter 21

German troops engaged in a surprise attack through Belgium and the Netherlands, during their push into France. French troops were overrun. The German army lost 150,000 soldiers, but the Allies lost over 360,000 men and the British army retreated to the French coast.

I sat on a kitchen chair watching steam rise from the saucepan. The steam, in my mind, turned to gunsmoke and I imagined Union and Confederate soldiers from Atlanta shooting their rifles at close range. I had read in *Gone with the Wind* how men, already near death, wounded and bleeding, had walked through the smoke like ghosts, dazed by the war, dazed by sudden attacks, afraid, and in great pain. I shuddered. Would I see wounded Belgians staggering through the haze outside my windows?

The house shuddered. Bits of plaster fell from the kitchen ceiling. Planes kept flying over the city. I tried to block out the sound, covering my ears with my hands, and then I began to hum a church hymn.

The vibrations from the planes caused the windows to rattle loudly. People wailed in despair outside on the street. Bombs fell on the city. I couldn't look. I didn't want this to be happening. I couldn't accept this was happening. Was the war going to kill us all? Was I going to die? Tears stung my eyes as I bit hard on my lip. I had to stay strong. I had to defend my father's house. I had to make soup.

I was an 18-year-old girl in May 1940. I had no idea that 40 miles away the largest tank battle in the history of the world was taking place between the Nazi Panzer divisions and the brave, but lightly equipped, Belgian army and French tanks.

I thought my armour was strong against Duessa the Witch. I thought I was clever, and would be safe in my house. I was Salomé and, like many other teenage girls, in love with Clark Gable. I was the daughter of the general.

But in reality, I was frightened. My Maginot Line wasn't working. My soup wasn't having the required effect. I couldn't bear to be in the house by myself. I saw the silhouettes of people rushing past the closed window shades: people fleeing their homes; little outlines of children's heads bobbing up and down; shadows without faces. People with names and histories flattened to indistinct grey shapes on my window shade.

'My name is Simone Lyon,' I said to the parade of shadows. 'My name is Simone. I am a brave Belgian woman.' I pretended that the people behind the window shade stopped and listened to me, in awe of my courage.

I had no idea that British and French troops had tried to help Belgium troops stop the invading army and tanks from advancing towards Brussels. I didn't know that on that day 2,500 Nazi aircraft had begun a bombing campaign against villages, airfields, and factories. I didn't know that over 16,000 Nazi paratroopers had landed in Rotterdam and The Hague. But I did know that I had to save my arms from the Nazis. I knelt on the floor thinking about Atlanta burning during the American Civil War, and I tried not to cry. I was going to be brave like Scarlet O'Hara.

There is a section in *Gone with the Wind* where Margaret Mitchell says that Scarlet O'Hara's suffering during the war was like a dream too horrible to be real. It felt as if I was in a horrible dream as I listened to the BBC. I heard the radio broadcast, and understood that Nazi troops were swarming into Belgium from the west. Then I heard another terrific explosion not far from the house.

The windows shook again, violently this time. The shadows moved past the window faster and faster. Brussels was under siege. German planes still passed over the city. Smoke bulged up in the distant sky, and then I heard a frantic knocking at the door.

I was afraid. Aunt Margaret had instructed me not to let anyone in. The knocking persisted. It was all too much: the bombs, the radio, the boiling water... the knocking. Even though Sergeant De Waden and my aunt had warned me to lock my door and not let anyone in, I grabbed the house key and raced to the hall hoping it was the sergeant, or my father. I turned the key and yanked open the heavy door. 'Hava!' I cried as she fell into my arms and wept.

'My father sent me,' Hava said as she leaned back and looked at me through her tears. There was dirt on her face. Her hair was matted. 'There's chaos everywhere. We heard the news about a possible invasion, and my father knew that you were alone. He wanted me to come to your house and see that you were safe. We didn't know the planes were coming. I was already through the park when the planes arrived.'

I tried to soothe my friend between my own tears; tears of joy because I was suddenly not alone. The only thing I could say to her was, 'Would you like some soup?'

We sat at the kitchen table in silence for some time, as if we were British gentlewomen taking afternoon tea. That is when I looked out of the window and saw that the next building was on fire. Orange and yellow flames seemed to be reaching out for my windowsill and I broke down, repeating again and again, 'My arms! Don't let them take my arms, Hava.' I crumpled to the floor. 'The Nazis, don't let them take my arms!' I began to shake. Poor Hava didn't know what to do.

Chapter 22

This is the BBC. The German army invaded Belgium and Holland early this morning. The armies of the Low Countries are resisting. An appeal for help has been made to the Allied Governments and Brussels says that Allied troops are moving to their support.

When I woke up it was dark except for a single lit candle on the bedroom dresser. At first I didn't know where I was. It was completely silent. No planes. No audible distress in the streets. No fires. My room was on the third floor of the house, filled with my books, piled on the floor in wobbly columns. Each pile denoted a category: poetry, journals, and novels. On the opposite wall from my bed hung my parents' wedding picture. In the candlelight it seemed as if my mother and father were floating in the frame, or perhaps it was my delirium. Hava said that I had spoken in my sleep a number of times.

I turned over and saw Hava sleeping in my reading chair beside the bed. I had witnessed the entire American Civil War in that chair, one chapter at a time.

'Hava?' I whispered. 'Hava?'

Hava moved her right hand to her face and rubbed her eyes.

'Hava?

She opened her eyes and looked at me with a sadness that I didn't immediately understand.

'Hava, are you alright?'

She pulled her thin legs up onto the chair and said, 'You were the one who fainted, and you're worried about me?'

'The bombing has stopped.' I looked at Hava again and remembered how she'd looked when I first met her at the Red Cross: confident and beautiful.

Hava stroked her cheek slowly with her left hand and said, 'I didn't know that I was a Jew until I was eight. It was my birthday and my father brought me to the carousel. I was riding a seahorse as my father stood behind the rope waving to me. I didn't dare wave back – I was afraid of letting go of the seahorse's head, even with one hand, fearing that I would fall.

'A boy was sitting on an ostrich right next to me. When he saw me looking at him, he said, "Jews don't ride seahorses."

'After the ride, walking hand in hand with my father under the linden trees, I asked him if I was a Jew. My father stopped walking, crouched next me and said, "Little one, my Hava, you have a sweet heart, and you love others, so yes, you are a Jew."

"But why can't I ride a seahorse?" I asked.

"What is this?" my father huffed. "Who told you that you can't ride a seahorse?"

'When I told my father about the boy on the ostrich, he lifted me up onto his shoulders and said, "Don't worry about him. He's God's problem."'

I sat up on my bed and asked Hava, 'Where are your parents and Benjamin?'

'They were going to the synagogue. My father insisted that I check on you, and bring you back there with me. We all left the house at the same time. When I got to the corner, I turned and looked at my family. They were all holding hands: my father, mama, and Benjamin in the middle. My father saw me at the corner and raised his hand to me. I raised my hand too, and then I ran through the park. Then the planes appeared and the bombs. We must go to the synagogue, Simone. We must go and find them, now that you're better.'

The summer before, Hava and I had visited museums to gaze at the paintings of beautiful horses, or fields of golden wheat. We'd admired the dress of a peasant and the royal vestments of a king. I had seen blue paintings of women looking out of a window, men in rowing boats, flowers as beautiful as jewels in a box, but among the most beautiful images I ever saw were the eyes of Hava in the candlelight that sad night, the shape of her cheeks, the lines in her face that etched an image of hope framed by her dishevelled hair.

'Yes, the synagogue. Of course,' I said, 'Like Tara.'

I had been to Hava's synagogue once before, and I understood why she felt it was a place of safety for her; a place she could return to again and again, like Tara, Scarlett O'Hara's home. We all have a place of safety in our memory, or in our daily lives, where we can push open the door and know that we are safe and welcome. Inside our home is a favourite room, a book remembered, a father planting roses, a cat licking its paws on the windowsill, God perhaps, the aroma of a favourite soup.

'Yes, the synagogue,' Hava said again, as she struggled to her feet. I placed the candle on the floor and reached out to her. She took my extended hand as she stood up slowly. 'Your hand is warm,' she said as she steadied herself. 'Okay, let's go.'

Before we left the room, I noticed Benjamin's drawing of God, with his green shirt and two orange kites, pinned to my wall. I grabbed the paper and Hava smiled saying, 'Remember, those aren't crosses; they're kites.' I looked at the happy God, the kites, and the green shirt, then I folded the drawing along its established creases and tucked it into my dress pocket.

'Let's go to the synagogue.'

We stepped out of my home. It was dark; the early hours of the morning. I felt for the first time the fear of death surrounding Hava and me. How was it possible? I thought as we ran through the streets. *How can one day be filled with picnics and opera, then the next day the sun is erased and the city is in flames, in so short of time?*

The streets were empty now. It seemed as if the city was asleep and the day had been a collection of nightmares strung together with planes, clouds, and the cries of mothers. I saw a small, torn Belgian flag hanging from a dark apartment window. *The synagogue. A place of safety. We needed a place of safety.*

'Are you sure your parents went to the synagogue?'

'Yes, Simone. Yes. I'm sure of it. They'll be at the synagogue. My father said they'd wait for me there. Let's hurry.'

We stopped in the middle of a wide, empty street. Hava looked into my eyes and repeated. 'He promised, Simone.'

'Which way, Hava? Which way to the synagogue?'

She looked at me as if she had forgotten the purpose of our being together in the middle of Brussels in the middle of the night, at the beginning of the Second World War, but then she squeezed my hand and pointed. 'This way.'

I thought about Van Gogh's painting, *Starry Night*, as we hurried through the dark streets of Brussels. There were no lights.

It seemed that most of the electricity in the city had been cut off. I had never seen the stars in Brussels because the city was always so bright. Even in the middle of the night, the street lights and fountains were usually illuminated. But at the very beginning of the war, Brussels had retreated into sudden hibernation, closed within itself.

Hava and I entered the park, that in the darkness looked like wilderness hidden under black capes. Trees bore down on us like ogres. Bushes became fat Nazi troops. The cool night air breathed down our necks.

Just as we were about to exit the park, a voice startled us.

'Halt! Stand where you are!' Hava stopped and stumbled backwards as if she had been struck in the face.

'Stop, I say.' We heard the bolt of a rifle being pushed into place. 'What are you doing here? It's forbidden. There's a curfew.'

'We're on our way to visit a sick friend,' I lied.

'Simone?' said the soldier.

'Sergeant De Waden?'

'Simone, what are you doing here? I told you to go home and stay there, and lock your door. The Germans have crossed the border. No one is safe. We have orders to arrest anyone who isn't in their home.'

'Is this your sergeant?' Hava asked as she looked through the darkness.

'Sergeant, this is my friend, Hava. We're on our way to meet her parents. She came for me, so I can be with them.'

'It's forbidden to walk the streets!' The poor sergeant didn't know what to do or what to say. His uniform said that he was to arrest us, but his heart said that he should escort us personally to safety … on his back if he could.

'Where do your parents live?' Sergeant De Waden asked Hava.

'We're not going to my house. We're meeting them at the synagogue.'

'The synagogue?' There was a change in his voice. 'That's not a place I think you should go, Simone.'

'We just have to meet her family,' I urged. 'Once we find them, we'll all go back to Hava's house. I promise.' Sergeant De Waden sighed.

'Fine, if you must. But I'll escort you there for your safety.'

I nodded, and as we walked through the streets of Brussels an odd sense of security arose among the aromas of the park flowers, and a calm descended from the suddenly subdued night. After all, Hava and I were under the protection of the Belgian army.

My sergeant walked between Hava and me with a confident stride. It was through Sergeant De Waden that I finally heard an update on where my father actually was.

'Your father is with the Dame Blanche, Simone; the Resistance. He'll fight the Germans in his own way now. I just hope that he'll be okay.'

Can this be true? I thought. *Could he be in danger?* Was my own private Maginot Line collapsing?

'Don't frighten her,' Hava said. 'The German soldiers are coming, that's enough for one night.'

I reached out into the darkness and touched Hava's hand. There was silence except for the sound of our shoes against the hard cobblestones. If I could have done so, I would have sung a song for Hava as we began this night walk in the newly artificial world that was crossing over into our lives. *Was my father okay?* I had to believe in that moment that he would be.

Poor Sergeant De Waden. He was built with brass buttons and orders, action and desire. I knew I was his desire, but I also knew the difference between the moonlight and the light from a man's urgency. When I pointed out how incongruous it was that the moon was so beautiful that night as the three of us walked to the synagogue, Sergeant De Waden lamented that it was a curse, a bad omen of what was to come. 'We don't need more light for the German Air Force. It would be better to blow up the moon.'

I wanted to tell the sergeant about Van Gogh's masterpiece *Starry Night*: how the moon was a part of the permanent picture; how no matter what happened, the moon would reappear; and that, to me, the moon was a pearl in the black sea of my own fears. But he would not have understood, so I was silent.

As we turned a corner, we saw movement in a doorway. I imagined it was a Nazi soldier. But then an old woman wearing a brown house smock stepped out onto the street with a straw broom.

As Sergeant De Waden, Hava, and I approached the woman, she began to sweep the pavement clear of broken glass, bits of wood, a child's shoe, and loose sheets of newspaper.

'Hello, madame,' I said.

The woman looked up from her broom, squinted and uttered just one word: '*Courage.*' She turned from us, stooped to her labour, and continued to sweep.

I remember how the broken pieces of glass jingled on the pavement. I remember seeing that the small shoe was torn on one side. I watched the soiled bits of newspaper roll under the pressure of the straw broom. It felt as if all that I knew of my city was being swept from the streets and pushed into the gutter.

Dawn had begun her work. Shadows disappeared slowly under the trees. The glow in the sky was not from bombs and fire, but from the sun's new alchemy on the dark earth, turning night into the gold of morning.

Hava pulled my hand gently and whispered, 'There it is.'

At the end of the street, the Great Synagogue of Brussels sat like a confident father towering over his children. It was coated in brick and hewn stones. A large, rose window was built in the centre of the arch; a large eye celebrating light, inviting it to enter the soul of the synagogue.

'Right, you girls are safe now,' Sergeant De Waden said. 'I'll leave you here. Remember, you cannot be out at night. There's a curfew.' He looked at me with a small smile, a nod of the head, and a slight bow.

'*Vive la Belgique,*' I said.

His smile disappeared as he glanced quickly at Hava. Then he saluted and walked away.

'Look, Simone,' Hava said pointing as we stopped opposite the large building. 'See under the glass window, carved in red marble, the Tablets from Moses, the Ten Commandments?' She let go of my hand and stood before the wide doors of the synagogue and began to rock back and forth on her heels. Her eyes were closed. She wrapped her arms around her body and said, 'Thou shalt honour thy father and mother.'

I put my arm around her. 'We will find them inside.'

Hava looked up at me and whispered again, 'Honour thy father and mother.'

'And Benjamin too,' I added with a smile.

She returned my smile, took my hand, and together we ran across the street and pushed open the large wooden doors of the synagogue.

CHAPTER 23

I was truly under Hitler's spell, that cannot be denied. I was impressed with him from the moment I first met him, in 1932. He had terrific power, especially in his eyes.
Joachim von Ribbentrop, 15 July, 1946, Foreign Minister of Nazi Germany, testifying at the Nuremberg Trials

Once, after reading *Romeo and Juliet* in Sister Bernadette's class, I met up with Hava at a small café. We drank our coffee, and as we walked to my house, she suggested that we act out the death scene. 'I can be Juliet,' she said as she closed her eyes, swaying back and forth on the pavement, and stabbing herself with an imaginary knife. 'O happy dagger! This is thy sheath; there rust, and let me die.'

Hava began to stagger on the pavement. She didn't look anything like Juliet of Shakespeare, but like Crazy Hava of Brussels.

'Hava,' I muttered, embarrassed, 'people are looking at you.'

Hava opened one eye and giggled. A man in a bowler hat with a newspaper under his arm stopped and said to her, 'Shakespeare is for serious-minded people.' Then he turned to me and said, 'And you, miss ... I'm sure your parents did not raise you to hang out with lunatics.'

The man with the bowler hat waved his newspaper in the air. 'Shameful!' he said.

'Let's do the death scene in your cellar,' Hava suggested. 'There are too many theatre critics around here.'

'There are too many army spies,' was my reply.

I remember that particular walk home, but not just because of the angry man. It was spring; the markets were full of tulips and early asparagus, plump mushrooms, tall rhubarb, spinach, and watercress. Trees expanded with green leaves. The trams seemed to clack against the road with a softer pitch. The sun made the buildings blush. Children leaned out of their prams as mothers gossiped. Old men with open collars sat on the avenue benches, probably thinking about other spring afternoons.

'I don't think my father would be happy about us playing in the cellar,' I said to Hava as she stopped suddenly in the middle of the pavement.

'Your father will never know we're down there, Simone. We both know the lines; we can just go there, set up the scenery quickly, and play out our dying scene.'

It was dark in the lowest level of my house. When Hava and I opened the cellar door, she suggested we take candles.

She went down first, her long hair touching the back of her neck. The candlelight wavered. Hava's shadow on the wall was wide and fat. I heard her hard shoes hitting each step. She turned, looked up at me and said, 'Maybe there are bodies buried down here.'

The cellar was dry and filled with empty boxes, a tool rack, a shelf of empty jam jars, and a long, flat work table.

'We can use the table as a bier,' Hava suggested.

'Or we could go back upstairs and have some tea instead,' I suggested.

'Tea?' Hava said as she began to form her long hair into a bun. 'We don't drink tea when we're dying, Simone.' She took a small piece of string from her pocket and tied her hair back. 'You can't be too pretty for death,' Hava said as she slipped off her shoes, and then stretched out on the low table. Her body fitted perfectly: her arms at her sides; her legs straight and parallel. She closed her eyes. 'Do I look dead?'

'You look like a Belgian girl stretched out on a dirty work bench.'

'I need a pillow,' Hava said as she lifted her head and looked around in the dim light. 'There, what's that in the corner?'

I walked to the corner and found several small, bulging burlap bags with the words 'coffee beans' stencilled on each. 'They're bags of coffee beans, Hava.'

'Well, I don't think Juliet used coffee beans as a pillow, but I don't think Shakespeare would mind.'

'How come you are playing Juliet? I don't want to be Romeo.'

Hava raised her hands and made a magician's gesture above her chest: 'Simone, in Shakespeare's day men played the role of Juliet. You can play the role of Romeo. Your voice is deeper than mine so it will be much easier for the audience to think of you as a boy.'

I laughed. 'I don't think spiders and dust make up a legitimate audience.'

'Just say your lines, Simone,' Hava said as she adjusted her coffee-bean pillow and closed her eyes. She looked like a sculpture in the candlelight: her body all curves and soft lines. I was all straight lines and flat. Perhaps I did make a better boy than a girl after all.

Hava and I knew the entire play by heart; it had been her idea to learn it. 'I want to die a thousand times in the arms of Romeo before I *actually* die,' Hava said as she handed me a copy of the play one afternoon. 'Let's memorize the entire play together.'

We never finished the dying scene in the cellar because, just as we began, the angry voice of my father echoed from the top of the stairs.

'What is going on down there? Simone? Is that you?'

Standing in the candlelight with Hava, I felt like we were two martyrs about to be engulfed in the flame of my father's torch; two city girls caught in a foolish escape into our imaginations. Hava and I in the shadows, surrounded by the protective black space as if prepared for a shower of anger – a shower that would not cleanse, but would separate her from me, and from my conservative father, who understood order and respect, uniforms and tradition.

Hava jumped off the table with such speed that she knocked over the candle and everything went dark, except for the light at the top of the staircase.

'Simone?'

'Yes?'

My father started to stomp down the wooden stairs. When he reached the bottom step there was a small click and the torch that he held firmly in his hand illuminated the cellar with a beam of yellow light. I turned, and there was Hava untying her hair and giggling.

'Hello, Miss Hava,' my father said as he aimed his light into my face. 'Simone, what are you doing down here in the dark?'

'We weren't in the dark, Papa. We had a candle.'

'Simone, you know what I am asking.'

'General Lyon,' Hava said as she stepped into the bright beam of the torch, 'Simone is doing a report for her science class about mould. We were looking for bits of mould on the cellar walls so she can look at it under the microscope at school.'

Hava stood in that light as if she were on stage. I was afraid she was going to bow, or that I was going to applaud her clever lie.

'The cellar is no place for young women. Come up, both of you. We'll have some tea and biscuits,' my father said.

As Hava and I walked up the stairs, and my father stepped into the kitchen, Hava whispered to me, 'I will never be afraid of the dark for as long as you are my friend.'

Chapter 24

Within the first days after their invasion of Belgium, the Nazi Party created laws that confiscated Jewish property and businesses. Jewish men and women were banned from many professions. Jewish families were frightened, threatened, and eventually taken to Auschwitz.

Now, the synagogue was like that dark cellar. As we stood before the great doors of the building, Hava turned and looked back to the empty streets. I will never forget her eyes at that moment: beautiful, brown, and filled with hope. She pushed the doors open with the full force of her body, sure she would find her father, mother, and Benjamin sitting in their favourite pew.

The doors opened like a blessing, two hands parting. We stepped into the sanctuary. There were no lights, no candles. From floor to ceiling, from wall to wall, a subdued light from the rose window created shadows. A grey-black gleam filled the synagogue with a quiet darkness. It was difficult to see, like an empty cave. Hava looked at me as if to ask, *'Where is everyone?'* I took her hand and we walked down the main aisle. The synagogue was Hava's Tara; her house of salvation.

'Where is everyone?' she finally asked aloud. I squeezed her hand and said nothing. In the far corner of the synagogue there was a little chair, and sitting in the little chair was an old man with a beard and a small book in his hand.

'That's Rabbi Menke,' Hava whispered.

As we approached the old man, I saw that he was stroking the book with his open palm and whispering a prayer: 'O Lord, grant that this night we may sleep in peace.'

The rabbi looked up at us through the dim light of the morning sunrise and said in a stronger voice, 'May your paths be free from all obstacles, from when you go out until you return home.' Then he lifted one hand, curled his fingers, and pointed first at Hava, and then at me. 'We need to protect each other and inspire each other to think and act only out of love.'

'Rabbi Menke … Do you know me, Rabbi Menke?' As Hava knelt before the old man, he placed his hand on her head.

'I do not remember,' he said.

'Rabbi Menke. Where is my mother?'

The man looked into her eyes, he looked up at me, and then returned his gaze to the face of my friend. 'I do not remember.'

'Where is my mother, and Benjamin, and my father?'

'Benjamin?' Rabbi Menke asked.

'Yes, and my father Yaakov. Yaakov Yosef Daniels, my father. I need to find my father.'

The rabbi looked up at and said, 'There's no one here. They are gone.'

I knelt before the old man and asked, 'But where, Rabbi? Where have they gone?'

'They are all gone. There's no one here. Not even their shadows.

There are no more shadows. Look, no shadows, not even ashes.' He waved his hand. 'You won't find anyone here. No praying. No singing. I am told a synagogue is burning in Przemysl, Poland, so people here are afraid. There are rumours the Nazis are coming.'

'But Rabbi Menke, where is my family?' Hava asked. 'They said they'd be here.' Then she broke down and wept into the rabbi's lap.

Rabbi Menke placed one of his wrinkled hands on her head as she cried. 'Many Jews in Antwerp have already fled to Cuba. Many in Brussels have already left.'

'But my mother and father wouldn't leave without me,' Hava said between tears.

Rabbi Menke placed his hand gently under Hava's chin, lifted her face up to the light, and returned to his prayers: 'Let us pray. Oh God, keep far from us all evil; may our paths be free from all obstacles from when we go out until we return home.'

Hava looked up as she heard the words 'until we return home'.

'Return home? Yes, of course. I'll go home. My mother will surely be there by now. The sun is out. She will have to prepare eggs for Papa. Benjamin has to be roused from his sleep. The day is beginning. He'll be going to school.' Hava looked at me and said, 'We must wake Benjamin. He needs to get ready for school.'

She stood up, leaned over, and kissed Rabbi Menke on his forehead. Then she turned and ran down the aisle, through the subdued light. When she reached the open doors she stopped, turned, and motioned for me to follow. I looked at Rabbi Menke.

He said, 'Be in peace.' Then I stood up slowly and walked through the synagogue, past the empty seats: one, two ... ten ... thirty ... a thousand ... a million ... six million empty seats.

When I reached Hava she took my hand and said, 'We must

hurry or there will be no eggs left. You know how Benjamin will eat six eggs if he's given the chance.'

She pulled my hand and we ran down the steps of the Great Synagogue and out into the twilight street. Black buildings stood at attention. The trees didn't move. An empty bicycle rack had been tipped on its side.

We stopped running for a moment when we both heard the loud engines of planes once again. Six large shadows flew overhead as we stood in the empty road.

As the planes disappeared, and silence returned for a moment, Hava let go of my hand and said, 'Do you hear that?' I stood beside her and together we just listened. Yes, there was a sound we thought we recognized. 'Birds?' Hava asked.

It sounded like pages flipping in a book, and then, thousands of leaves began falling from the sky: leaves; thousands and thousands of yellow leaves.

Hava walked into the middle of the street and looked up at the early morning sky. She spread out her arms and turned slowly, round and round and round, under the falling leaves. I held my arms close to my chest. It was a cold morning.

'Simone,' Hava called out, 'look at the leaves. Aren't they beautiful?'

They were beautiful, light-yellow leaves: maple leaves? As they floated to the ground, I realized that they weren't ordinary maple leaves, but leaves made from thin paper. I looked up into the sky and watched the leaves twist and swirl through the air, and land on the buildings, the streets, and the bushes. Hava stopped suddenly, leaned over, and picked up a single leaf.

'Look, Simone,' she said as she offered me the leaf. 'Look.'

Printed on the paper leaf, above the skull of a soldier wearing a helmet, were these words:

In autumn the leaves fall.
We fall with them. In the spring
nobody will remember the dead leaves
any more than the dead soldiers.
Life will pass over your graves.

Below these words I saw the crooked cross of a black swastika. I looked at this symbol, at the skull of the soldier. I reread the words. I thought about my father and my mother's grave. I thought about dead soldiers and the black planes. I held the leaf in my hand and ran my finger over the black cross, the mark of death.

It was one of the most effective leaflets that Hitler dropped on the people of Europe during the war. A simple message: no one cared if we died.

The Nazi leaves soon covered the roads and pavements as they continued to fall from the distant planes.

We sat in the middle of the street as the last leaves fluttered down and then all was silent once again until Hava whispered, 'My family. We have to hurry.' She stood up and began to run.

The propaganda pamphlets rustled around her feet as she ran over them. They seemed to chase her as she ran down the street towards the square. I stood and called her name again and again, 'Hava! Hava!' but she did not stop.

More planes roared overhead. In the distance more bombs exploded and seconds later plumes of black smoke rose from behind the distant buildings. I could smell burning and imagined the heat of the flames against my cheeks.

CHAPTER 25

In red we see the social idea of the movement, in white the nationalistic idea, in the swastika the mission of the struggle for the victory of the Aryan man, and, by the same token, the victory of the idea of creative work, which as such always has been and always will be anti-Semitic.
Adolf Hitler, *Mein Kampf*, speaking of the Nazi flag

More bombs landed closer as the surrounding buildings shook. Hundreds of windows shattered at the same time. Splintered glass rained down on me. Vicious shards covered the street. Bricks shot into the air. The ground shook with each thump of an exploding bomb. 'Hava!' I called after her, as my friend ran and ran.

I had no one to run to. My father was with the Resistance. In that moment, Hava's family had become my surrogate family: my mother, father, brother. I began to run again, hoping to catch up with her.

When I finally reached her, Hava was standing at the edge of the square. I didn't know why she'd stopped. I was out of breath, my legs hurt. I looked at Hava, she looked at me and then, without a word, she pointed towards the building across the square.

Outside a window someone had draped a giant red flag with

a white circle, and in the white circle was a black swastika. I had never seen the Nazi flag in real life before. Of course, I had seen the image in my school books in flat black and white pictures in the newspaper, and on the propaganda leaves, but here, hanging above our heads, colours illuminated in the morning sun, it was an ominous, eerie presence that terrified me. The flag hung motionless. Hava and I stood before it and stared.

'What does it mean, Simone? Why is it here?'

The flag bulged outward in a sudden gust of wind, flapping in a mocking wave above the square.

'Is it a warning, Hava? Do we have to surrender? Is it a death flag?'

A small, horse-drawn wagon appeared carrying chairs, blankets, pots, and a stove. Sitting beside an old man at the front, an old woman with a blue scarf wrapped around her head held a thin dog on her lap.

Men pulled at the horses' reins, urging them forward, out of their way. Children clutched suitcases and ragdolls. It was as though the square had cracked open, and people started spilling out of a bowl that was breaking.

A siren blew, a wailing, plaintive sound muffled by the sudden cries of children. Mothers called out to the men to hurry.

'Where are you going?' I asked a woman with a large suitcase.

'Going? We're leaving Brussels. The Germans are coming. Run! We must all leave the city!'

A man pointed to the flag, shaking his fist. 'This is no longer Belgium!' he declared angrily.

'Take what you can!' another man shouted. 'Go west! Go south! You'll be safe in France. There are no Germans in France. Escape while you can!'

CHAPTER 26

At that time I believed in the Führer Principle because to me it meant that the best one should be the leader. If the leader is good and responsible, then the government is good.
Walther Funk, German Minister of Economics, 31 March 1946, from the Nuremberg trials

Someone tore down the Nazi flag. Hava and I watched it descend and flatten onto the cobblestone in a deceptively soft manner. Three men stopped running and stood before the fallen flag. One of them pulled a small box of matches from his pocket, struck a match on the side of the box, and touched the edge of the flag. It was quickly engulfed in flames, and swiftly reduced to ash.

It seemed that all of Brussels swirled around us like a cyclone: a tumult of people held hands, rushed down the streets, twisted in the crowd. Hundreds of people blown from their homes, uprooted from their lives, and callously tossed aside.

Hava and I stood in the eye of the storm, briefly protected from the threat of guns, bayonets, slaughter, and death. Then she whispered, 'I want to go home.'

Where is my father? I wondered to myself. We sprinted together through the streets of Brussels at the beginning of the Second World War, among the thousands of refugees spilling out of their homes, trying to get ahead of Hitler's advancing army, trying to dodge the approaching machine-gun fire and bombs from the Luftwaffe.

Hava was convinced that her family had returned home from the synagogue. 'They must have gone home when they found the synagogue empty. They would never leave me. Where else would they go?'

We made our way through a sea of sorrow and fear. Horses skittered nervously, agitated by the noise and the crowds. Children howled their distress, not comprehending the panic. A man smoking a cigar carried a poodle in one arm and a violin in the other. A woman pushed a wheelbarrow filled with books.

I stood for a moment on the edge of a fountain and looked out over the heads of people. As far as I could see there was chaos. Like oil from a motor car that had spilled onto a wet road, everything on that first morning of the war tried to mix in with the new world, but failed, finding resistance – like oil floating on rainwater.

I jumped from the wall and realized I had lost Hava. She had been swept up in the crowd.

'Hava,' I called. 'Hava!' I jumped up and down trying to spot her blonde hair in the throng of people. 'Hava!'

I remembered where she lived, and knew the streets to take, but it was like trying to walk in a vat of treacle. People were packed tightly in the streets. Fear choked the movement of every step, and every heartbeat. My legs felt heavy, my arms weak. I pushed my hair from my face. Each step forward was a challenge. People pushed me from behind, from the side. I felt like a puppet, my movements orchestrated by the machinations of others – people trying to escape, trying to save themselves. More planes flew overhead. More blasts. More destruction. The dragon had been unleashed.

As I approached the end of the square, I felt a firm grip on my shoulder. 'Hava!' I gasped in relief, as I twirled around. 'Hava?'

'What are you doing here?' a voice of command and authority barked at me. 'What are you doing *here?*' Sergeant De Waden asked again, his tone laden with anger and frustration. I tried to smile. His boots were polished, his uniform crisp. The visor of his hat was pulled nearly over his eyes. I had always been taught that if you hid your eyes, you hid your soul.

'We are trying to get everyone to return to their homes. They'll be safer there, inside.'

'But the Nazis are coming,' I said as I rubbed my arms. 'They're coming! Everyone says we need to leave!'

'The Nazis won't harm us if we listen to them.' Sergeant De Waden said stiffly.

I looked at this boy in a man's uniform, and for the first time I did not like what I saw.

'The Nazis won't harm us?' I repeated in disbelief. 'Is this not *harm?*' I pointed to a little girl dragging a suitcase, and the frightened mob swarming around us.

'You are all running for nothing,' De Waden said as I watched the girl disappear into the crowd.

'Nothing? They shot my father in the First World War, and now this? Invading our country?'

'Your father belongs to the old world of Resistance, the underground, Simone. This is the new world now. I have given up believing in resistance. The Germans are coming and we can't stop them, so we might as well accept the new order, and give up our struggle. It's safer that way – to do as they say. Where is your friend, Simone?'

'But the war has only begun. How can you say *give up*?' I couldn't believe what I was hearing from the mouth of this man, my horse-riding companion, a man I thought I might have loved.

'Look, Simone. Look up! Those are not Belgian planes. You must go back home! Where is your friend?' he repeated.

'I'm helping her find her family. They weren't at the synagogue. They've disappeared.'

'She's Jewish. You're better off keeping your distance from her. Go back to your house.'

And there it was. I wanted to shake my wooden rattle, my gragger, in disgust.

'Yes, she's Jewish,' I said as I looked directly into the eyes of the man hidden under a black visor. 'She's my friend. And she needs me.'

And I need her, I thought.

'The German troops have already crossed the border. Go home. It will be safer for you there. Just go home and I'll check up on you when I can.'

And just like that, he was gone again, and I was left alone in maelstrom.

Chapter 27

The German forces advanced rapidly. Holland fell quickly as the Dutch tried to defend their country with outdated First World War weapons. Belgium held out against the Nazi invasion for eighteen days against overwhelming odds.

Suddenly, a distant hum caught on the breeze; a persistent drone that grew louder and closer, like the vicious onslaught of a swarm of bees.

Pandemonium ensued. Children wailed. People shouted, 'Get down! Get down!'

I looked up and no longer saw the clouds and spring leaves, but something much darker that seemed to shroud the entire city. Outstretched wings soared high above my head, and what looked like the belly of a dragon.

I broke away from the mob, pushing my way between men in clogs and woman carrying crying children and baskets of bread, forcing my way towards Hava's house.

The plane swooped lower, lining itself up above the straight road leading to the square. Something ricocheted past my head and thudded into the ground at my feet. More projectiles hurtled through the air, missing me by a whisper, others not so fortunate. Bullets sprayed indiscriminately from guns attached beneath the wings of the aircraft. The gunner visible from below, unmoved, relentless ... able to see the frantic expressions of those who ran for cover; the faces of those he targeted: women, children, infants ... innocents.

I ran and managed to cower in a doorway, just as the plane turned round and came again. Once more bullets ripped through the air, through those unable to find protection.

Then the bullets stopped and the plane disappeared. All was silent for a brief moment, as if the world took a deep breath. And then there was a scream. It was almost as if the wheels of a train had locked and strained against the railway tracks, a high-pitched sound like the wail of metal against metal. Tragedy embodied that scream. Horror conveyed in a singled, anguished cry.

Before me, the cobblestones ran red with blood. The wounded moaned. Others keened their loss, clutching their lifeless loved ones to them. I thought again of the sergeant's words: *The Nazis won't harm us if we listen to them.*

When did we have the chance to listen? The enemy had spoken, not in words but actions. No one was safe.

Run! I thought. *Run! Run!* They must not get me.

I knew Hava would be in her house. I knew that was where she would be.

I ran down a familiar side street. I could see the windows of Hava's home. They were dark.

Chapter 28

The battle beginning today will decide the fate of the German
nation for the next thousand years.
Adolf Hitler's proclamation to the soldiers on the Western
Front, 10 May 1940

I have never liked the dark. I feel as if I am in a closed box and the only way out is to find a bit of light. That is why I love the stars. They always seem to say, 'This way.'

The city lights were extinguished. German planes continued to fly throughout the dark morning. I heard voices in the streets.

I had memorized a poem, in English, for Sister Bernadette, 'The Light of Stars' by Longfellow. I still remember a section:

> *Oh, fear not in a world like this,*
> *And thou shalt know erelong,*
> *Know how sublime a thing it is*
> *To suffer and be strong.*

One night, Hava and I were walking home from the opera when she pointed out the appearance of the first star in the dark sky. I told her it was not really a star, but the planet Venus. I was proud to tell her this because for once I was teaching her something she did not know.

'It was named after the Roman goddess of beauty and love,' I said as we walked through the park.

Hava took off her shoes and socks and said, 'Let's dance on the surface of Venus.'

'Hava,' I said. 'People will …'

She cut me short. 'Oh, Simone, stop worrying about what other people think. Someday you will want to be brave, eat chocolate all day, read D. H. Lawrence in church … and you will no longer care what others think.' Hava ran through the park, clapping her shoes above her head and whooping loudly.

At that time, the star of Hava's world was not Venus but the opera singer, John Charles Tillman, the love of her dreams.

Back then, Hava and I had no fear of the world. I feared others' disapproval, but not the world, and I did not know how sublime a thing it was to suffer and be strong … not yet.

Sister Bernadette had taught us that fire begins when a material that can burn is combined with something packed with oxygen and is exposed to heat. 'In a chain reaction, the fire burns and burns – like sin,' Sister Bernadette added. 'Like sin, which burns in your heart and causes a chain reaction, until your heart is nothing but a black, charred mass from the devil's oven.'

When I finally reached Hava's home that morning, I grabbed the cold, brass door knocker and knocked once, then twice. There was no response.

'Hello!' I called through the door. 'Monsieur Daniels? Madame Daniels? Hello? Hava?'

Silence. I turned the doorknob. The door was not locked. 'Monsieur Daniels? Hava?'

Weak sunlight filtered into the silent rooms, pearl light, blue light, nothing like the light of Venus or the opera. 'Hava?'

In the corner of the large room I saw her sitting on the floor, knees pulled up to her chest, head in her arms. Her legs were covered by her plain, dark dress.

'Hava?'

I found a candle and some matches. As I struck a match, a small cloud of smoke rose to the ceiling. The smell of sulphur hung in the air. The flame illuminated my hand. I lit the black wick as the flame leapt willingly from the match to the top of the candle. I carried it across the room as the candlelight danced in the darkness.

I lowered the candle and knelt next to my friend.

'Hava?'

She lifted her head and looked at me. 'Your face is yellow, Simone,' she whispered. I did not recognize the voice. When Hava spoke, you could usually imagine that you were at a circus and she was the ringmaster. But there, in the light of the candle, Hava's whisper was weak. 'They're gone.' She waved her hand in a wide, broad gesture towards the empty room. 'They're gone.'

'Perhaps they're visiting relatives.' I said quietly. 'Perhaps they were shopping when the planes arrived and now they're with relatives or friends.'

Hava stared at me. 'Let's pretend the moon is burning. Let's go swimming.'

'Hava, are you all right?'

'The moon, the cow ... let's jump over the moon and go swimming, Simone.'

Hava and I had always loved the moon. Sometimes we rolled old newspapers into pretend telescopes and looked directly into the moonlight.

'I see John Charles Tillman,' she'd say.

'I see Clark Gable,' I'd say.

I remember when Hava and I went swimming in Ixelles Pond. We dared each other to leap from a large rock and dive into the cool water. We took turns: back dives, flips, shallow dives, cannonballs, belly flops, all accompanied by much laughter.

The real idea was to impress a boy we knew, André Van Acker, the butcher's son. We knew he liked to fish at the pond early on Saturday evenings. We knew his skin was bronze and his hair the colour of wheat. Each time we swam close to where he sat, André complained that we were disturbing the fish. 'Go away,' he said irritably.

Hava and I pretended that we had turned ourselves into fish and swam closer to the boy with the fishing rod in his hand. André Van Acker reeled in his line, stood up, placed his fishing pole on his shoulder like a soldier going off to war, and then said, 'You should be ashamed of yourself, Simone Lyon.' Then he walked away into the undergrowth and disappeared.

'You see, Simone! Too many people know you and are always turning a dream into a dull Saturday night.'

That's when I jumped into the water. The moon had just risen into the early night sky. When I rose to the surface, Hava was standing on the rock in the fresh moonlight. She looked out at me and said, 'I salute you, Daughter of the General.' Then she too jumped into the water, and we swam together like newborn dolphins, our skin rippled with goose bumps.

The moon is one of the saddest objects in the sky, for it seems to go through much pain as it changes shape, enduring a passive position at the mercy of the brave sun. As the German invasion cast an evil melancholy over everything we had taken for granted, now we too found ourselves at the mercy of events beyond our ability to resist or comprehend.

PART IV: EVACUATION

CHAPTER 29

Thousands of Belgian refugees, trying to escape the Nazi invasion,
took to the Brussels–Louvain road, fleeing westward.

I didn't realize how animated objects become in a house filled with people. Tea cups jiggle on plates. Chairs move forwards and backwards under the leaf of a table. Flowers arrange themselves with dignity in a glass vase. Peanut shells tumble into a flat hand, swept suddenly into a wastepaper basket. But without people, a straw broom becomes a monument, as solid and motionless as an obelisk. Shoes seem cemented to the floor. Pencils, books, umbrellas, shawls ... they all seem to be dead.

Hava sat on the floor in her parents' home, willing the silk robe to jump onto the warm shoulders of her mother, aching to see the little paper crown jump up and adorn the beautifully shaped head of her brother. 'Where are they?' Hava asked repeatedly.

'Perhaps they're with friends?' I suggested again. 'The Arnoffs, or the Bergmanns live near the synagogue. Perhaps they're there. Sergeant De Waden said that the Germans were already across the border, heading this way into Brussels. We must leave!'

More planes marred the morning sky. The windows began to rattle under the thrum of their latest approach. I looked outside and saw an intermittent glow rise and fall over the northern section of the city.

'Hitler is very close, Hava! Pack some clothes and come with me. We'll go to my house. I need to collect some things as well. We can't stay here. We'll be killed.'. A German invasion was no longer a theoretical possibility. It was happening. People were dying in the streets. We needed to leave. But Hava wasn't moving. She seemed to mirror the inanimate household objects. She didn't look up at me. She didn't move her hands. She just sat on the floor like a brass Buddha, immobile, expressionless.

'Hava!' I pleaded with her. 'We can't stay here! Hava!'

I slumped down beside her and spoke slowly and directly. 'Hava. The Germans are coming. We can't stay here. Find a bag and some clothes. Do you know if your parents have any money in the house?'

Hava finally looked up at me and said, 'Yes, of course. Perhaps they're with the Bergmanns. I know the Bergmanns. They sit next to us in the synagogue. We can go to their home and look for my parents.'

The windows rattled again, tormented by the blasts of the latest bombing raid. 'Hava,' I begged. 'There's no time. We must hurry.'

Chapter 30

Many Belgian convents hid Jewish children during the Nazi occupation of 1940–1945, presenting them as Catholics. Among these institutions were the Franciscan Sisters in Bruges, the Sisters of Don Bosco in Courtrai, and the Sisters of Saint Mary near Brussels.

Hava stood up, her hair over her face, her shoulders slumped. I stepped up to my friend, brushed back her hair, and as she leaned into me, I whispered, 'All will be well, but we must go. Your family isn't here, but we'll find them. We need to hurry. I need to get something from my house.'

Hava, the beautiful Jewish girl, wept silently in my arms. Then she looked up and licked one of her tears. 'It tastes salty.' Hava of the opera. Hava Juliet. Hava Salomé. A Jewish girl with salty tears.

'Come on. We must hurry,' I said gently.

'Yes, okay. Let's go back to your house, Simone.'

Once in the crowded, afternoon streets, my renewed confidence quickly vanished. I wanted to be brave for Hava, but the noise, the chaos, the apprehension in the air, all filled me with a sudden and overwhelming anxiety.

As I stood on the street corner not knowing where to turn, a man nearly knocked me down. 'Run, you silly girl,' he yelled. 'Run! The Germans are coming!'

My mind spun, dizzy with helplessness. An ambulance squealed past. *We are Belgian*, I thought. *We are strong. We must endure. We must find someone to help us.* Just then, I thought about Sister Bernadette. *The convent! Sister Bernadette will protect us. She will know what to do.*

My panic subsided. I stood still and adjusted the sleeves of my dress. *I will pretend that Hava and I are just visiting a friend. I will pretend that this is an ordinary day and we are just visiting Sister Bernadette.* I grabbed Hava's arm and said, 'Maybe my teacher can help us. The convent should be safe, and if she's there, I know she'll help us.' Hava nodded, looking dazed at the surrounding confusion, but with renewed hope to continue our journey.

I knew my way to the convent. It was across the street from my school, an old building with many floors. When I knocked on the door, there was no answer. I looked back at the school. It was dark. The gates were closed. Everything seemed to have stopped as soon as the planes arrived. I stood at the convent door hoping someone would hear us.

'Knock again,' Hava suggested.

I turned and knocked again. 'We are brave Belgians,' I muttered to myself.

'Yes? May I help you?' a harsh voice called from behind the door.

'I am Simone Lyon. I'm a student at the school. Is Sister Bernadette here?'

Silence.

'She's my teacher. The planes ... the bombs ... I must speak to

Sister Bernadette. We need her help … please …' And then like the child I was, I just cried, squeezing my eyes shut, trying to prevent the tears from sliding down my cheeks. In that moment, it felt as if all of Belgium wept with me.

When I opened my eyes, the door was unbolted and there was Sister Bernadette. 'Come in, my child. Come, Simone.' I fell into her arms. The aroma of her cloth habit, the tenderness of her embrace, made me nearly say 'Mother'. And I cried some more.

'I don't know where my father is,' I said finally between sobs. 'You told me he was working at the Foreign Ministry, but I don't know where he is. My aunt went back to Luxembourg. We can't find Hava's parents; the synagogue was empty. Oh, Sister Bernadette, the planes … Before he left, my father said if the planes came, the war would begin. The planes and bombs … I'm trying to be brave, but I don't know what to do. We don't know what to do.'

Sister Bernadette unfolded her arms from around my shoulder, and produced a handkerchief from under her robe. 'Simone, you are not alone. Who is this with you?' Hava stood patiently outside in her simple dress, a small smile on her lips.

'Sister, this is Hava Daniels.' I pulled Hava closer. 'She's my friend. We tried to find her parents and brother at the synagogue, where they said that they'd be waiting for us, but no one was there. Just the rabbi, all alone. They weren't at her home either. We don't know where they are.'

'Come with me, Simone. And Hava, you too, you are also welcome, always welcome. You need something to eat, some hot soup. We cannot fight the war on empty stomachs.'

At the word 'soup' I smiled meekly, thinking about my Maginot Line, thinking about my own war soup. 'We would love soup, Sister.'

Sister Bernadette led us down a dark hall. On the wall hung pictures of saints: Joan of Arc, Saint Thérèse of Lisieux, Saint Elizabeth of Hungary. 'Now, girls, *there* are examples of brave women. Let's be brave women and have some soup.' With a small wave of her hand, Sister Bernadette pushed open a swinging door, took my hand and Hava's hand and smiled. 'Welcome,' she said, 'to a bit of hope.'

Sitting at a long table were four children, each with a yellow napkin attached to their necks, each with a bowl of hot soup, steam rising from each bowl. Sister Bernadette looked down the length of the table and said 'Children, say hello to Mademoiselle Lyon, and her friend Mademoiselle Daniels.'

In unison, the children called out politely '*Bonjour*, Mademoiselle Lyon. *Bonjour*, Mademoiselle Daniels.' A girl with pigtails stood up from her seat, walked over to me, and pulled off her yellow napkin. 'Here, mademoiselle, so you won't spill soup on your beautiful dress.' The child handed me the napkin, curtsied and ran back to her seat.

As I held the napkin in my hand, I turned to Sister Bernadette. 'Do you have a little school right here in the convent?'

'We have a secret,' Sister Bernadette whispered. 'Come with me.' Then she turned and said to the children, 'I will take our new friends to the kitchen to get them each a bowl and help put on their napkins.'

As Hava and I followed Sister Bernadette, I watched for a moment as all four children blew into their bowls, some taking small sips with their spoons, other stirring the soup. The sound of the spoons hitting their bowls reminded me of broken bells tolling.

I asked, 'Where did the children come from?'

'They're our secret,' Sister Bernadette answered. 'They're from the neighbourhood. We weren't expecting the war to start so soon, but there were rumours. We have nuns in Germany and they sent us letters about Hitler and Russia invading Poland. Apparently, Hitler's navy sank a British liner, the SS *Athenia*. Priests have been publicly executed in Poland, and all Jewish businesses in Germany have been closed.' Sister Bernadette took the yellow napkin from my hand and began to knot it gently around my neck.

'They're all Jewish children. Their parents asked if we could keep them here in secret and pretend that they're Christian orphans. Their mothers and fathers know what's happening in Germany to the Jews. When the planes arrived this morning, the parents arrived with their children. It's been prearranged for them to stay here as long as they need to.'

'They look so brave sipping their soup.'

'They are innocent. They have been told that they will be with us for a long holiday.'

'But where are their parents?' Hava asked hopefully.

Sister Bernadette pulled out another yellow napkin from a drawer, and as she adjusted it around Hava's neck she looked into her eyes and said, 'We don't know where they are. They said that they will come back when they can. They asked that we pretend their children are Christian. That's all I know.'

When we returned to the dining room, the children looked up. One girl with a bow in her hair called out, 'Mademoiselle Lyon, you look lovely in your yellow napkin.' Another child, a boy with freckles, patted the empty chair beside him. 'Mademoiselle Daniels, come and sit here.'

As Hava and I took our seats, Sister Bernadette placed bowls of soup before us. 'Do as the children do. Blow on the soup. It's very hot.'

The boy said, 'Like this, mademoiselle,' then he leaned forward, his mouth just at the edge of his bowl, and gently blew across the top of the soup. 'It's like the wind. Blow like you're a breeze, Mademoiselle Daniels. Pretend the soup is the ocean.'

'Like this?' Hava asked, and then I, too, leaned over and blew like the wind across the surface of the sea.

'When you're finished with your soup, Mademoiselle Lyon,' a girl in a red dress chimed in, 'you should lift your napkin and wipe your lips like a lady. My mother says we always have to wipe our lips like ladies, like this,' and the little girl lifted the edge of her napkin, pursed her lips, and gently tapped her mouth. Just then, a vast explosion shook the building, accompanied by the drone of planes overhead.

But the children continued blowing calmly on their soup. I gasped and looked up. Sister Bernadette lowered her eyes a bit and said gently, 'The children, Simone. Think of the children.'

Another blast. More planes. I leaned over my soup and blew and blew.

'We're here on holiday,' the girl with the bow in her hair said.

And again, there was silence. No bombs. No aircraft. After the soup the children, one by one, walked their empty bowls to the kitchen sink. Hava and I did too.

'Now, off you go with Sister Thérèse,' Sister Bernadette called out with a clap of her hands. 'Say good bye to Mademoiselle Lyon and Mademoiselle Daniels.'

As each child shook our hands, another nun ushered the group out of the dining room, and they disappeared through the door towards the dark hall of brave women.

'Hava, you might like to accompany them,' Sister Bernadette said kindly. Hava nodded and followed the children into the hall.

'Simone,' Sister Bernadette turned to me. 'Your father might not return for some time. The war has begun, and he's part of the Resistance. Here at the convent we will play our part. But you must also play your part. You must be brave and stay at your home, like your father told you. You'll be safe there. Look how brave these children are. You must be brave too.'

'But what about Hava's family? What should we do?'

'You can't save everyone, Simone.'

'No, sister, but I can try.'

'That's all any of us can do,' she said. 'Listen.'

From a room nearby, the children's voices rose in unison, as they began reciting a Jewish prayer.

'Here, O Israel: the Lord our God, the Lord is One
Hear, O Israel: the Lord our God, the Lord is One.
Praised is the Lord by day and praised by night,
Praised when we lie down and praised when we rise up.

I place my spirit in His care, when I wake as when I sleep.
God is with me, I shall not fear, body and spirit in His keep.'

In the background, Hava's voice could also be heard, as she recited the words with the children.

Minutes later, she walked back into the room and smiled gratefully at Sister Bernadette. 'It's the bedtime prayer version of the Shema for children,' she said. 'We ask God for peace and protection in the evening. It may not yet be fully night, but it feels like the end of the day.' She closed her eyes and repeated the last line again: 'God is with me, I shall not fear, body and spirit in His keep.'

'It is a beautiful prayer,' agreed Sister Bernadette, 'but I will need to teach them the *Hail Mary* if we if we are going to pretend that they're Christian children.'

At the door to the convent, Sister Bernadette once again held my hand and said, 'You're not alone. God is with you both.'

We thanked Sister Bernadette for the soup and her calm reassurance and as she closed the door, and we walked down the steps, I thought about the pictures of brave women hanging in the tranquil hallway of the convent.

Chapter 31

It is estimated that between 220,000 and 500,000 Romany people were
killed by the Nazis and their collaborators between 1939 and 1945.

By the time Hava and I reached my side of the city the moon was out, the early evening light a pale blue. I looked at the shadows of trees branching out, their wide shapes dusting the buildings. Tendrils of low mist caressed the ground.

The people in the streets seemed less frantic. There was an odd moment of calm.

'The silence, Simone,' Hava exclaimed. 'Do you hear the silence?'

There was no sound: no cars, no one selling bread. The bakery, the fishmonger, the butcher all closed, their empty windows covered with dark shutters.

'We must hurry.'

Hava and I walked briskly beside each other, her hand in mine; the hand of a pianist, an artist, or potter; the hand that washed her hair, picked lilacs, held a book or two. Hava could have been a conductor of a grand symphony. I was grateful she was my friend.

As we walked there was a sudden, vague jingling in the distance.

'Do you hear that, Simone?'

We stopped walking. Hava let go of my hand and held her hand to her ear. 'I hear them!'

'Who?'

'Listen, Simone. They're getting closer.'

There was a distinct jingle and jangle. Bayonets? Helmets? Belts of bullets and brass medals on proud chests? I folded my arms, ready to protect my arms, ready to flee the advancing Nazis troops.

'They will not cut off my arms, Hava. I won't let them.'

'Who?' Hava said.

'The Nazi soldiers. They're coming, I hear them too.'

The approaching noise included wheels against the cobblestones, pots and pans clanking together, the hooves of horses in a slow cadence.

'Simone, they aren't soldiers. They're gypsies!'

I had been on my way to school the last time I'd seen them, before the war began: two brightly painted horse-drawn wagons full of gypsies.

The wooden wheels bounced on the cobblestones and the buckets and tools that hung from the rear made a magical clatter. The horses had paper flowers stuck in their harnesses, just over their ears. Beautiful brown women, their heads wrapped in colourful silk scarves, leaned out of the small windows. Barefooted, curly headed children ran alongside.

I had been enchanted! For a girl painfully conscious of the narrow limits of home and school, the gypsies had brought awareness of the open road, the reality of other, more exotic cultures … the possibility of freedom.

'Look, Simone. Gypsies!' Hava repeated, as a brightly coloured wagon appeared under the linden trees; a brightly coloured wagon that looked like a little house on large wagon wheels. The wheels were painted yellow. The side of the 'house' was decorated with scrolls of swirls and lines. I remember the images of fruit and horses, birds and vines. The paint was maroon, dark blue, and green. Two strong, colourful horses pulled the wagon through the rising mist. A man sat high atop the wagon, guiding the horses with reins that were entwined with strings of little bells.

'I don't think they'll hurt your arms, Simone,' Hava said as we watched from the side of the road.

The wagon made its way up the street and as its shadow passed over Hava and me, the man at the reins looked down, nodded, and drove on. As it continued, a small door at the back of the wagon opened and a girl, wearing a bright purple dress and a crown of wildflowers, stood in the door frame. She waved, smiled, and then blew us a kiss.

CHAPTER 32

Julius Schreck, an early confidant of Hitler in the Nazi Party, developed the use of the skull and crossbones on the military caps of Hitler's bodyguards – the Stabswache, the Storm Detachment. This special unit evolved into the brutal special unit, the Schutzstaffel, the Protection Squad – also known as the 'SS'.

When we arrived at my house, we were both so exhausted that we managed to sleep through the night. The next morning we found Sergeant De Waden sitting on the doorstep.

'I was worried about you.' he said. 'I've been ordered to the front. The Germans are coming with their tanks and their trucks filled with soldiers. I was wrong – we aren't safe. Their paratroopers are dropping from the sky. The Albert Canal fortification has already been taken, and the Luftwaffe destroyed all of our planes at Schaffen Airfield. The border has been breached. They're coming!'

I looked at Sergeant De Waden's lips as he spoke to us about the unfolding war. They were thin, soft, the colour of raw beef.

The streets were already crowded with thousands of people evacuating the city. I remember seeing a man leading a horse attached to a country hay wagon loaded with luggage, three children, and an old piano. I'll never forget that piano – a black grand piano strapped to a hay wagon – as if challenging the German planes to destroy such an instrument of beauty.

'They have fast planes – Stukas,' Sergeant De Waden continued. 'The pilots are shooting civilians. And it's said that Rommel is leading the way.' He stared at the ground.

Everyone knew of Rommel, the greatest German general. My father thought he was a turnip.

'I'll take you to the train station,' Sergeant De Waden continued. 'The trains are still running, but I can't say for how long. I thought you'd be safe at home, but I see now that you must leave. Pack what you can, and I'll take you to the station. Hurry!'

He waited outside. There were no children asking about my father's horse. Hava and I rushed back into the house. 'I'll pack quickly,' I motioned to Hava. 'You go to the kitchen and see what food we might be able to bring.'

As Hava rushed down the narrow hall, I ran upstairs to my bedroom. I knew exactly what I wanted to take: my journal, my yellow dress, my blue dress, my shoes, my black suitcase with brass hinges, my sheets, and my pillows. I wanted to take those dresses because when my father had been promoted, I had been able, for the first time, to buy some new clothes: a yellow dress from Paris; a pair of leather walking shoes from London, and a blue dress from Brussels. I'd had plans of being a woman of the world at eighteen, and I thought I had to look the part. I wanted to shock the world with my fancy dresses. But the world was about to shock me.

I have no idea why I wanted to take my sheets and pillows. I quickly folded the dresses and gently placed them into the suitcase, and then I hurriedly tossed in the rest, slammed the suitcase shut, and secured the brass lock.

'Simone! You must hurry,' Sergeant De Waden called from downstairs. 'We must go now. They're coming!' He rushed back into the street to check on the chaos.

I dragged the suitcase down the stairs, and it made a loud clump, clump, clump. Poor Hava. She came running from the kitchen with a loaf of bread in her hand, thinking I had fallen down the stairs.

'Are you alright?' Hava asked as the front door opened. Sergeant De Waden had heard the same noise and run inside.

'I heard a crash. Are you alright, Simone?'

When I explained about the suitcase and sheets, we all started to laugh, and then a loud explosion shook the house.

'Come on. We must hurry,' Sergeant De Waden said as he lifted my suitcase and carried it through the door.

Hava and I gathered our provisions, her little suitcase, some bread and some cheese, and just before we followed the sergeant through the front door, I gasped. 'Wait, Hava! Wait!'

I dropped the bread and ran back up the stairs, down the hall, opened the top drawer of the dresser, reached in reverently, picked up my father's Croix de Guerre, and buried it in my pocket alongside Benjamin's drawing.

'Simone, hurry! We must leave!'

I ran back through the house and locked the front door behind me, perhaps for the last time.

When we walked outside the sun was bright and the sky clear except for small black dots high above us, planes flying over the city, their wings spread out like the arms of the devil.

'Get in!' Sergeant De Waden shouted as he slammed the boot of the car. The car had balloon tyres. That is what I remember – the tyres were white and thick.

Hava sat in the back with her suitcase on her lap. I sat in the front, holding our food.

Just as Sergeant De Waden closed the car door, Nicole appeared. She just looked at me as the car began to roll away. I looked back at her. She didn't smile. She didn't wave.

As we drove through the streets of Brussels, I felt like a string puppet tethered to the planes above me. If the car made a right onto the boulevard, it seemed as if the planes turned in the sky above us. If we zoomed to the left, the planes were right there.

A huge number of people were leaving the city using cars, bicycles, and wagons. Many people simply began to walk out of Brussels into the countryside.

A man pushed a bicycle, on which sat a little boy in a grey suit ready, it seemed, to attend church. A woman followed behind wearing an elegant red coat. She looked at me as I sat in the seat of the car with balloon tyres and I turned away.

I didn't know where we were going. To the train station, yes, but beyond that we had no idea. Sergeant De Waden, using his military influence, had arranged for two train tickets for Hava and me. He didn't know where the train was going. All we knew was that we were escaping the invasion. The point was to flee Brussels in any way possible, as quickly as possible.

As we drove through that sombre morning scene, the German army advanced like lightning, splitting Belgium asunder, without mercy. Artillery tracked across the sky, slamming into buildings, reducing beautiful facades to rubble. Shattered stone lintels reached upwards like supplicating fingers, silhouetted eerily against a skyline that glowed red with fire and flame. Church steeples wreathed in smoke and dust guided crying children and families towards the city limits, before they fell. One by one, Brussels' landmarks collapsed like dominoes, disappearing in the wake of the evacuees as they left behind everything they had known. The city was collapsing.

Our car zigzagged between the broken threads of a dying world, and when we reached the train station, I thought we would be swallowed up by the advancing army for sure. So many people had had the same idea – escape by train.

As I stepped out of the car, Sergeant De Waden yanked my suitcase from the boot. I stood on the suitcase to try and see what was happening, while he helped Hava. No matter where I looked, people surged together, shuffling back and forth: the tops of their heads, hats, scarves, luggage, hands waving in the air. No one, it seemed, was moving forward.

'Sergeant!' I called to him. 'Sergeant, it's impossible. There are too many people!'

Hava looked left and right. People bumped into her, twisted her around. She dropped her suitcase, scrambled for it quickly, then stood up like a post, stiff and firm.

'Hava, take my hand! My hand, Hava. Take my hand!'

Her soft white hand reached out to me through the crowd and the panicked chatter. I grabbed it and locked into her palm and fingers. Sergeant De Waden pulled out a whistle from his pocket and blew; a loud, long strident squeal of authority. The people around us suddenly stopped moving, and then my sergeant blew his whistle again and again after every fifth or sixth step. People before us stopped, turned and, seeing a military uniform, stepped aside as Sergeant De Waden, Hava, and I made our way to the train.

How foolish I was to drag that suitcase behind me. You would have thought that I was pulling a treasure chest. Finally, Hava said, 'Simone, let the suitcase go! Drop the suitcase!'

She pulled on my hand as I held the handle of the suitcase, refusing to release it.

'You can't take it with you, Simone! Let it go!'

And so I did. It was immediately swallowed by the crowd behind us, and as we took a few steps, I suddenly remembered: my journal!

'I have to go back, Hava!'

'Are you crazy, Simone? The Germans are coming! Your house is probably burning as we speak! You can't go back!'

'Not to the house. I left my journal in my suitcase. I need to get my journal!' I let go of Hava's hand, and disappeared back into the tumult.

CHAPTER 33

As Belgium collapsed under the Nazi invasion, its government was able to negotiate a plan with Hitler: Belgian factories would only produce what was needed for the population, and not military equipment for Germany. So, Berlin instituted the compulsory deportation of 200,000 Belgian workers to Germany. This was one reason so many Belgian citizens tried to flee the country and/or go into hiding.

To my right, the black engine of the train wheezed, exhaling steam, and churning coal; a creature low on the tracks, like a serpent anxious to swallow me. But before I succumbed to its venomous bite, I had to find my journal.

My journal had always been my secret companion. Since I could write, I had catalogued things that had happened to me, recorded events in my life from when I was a child, as I had transformed from a small, ugly larva to a not-quite-beautiful 18-year-old butterfly.

I *had* to find my suitcase and recover my journal.

I pushed my way through the crowd, back to where I thought I left the suitcase. And there it was, broken apart, my sheets strewn on the cobblestones like abandoned sails, ripped, covered with dirt and mud. I saw one of my pillows trampled, shredded like paper, my other pillow embraced by a man wearing a dinner suit and a top hat. He looked like John Charles Tillman, and I half-expected him to sing.

I looked again at the man in the dinner suit. He was hugging my pillow as if it were a woman, his mother, or his soul perhaps. His eyes were closed and he swayed back and forth, pressed against the back of the pillow.

Under the man's clenched hands was my journal.

Planes continued to fly overhead, their mechanical hum competing with the *chug, chug, chug* of the train's engine. My heart thumped inside me.

'*Monsieur!*' I cried out as I stood before the man. '*Monsieur!*'

He seemed to be in a trance. Flames crackled from a dress shop opposite the train station.

'Monsieur, can I speak to you for a moment?' I tapped his shoulder.

The man opened his eyes and said, 'Ah, Matilda, you've come to get me.'

To my left, two men carried a woman on a stretcher. Across the street, in the dress-shop window, two mannequins in silver evening gowns caught fire, the flames providing a relentless golden backdrop. Ash drifted down from shop's burning roof.

'*Non*, monsieur. I'm not Matilda. My name is Simone. You have my little book.'

'It is so nice dancing here with you, Matilda.' The man closed his eyes, hugged my pillow and began to sway back and forth again.

Fire crept up the legs of the mannequins.

'Monsieur, can I have my book? You have my book in your hand.' I touched the back of the man's smooth hands.

He opened his eyes again, looked at me and said, 'Matilda, after all these years, I've missed you so.'

The mannequin to the left fell forward, and crashed through the dress-shop window. Glass exploded outwards, followed by a draught of hot air. The man in the dinner suit closed his eyes, and as I touched his hand again, he released my journal, took my hand, and held it tightly. He opened his eyes.

As I looked at him, more planes flew overhead, casting their deadly shadows above the flames. The man leaned over, kissed my hand, and said, 'I'll see you tonight, Matilda, when I return from the office.'

'I'll be waiting for you,' I whispered.

The dress shop imploded as the walls and roof collapsed, setting light to the bakery next door as it fell.

'Simone!' Hava yelled from a distance. I saw her, and then I didn't. Then I saw her again. As people rushed between us, she waved and jumped up to see me better. 'Simone! The train!'

The train's engine exhaled great amounts of steam. The whistle blew. I forced my way through the throng, to reach Hava. 'I've got my journal.' I waved it above my head.

She grabbed my hand and pulled me through the crowd, pulling so hard that I thought I would end up looking like the Venus de Milo after all.

Jack and Jill went up the hill to fetch a pail of water. That is what I remembered as Hava and I held hands and ran to the side of the train. Like a bull, the train bellowed, inhaling and exhaling smoke. The heat of the steam billowed around my legs, as we managed to reach the first car behind the engine. I wanted to touch the side of the train, to feel its skin, its heart; to tame the beast and beg it to take us away from the planes. People pushed us from behind; others were crushed ahead of us. The conductor tried to maintain order.

'We must get on the train!' Hava yelled. 'We must.'

Jack fell down and broke his crown, and Jill came tumbling after. Either I was going to tumble and break my crown, or Hava was going to tumble and break hers. It was clear that we were not getting on that train. The engine settled into a steady huff, huff, huff. Steam poured from its nose. There was a sudden lurch, as the engine's large wheels began to spin, then stopped.

'Step aside!' someone ordered. 'Step aside!' Hava squeezed my hand. We stood in place, immobile with horror and disappointment. *Jack and Jill.*

'Step aside! Step aside!' The voice increased in intensity, followed by a loud whistle. 'I command you to step aside.' People behind us made room for a man in uniform, a soldier, a man with a whistle: Sergeant De Waden. 'I said, step aside.' He blew his whistle once more.

Sergeant De Waden walked right up to me, looked into my eyes, and said in a voice much louder than necessary, 'You are the daughter of Major General Joseph Lyon?'

'Sergeant, you know who—'

'Mademoiselle, I asked you a question,' he repeated, making sure the conductor heard him. 'Are you Simone Lyon, daughter of Major General Joseph Lyon?'

A woman carrying a brown piece of luggage leaned over and said, 'I saw your father on his horse in the king's garden.'

A man with a beard and a purple handkerchief protruding from his shirt called out '*Vive la Belgique!*' and he tried to pat my shoulder, but Sergeant De Waden pushed him aside.

The conductor then raised his voice: 'Make way for the general's daughter!'

Hava and I began walking slowly towards the small steps that led onto the train. It seemed that everything had stopped. People stopped pushing. What I thought was the train's heart was my own heart banging inside my chest. Hava let go of my hand and stepped up on to the train.

I turned to Sergeant De Waden before following her in and said, 'You bought two tickets. You bought one for Hava too. I thought you warned me to stay away from her because of who she is.'

Steam from the train filled the platform.

'I knew I'd have an easier time convincing you to leave if she was leaving too. Also, I know what she means to you, and I wanted to honour that. I wanted to honour you, Simone Lyon.' And then finally he kissed me, before pushing me gently, but firmly, on to the train.

I took a step, then a second, and when I stood just inside the train, I turned around. There was a sudden roar. People clapped. People exclaimed, '*Vive la Belgique!*' 'Long live General Lyon!' 'Long live the general!' Then they began to wave their hands and I looked at the people with compassion as the bakery continued to burn.

Sergeant De Waden didn't wave. He just stared at me.

The train lurched forward once again, but this time the wheels engaged. I waved back to the crowd, which had suddenly turned back into individuals: children wearing brown hats; women in long black coats; men carrying sacks on their shoulders.

I looked down at Sergeant De Waden. He looked up at me and smiled. I smiled back and bowed my head slightly, grateful for what he had done.

I never saw him again. He died in the Battle of the Bulge, and was found curled up in a ditch, with a bullet in his chest.

Chapter 34

Many Jews and Romanies were spared the concentration camps because of the Belgian Resistance. One group, the Comité de Défense des Juifs, successfully attacked a train carrying over 1,500 Belgian Jews on the way to Auschwitz.

'Mademoiselle Lyon,' the conductor said, as he touched my shoulder, 'Your friend is in her seat waiting for you. Some people gave up their seats for you.' He smiled and led me to my seat next to Hava, who was looking out of the window.

As the train gained speed, trees, people, and buildings began to blur into each other. No one spoke. We were escaping. We were leaving Brussels. We did not know where the train was going, but I did know we were going west, in the direction of the setting sun and the sea. East was Germany, Hitler, the invasion, the attacking soldiers. West, we were going west. No one spoke. I saw a man smoking, his lips were shaking, making his cigarette bob up and down. A woman leaned her head against the widow, her cheeks stained with silent tears. The conductor slowly adjusted his necktie, exhaustion etched into his face. My legs felt cold against the hard seat and I was glad Hava was with me.

The train rumbled onwards, jerking slowly and swaying from side to side along the tracks. My eyes became heavy and my fears subsided a bit. When chased by a dragon, you have to find a place of safety and rest, renew your strength, and eat a little. Somehow, I had dropped our food in the confusion of reaching the train, so Hava and I had nothing to eat, but at least we could rest as it seemed we were pulling away from the dragon's fire.

Hava leaned her head against the window. I leaned my head back against the seat and closed my eyes. I wanted to sleep. I had to sleep, but then I heard Hava. She whispered my name. And then she began to speak.

I opened my eyes.

'Where are they?'

'Who, Hava?'

'My parents. Is my father here?'

'Hava, we're on the train. Your father isn't with us.'

'Did my mother remember to bring us liquorice?'

'Hava?'

She looked at me. Her eyes were glassy, her cheeks sunken.

'Do you have any liquorice, Simone?'

'No, I have no liquorice.'

'Ask my mother. She always has liquorice in her bag.'

'She's not here, Hava. She's with your father.'

Hava closed her eyes again, and leaned her head back against the window glass. Behind her, trees and hayfields blurred past like modern paintings.

Then, for no reason it seemed, Hava began to tell me the story of Rosh Hashanah. The wheels of the train created the background cadence of her words; the houses, trees, factories, and fields passing by added to the motion in Hava's story. She was half-asleep, dreaming, speaking.

'Rosh Hashanah is when we practise *tashlikh*. It means "casting off". On the afternoon of Rosh Hashanah last year, I took Benjamin to the duck pond in the park. You're supposed to find flowing water, a stream, a river, even the sea. But with no flowing water in the city, I decided the duck pond in the park was good enough. On Rosh Hashanah we cast off our sins. We throw bits of bread into the water, sending off our sins from the previous year.

'Benjamin and I carried bread in a small basket to the pond. Anyone would have thought we were there to feed the ducks, but we were really there for atonement. Well, I was there for atonement. Benjamin really did just want to feed the ducks.'

The train car jostled back and forth.

'*Tashlikh*, Simone, *tashlikh*. When we throw the bread into the water, when we throw our year's sins into the water, we say the words from Micah: *Who is a God like you, who pardons sin and forgives the transgression of the remnant of his inheritance?* I asked for God's forgiveness.'

'Hava, I don't understand,' I said, wishing I could reassure her.

'Simone, where's my father? Where are Benjamin and my mother? The rabbi said that they were gone. Where's forgiveness? Where are they?'

Hava looked at me as if I were a sage with answers. Then she leaned back once again and closed her eyes. We were moving in time, in colour, to the sound of the train, moving west towards the sea.

Shortly after her story, the bombing raids started again. I hadn't expected bombs or planes. I thought that once we had escaped Brussels, we would be able to outrun the Germans. At first, I thought the dull thud was a mechanical error in the engine. It sounded like someone had dropped a heavy sack in the next carriage. When it happened a second time, we heard screams coming from another car. The train slowed. The shadow of a plane rippled over the distant field; the shape of its wings bent with the hills, its dark tail swaying back and forth as it moved over the trees.

I remember the conductor as he walked through the carriage. His uniform was clean and blue. His cap was round, flat on the top, his visor giving him just enough authority to suggest he had everything under control. He looked at me and said, 'The Nazis have captured Eben-Emael.' That was the second day of the German invasion: 11 May 1940.

I sighed and looked out of the train window. Shadow after shadow of planes sped over the landscape. The trees were wounded, some blown apart to the roots. Telegraph polls were slumped, their wires cut and dangling to the ground. It felt as if Belgium had been ransacked by a plague. My momentary sense of calm gave way to a new rush of dread.

Hava looked up at the diseased sky. 'The monkeys, Simone! Remember the witch's monkeys in the Land of Oz?' Would we be caught, like Dorothy?

We heard the voice of the train conductor in the distance arguing with a passenger. The train stopped. The black aircraft kept flying overhead.

'Monkeys,' Hava said as she closed her eyes in fear. The planes droned above us, biting the air. 'They're coming closer. We can't hide in the train, Simone.'

The conductor re-entered our carriage. 'We can't continue. There's word the tracks have been blown up. We must evacuate.'

'Where are we?' I asked the conductor.

'Roeselare.'

Then he pulled out a silver whistle from his pocket, blew into it three times, and announced as he walked through the train, 'Everybody out. End of the line. Everybody out. End of the line.'

'Roeselare!' I turned to Hava. 'My cousin lives in Roeselare. She'll help us.'

My cousin, Marie Armel, was eighteen years older than I was. She was my father's niece. Both my uncle and aunt had died in a car accident when Marie was twenty-five, and she had inherited their house on the outskirts of Roeselare, as well as some money. She was a banker and an influential citizen of the town.

'She has a large home, Hava. I visited there once as a girl.'

Just as we stepped down from the train, a German plane dived overhead, its machine gun opening fire rapidly and viciously. Bullets flew in all directions, pelting the train, shattering the windows. People ducked and cried out in fear. A piece of glass cut my cheek. I grabbed Hava's hand. 'Run!' I gasped.

Hava and I rushed down a small hill, through a narrow field, and towards the dark woods. I saw another plane in the distant sky, dropping lower and lower. Hava picked up a rock and threw it in the air as if believing she could hit the plane and knock it from the sky. The pilot began shooting; I saw a man to my left fall as bullets tore through his body. A woman jumped into a ditch and threw herself over a little girl in a blue jacket. I yanked Hava's hand as we ran across the field and into a thick grove of peach trees.

The train was exposed like a defenceless snake in the road.

People didn't know whether to stay inside, or jump and run. The train's engine still churned and groaned. More planes flew overhead, shooting and snarling. People screamed. That's when Hava began to laugh.

Blood oozed from a woman's leg. Children were crying. But Hava laughed. She stood up and reached for a branch. 'It's so beautiful,' she said. 'Look at the peach blossom. It's really beautiful. My mother always celebrates New Year of the Trees. It's a minor festival, Tu B'Shevat. She buys spring fruit: a piece for Benjamin and one for me. Then Benjamin and I go from door to door collecting money to plant trees. We celebrate the trees. See how beautiful it is? Stand up, Simone. Look at the peach blossom.'

A flash of light spread over the horizon. Explosions rocked the ground. We felt the tremor under our feet where we hid.

'My mother cuts the blossoms and makes a bouquet for the table. When the flowers bloom, we know spring has arrived. I'll take her some peach blossoms, Simone. She'll be waiting for us when we go home.'

Hava reached up and broke off a small branch covered in delicate pink blossom like bits of candy floss.

A bomb smashed into the last carriage on the train, throwing shrapnel into the air which rained down on those still trying to escape. Hava looked out across the field as flames engulfed the train. 'My mother says that we have to take care of the world.'

The blazing wreckage was reflected in Hava's eyes, and we felt the heat against our bodies. The train carriages burned one by one. First the inside filled with smoke, and then the roof caught fire and smoke billowed upward: black smoke, a long plume of smoke, burning the arms of the seats, shattering and melting the windows. The outside skin of the train first turned a glossy black, then ignited. A sudden down-draught caused the smoke to move flat along the ground, closer and closer to us, until it embraced us, surrounded us. The fire burned bright and furious. Hava and I began to cough. Once again, I grabbed her hand and pulled her deeper into the woods.

'You can tell me more later, Hava,' I said as we ran.

The acrid smell of burning followed us. As I looked back, flames danced beyond and between the trees. The flickering light pushed forward, trying to reach us. The smoke followed like a wolf on padded feet, silent, deadly – Nazi smoke. We ran, pushing branches out of our way, stumbling over roots and stones. Hundreds of people ran alongside us through the woods, trying to escape the fire, the smoke ... the German planes shooting at us. Coughing, choking, we ran.

As the people scattered, and we were suddenly alone, I heard the soft sound of running water. Just beyond a small ridge, we found a silver stream.

I remembered a story Hava had told me the first time she and I drank water together from the fountain pool in our town square: 'There was a rabbi. Two hundred years ago he wrote, "If we walked in the woods and a spring appeared just when we became thirsty, we would call it a *miracle*. And if we became thirsty at just that same point again, and again the spring appeared, we would call it a *coincidence*. But if the spring were always there, we'd take it for granted and cease to notice it. Is that not miraculous still?"'

I believed in miracles. I still do. The train was burning. Hava and I were exhausted, thirsty, and afraid. Finding that stream of water seemed like a miracle to me. Hava leaned over, cupped her hands, and scooped the cool water into her mouth again and again. It dripped down her chin. Her face was wet. She was crying.

'The rabbi said they were gone. Where could they have gone?' She looked up at me. I knelt beside Hava, my friend, and held her against me as she wept.

'We'll go to Roeselare, Hava. My cousin, Marie Armel, lives in Roeselare. It's not far from here.'

Chapter 35

Hitler authorized the killing of mentally and physically disabled children and adults to protect the 'purity' of the Aryan race and the Nazi dreams. By August 1941, as a result of the programme, over 70,000 disabled German and Austrian individuals had been given lethal injections or had been murdered in the gas chambers.

As we sat by the stream, Hava washed her face. 'The Germans won't find a filthy Jewish girl lost in the woods. I will look pretty, and dignified.'

As she scrubbed her cheeks, I thought back to another day not too long ago, when Hava had been determined to look pretty. She had showed up at my door that day with a box under her arm.

'We're going to make ourselves beautiful,' she announced as she pulled from the box a boiled beetroot, a canister of tea, and a pencil. I laughed.

'Beautiful?'

Hava ignored my scepticism as she grabbed a cup and a rag from the counter. She placed the boiled beetroot in the rag, and held it over the cup.

'Now watch, Simone.' She squeezed the beetroot, and as she did, its juice seeped through the fabric and into the cup. 'I read an article about American girls and how there isn't much red lipstick available. So, they use beetroot juice and rub it on their lips.'

'Hava.' I said rolling my eyes, 'I am not rubbing beetroot juice on my lips.' But as I spoke, Hava dipped her finger into the juice and rubbed it slowly onto her lips, which gradually acquired a deeper red, a blush.

She tilted her head a bit, modelling her new look, and asked, 'So what do you think?'

I dipped my finger into the beetroot juice and slowly rubbed it onto my lips. 'I think even Clark Gable would be impressed.' Hava giggled.

Then we made tea, because Hava had read that if we rubbed tea onto our legs, they'd turn a shade darker and make it seem like we were wearing stockings. She also drew a line on the back of my legs with the pencil, which added to the stocking illusion.

We stood before the mirror in the hall. Our lips were red, our legs tanned. I wished that my hair looked like Greta Garbo's.

'Now we need to smoke and read Hemingway,' Hava declared with conviction.

'What!' I laughed as she stretched out on the couch and pretended to smoke a cigarette. And, just like that, we were two American girls at a party of the Great Gatsby; sophisticated women with red lips and expensive stockings. And I did feel beautiful that day.

Now, by the stream, Hava wet her hands once again and gently washed my face.

'You could use some bright red lipstick, Simone,' she said as she stood up, reached down, and pulled me to my feet. 'We'll not be dirty when the Nazis capture us. We'll be elegant Belgian women.'

Although I could still smell the burning train, and the metallic-tasting air scratched at the back of our throats, I tried to convince Hava that we were not going to be captured, that we were going to find my cousin. 'She'll help us, and feed us, and give us advice. She's a banker.'

'Okay, Simone. Let's go and find your cousin.'

I was relieved at Hava's new-found courage.

'We must look for the steeple,' I urged. 'My father said that if we're ever lost, we just have to look to the horizon for a steeple and we'll find our way.'

'Simone, all I can see is smoke and trees.'

'This way. I'm sure Roeselare is in the east. Look at the sun. We'll walk east, this way.' I pointed. It was as good a direction as any, with the burning train to our backs and the woods to hide us from the planes.

And so we ran east.

I stumbled once and bruised my knee. Hava stopped and extended her hand to me saying, 'Come on. We must hurry before the planes return.'

I stood up and brushed the dirt from my legs. It seemed as if Hava and I had been running from the Nazis for weeks, when it had only been a single day.

As we hiked deeper into the woods, we realized that the dense trees blocked the sinking sun and we were walking in near darkness. Thick bushes grabbed us, trees leaned over like angry gods, the rotten leaves of the previous autumn made the ground unstable.

We were lost.

I placed my hand on my chest to feel my heartbeat as Hava walked ahead of me, pushing low branches aside. Now and again she turned and said, simply, 'Okay?'

And each time I answered, 'Okay.'

It was obvious that we would not find Roeselare before nightfall. I stumbled once again, tripping on an exposed root. 'Hava!'

She was immediately at my side, helping me to stand when I said, 'Look, there, through the trees. A light.'

Hava turned to where I pointed and the two of us stood still, looking at the small flicker of light that winked between the trees.

'Is it a lantern, Hava?'

'Maybe it's the moon.'

'Maybe it's a coven of witches,' I teased.

'It can't be witches. They've probably all flown to London already.' I wished right then that we could hop on two magic broomsticks and fly to London, escaping the invasion that followed us like a hungry wolf.

'It's a house, Simone! There, in the clearing.'

As we approached the light, the trees thinned, a field opened, and a small house with a red roof appeared in the growing dusk. I wanted to run towards the house, but Hava held my hand and gently pulled me back.

'We don't know who lives there, Simone.'

'All I know is it isn't Hitler and we're wet, tired, and hungry, Hava. So, you can follow me or fly on a broomstick to London.' I shook her hand loose, began to run, and soon Hava was at my heels.

When we reached the house, I felt as if we were invaders, stepping into a fairy tale we were forbidden to enter, but I knocked on the door anyway.

Smoke curled from the chimney. Two small windows stared at us with tired, dim eyes. There was no sound from within.

Hava stepped in front of me and pounded on the door. 'Hello? Hello?'

From deep inside the house rose a voice like the growl of a bear. 'What do you want?'

I jumped away from the door as if it were about to burst into flames. Hava stood her ground. 'We are Belgian girls. We're running away from the war.'

Silence.

I bent down and picked up a stone. 'Tell him our names.'

'Our train was bombed. My name is Hava and I'm with my friend Simone.'

'Go away,' said the bear, his voice slow and deep.

I stepped in front of Hava with the stone ready in my hand. 'Monsieur! We are hungry and lost. Please help us.'

Silence.

A distant explosion.

Silence.

'My name is Simone Lyon! My father ...' But before I could continue, Hava and I heard the turn of a heavy lock and the door opened slowly.

'My father is General Joseph Lyon,' I stated determinedly.

'Did your father teach you to throw stones at old men?' the figure at the door asked, glancing at the stone in my hand. I looked down at my hand as Hava grabbed the rock and tossed into the bushes.

The bear turned out to be a short man with a wrinkled face, his body bent, his hair dishevelled. He studied us, and then sighed, 'You look like strong Belgians. Come in. Close the door.'

The front room had a table covered in a green cloth with stars embroidered on the edges. There were four chairs, an outdated calendar on one wall, and a cuckoo clock on another.

'I can offer you bread and stew. But you must stay here, at this table. Then you must go.'

'We have nowhere to go tonight,' I said. 'We were on our way to Roeselare but we got lost.'

The old man nodded. 'I'm Jacques Dormond, just a woodcutter.' He gestured towards the table.

'Do you think it's safe?' I whispered to Hava. She shrugged as she pulled up a chair, so I took a seat beside her.

Just then, the cuckoo clock struck seven. A small white and blue bird popped out from a door at the peak of the clock. *Cuckoo. Cuckoo. Cuckoo.* At the fourth call of the bird, a husky, low laughter followed, and continued to follow the fifth *cuckoo*, the sixth *cuckoo*, the seventh *cuckoo*.

'Ignore that. Here … your stew.'

But the laughter continued from the inner room: a guttural laughter, laughter filled with the sound of drool and grunts and spit.

Hava stood up from the table. 'Monsieur Dormond!' she entreated. 'Someone is choking in the next room!'

'It's nothing. Please, sit.'

Once again there was laughter, then a loud outburst of coughing.

'It's nothing. It's just my son. He likes the bird in the clock.'

But when the laughter in the other room turned into gasping, one gasp after another, Monsieur Dormond rushed to the other room. Hava and I saw him lean over a chair and, as we stepped quietly to the room's entrance, we found Monsieur Dormond cradling a distorted figure in his arms. Was it a child? A man? We could not tell.

Monsieur Dormond looked up at us. 'Here, this is Joff. He's my son.'

Sitting in a wooden chair in the middle of the room was the bent figure of a young man. His hair tumbled over his face. He had no shoes. His feet were twisted. 'Whenever the clock strikes the hour, he laughs. That's the only time he ever laughs.'

I was repulsed. This man, this half-man, drooled again, gurgled, and spat on the floor, then gasped. 'He just needs a spoonful of his medication,' Monsieur Dormond sighed, reaching to the nightstand for a bottle and a spoon.

I stood to one side, watching Joff rock back and forth in the chair. He looked up at me and grinned, his teeth crooked, his face like a rabid dog.

Hava quietly approached Monsieur Dormond. 'Can I do that?' She asked easily, with freedom, with compassion.

Monsieur Dormond hesitated, then handed Hava the bottle and spoon. 'A spoonful when Joff begins to gasp is all he needs. He'll open his mouth for you; just touch the tip of the spoon to his lips.' Hava uncorked the little bottle and slowly poured a dose of medicine into the spoon. 'Yes, like that.'

'Here, Joff. For you.' Hava gently touched the spoon to Joff's lips. I looked at Hava's eyes as she held the spoon firmly in her hand. I noticed in them a tenderness, a light, and her face seemed to change to something angelic.

Joff opened his mouth. His face contorted. She brushed back his hair gently. Joff closed his lips around the spoon, swallowed the medication, and then reached up to touch Hava's hair.

'No, no Joff,' his father scolded.

'It's okay. He can touch my hair.'

A crooked hand with twisted fingers rose from the crumpled man in the chair. Like a knot of rope, Joff rolled his hand over

Hava's head using his knuckles instead of his fingers to touch her hair. A thin smile appeared across his pale face.

'Thank you, Belgian girl. Joff doesn't smile often.'

I felt like a sinner watching how comfortable Hava was with Joff. Hava, my friend.

'Joff must sleep now. Will you help me carry him to his bed? It's why I was glad that you looked strong. I hurt my shoulder this afternoon splitting wood. I could use the help.'

'How?' Hava asked.

'Go behind him, behind the chair, and place your hands under his arms. And you,' Monsieur Dormond pointed at me, 'place your hands under his thighs, and then you can both lift him to the bed.'

Joff felt like a light bag made of bones and hair. He gurgled and shook. As Hava and I carried him to his small bed in the corner, Monsieur Dormond called out instructions. 'To the left a bit, now parallel to the bed. Closer to the side. Place him gently on the mattress, on his side. Joff likes to sleep on his side.'

As Joff rested his head on a pillow, he closed his eyes and slept. We watched Monsieur Dormond pull a thin blanket up to his son's shoulders. 'He was born like this. His mother died in childbirth. I thought Joff would die too, but look at him now, 26 years old. He laughs when he hears the cuckoo clock. Now, eat your bread and stew.'

Hava and I ate, and slept that night in a small loft above the house. The next morning, we found a note on the table:

Joff sleeps until noon. I had to make an early delivery of wood to the local school. I have little, but you are welcome to take what bread is left, and there's cheese. Mademoiselle Lyon, when Joff was born, there was an article about your father's wound and what he did for Belgium in the trenches. He gave me the courage to love Joff. Take the path beyond the house. It will lead you to a stream. Follow it and it will take you straight to Roeselare. Mademoiselle Daniels, thank you for your tenderness towards my son.

CHAPTER 36

The German army would soon break through at Sedan. This was
the reason for the panic in Brussels. This was the reason why two
million refugees had fled, in fear of the invading Nazi troops and
its heavy artillery; why the roads were clogged with thousands and
thousands of people running away, attempting to save themselves and
their families. And to add to the chaos, British and French forces were
coming from the east to fight the Germans.

That morning, after we left the cottage, Hava and I reached the
stream. We ate the small bits of bread and cheese Monsieur
Dormond had left us, and Hava washed her face again, repeating her
conviction: 'The Germans won't find a filthy Jewish girl.'

I asked Hava, 'How come you were you so comfortable with
Joff, his distorted face, all that drool and spit?'

She shrugged. 'He made me smile.'

The woods in May had a pungent aroma of soil and forgotten
leaves oozing into the earth after the winter thaw. The bark on
the trees was wet and dark. Mist rose from the ground. We started
seeing other people, moving quickly among the trees, appearing

and disappearing in the fog, carrying suitcases, babies. A man came upon us suddenly, a silver candelabra clutched in his right hand. He stepped close to me and said, 'All that lives must die', and then he disappeared into the trees, raising his candelabra above his head like a trophy.

Hava and I walked in those woods together, hand in hand, like children in a Russian fairy tale. Mushrooms seemed to guide our way. The oak trees were old, stiff, and thick. The roots of pine trees bulged up from the ground. The more we walked, the smaller I felt. The undergrowth was dense. The ferns were the size of elephant ears. There was little colour: just grey, black. Through the tops of the trees, I could see the blue morning sky, and I thought that somewhere in the world, people were sitting on beaches on hot sand under a blue tropical sky.

We continued to walk down the sloped terrain, passing patches of wild grass and then tangled trees again. Then, the woods opened and there were hundreds of daffodils scattered in the open spaces, clustered in groups like gossips at a party.

How ironic, I thought. *The arrival of spring and the arrival of the Nazis.*

Hava saw it first, the top of a red roof through the trees. 'Like Tara,' she said. 'Like Tara ... still standing. Roeselare!'

The small city unfurled like a quilted blanket as Hava and I trudged out of the woods and into the streets. People were in a rush, but there didn't seem to be any panic, nor people leaving the city. Belgian flags were draped from the windows of apartment buildings. A boy on a blue bicycle hurried past us as he urged on a little girl who lagged behind on her red bicycle. 'You're too slow, Veronique! Let's go!'

Hava looked at herself in the window of a bakery and adjusted her hair. The shelves in the bakery were empty. A woman with a bucket of freshly cut chicken heads stepped out of the next shop.

'Are you a gypsy?' the woman asked as she looked at me.

'No, madame,' I said. 'I'm from Brussels. Our train stopped. There were bombs.'

The woman looked at my dirty dress. 'We don't want trouble here.'

'Tell her who you are,' Hava said as she stood beside me.

'And you? Are you a gypsy?'

Hava stepped up and said, 'No, madame. I am a Jew.'

'What's your name?' the woman said turning back to me. She placed the bucket of chicken heads onto the ground and took out a small pad and pencil.

I looked at Hava, and then I said to the woman, 'I'm Simone Lyon. I'm the daughter of Major General Joseph Lyon.'

The woman lowered her pencil and looked up. 'General Lyon?'

'Yes, madame.'

'Can you prove you are his daughter?'

I reached into the pocket of my skirt and pulled out my father's Croix de Guerre. His name was engraved on the reverse side: Joseph Lyon.

I handed the medal to the woman. She reached out with her wrinkled hand. I noticed the dirt under her fingernails as she ran her fingers over the cross and the crown. When she turned the medal over and saw my father's name, she said, 'He is a great man. He used a shovel to save Belgium.' She looked at me, then at Hava and, as she handed back the medal, she said, 'Wait here.'

The woman turned and walked back into the empty shop. Hava was surprised that I had the medal.

'You always say that my father has army spies all over the world keeping an eye on me. I figured if that were true, and I needed to prove to someone who could help us that I was his daughter, that this might help.' I stuffed the medal back into my pocket.

The woman returned and handed me a loaf of bread and a chocolate bar. 'Take this.' She glanced at Hava, and then said to me, 'Be careful.'

I thanked the woman as she picked up her bucket of chicken heads and walked down the street in the dim morning light, hunched, grey, the bucket in her left hand, her right arm swinging slightly with the movement of her heavy body.

Hava and I walked for a few moments, looking for a place to rest and eat our bread and chocolate. We were tired and hungry. 'There,' Hava pointed, 'on the steps of that building.'

Across the street sat a large building with columns, tall, wide windows, and steps made of marble. The steps were empty, so we took our seats at the top where the sun bathed them with warmth. I broke the bread in half.

'I'm not a gypsy, Simone. I'm a Jew.'

'But you still need to eat, Hava.'

'That woman didn't speak to me. I was invisible to her.'

'We are all invisible to people who are blind, Hava.'

We ate our bread in silence, and as we finished, we leaned back against the wall, the sun and breadcrumbs on our dresses. Then Hava spoke.

'When I was little my father taught me about Kiddush Levanah, the blessing of the moon. He said that blessing the moon is like saying hello to God, and that each new moon reminds us of creation, how everything was born from the darkness. The light was born, like the moon being born in the night.'

Hava's dress clung to her body like a collapsed silken tent, conforming to the shape of her shoulders and hips; her arms white, like alabaster, or marble, or covered with a fine white powder.

'My father says the universe is a masterpiece,' Hava continued. 'Often we walk to the park to greet the new moon. We stand together, my father and I, facing east with our prayer books in our hands, and then we recite Psalm 148. And here's the fun part ...' Hava stood up. 'We lift our heels three times and talk to the moon. We say: "Blessed is your Maker; blessed is He who formed you ... Just as I leap toward you but cannot touch you, so may all my enemies be unable to touch me harmfully ..."'

Hava lifted her heels three times. 'See? Even as we cannot touch the moon, so our enemies cannot touch us. And my father always reminds me that when we say such prayers, we speak about our enemies, so we must also speak of peace.'

Hava closed her eyes. I unwrapped the chocolate bar and placed a piece on the flat of her palm. It was as if I had placed the entire world on her hand: she pulled it to her lips, licked it once, and then popped it into her mouth. The chocolate tasted sweet, warm.

'What are you two doing here?' Two men in military uniforms that I did not recognize stepped out of the building. One man had a moustache, the other a riding crop and a briefcase.

'This is a military post, not a ladies' lounge.'

I asked the soldier with the moustache if he knew how to get to Rue St Germaine, my cousin's street. He glared down at us, then sighed.

'Go straight down there, and take the third street on your right.' I was going to thank him, but he turned abruptly and marched off with his companion down the long steps.

As we walked, I told Hava about Marie Armel. 'She's very

smart. She seems to know things about the world.'

'I hope she knows how to make pea soup. I would love pea soup. I'm so hungry, Simone.'

When we reached Rue St Germaine, I looked down the street. 'There's her house! It's the one with the yellow door. That one!'

CHAPTER 37

Berlin ordered that identification cards of Jews in Belgium be specially
marked, and ordered the immediate dismissal of Jews from government
employment. Jews could no longer be teachers, lawyers, or journalists.

I was so grateful to see that yellow door.

As Hava and I stood before Marie's house, she looked at me. I
looked at her. I wanted to cry, but instead, I knocked on the door.

A voice from within the house called out. 'Yes?'

'Marie Armel?'

'Yes? What do you want?'

'It's Simone Lyon. Your cousin Simone.'

The lock was released from the other side with a small metal
click. Marie looked out through the partially opened the door.
'Simone?' She opened the door wider. 'What are you doing here?'

I rubbed my arms as I stood at the door. 'The Germans have
bombed Brussels. We took a train.' When I said 'we', Marie looked
to my left and eyed Hava.

'This is Hava, my friend. She escaped with me.'

Marie looked at me again, but didn't smile. 'Come in.'

Under my first step into the foyer, my heel clicked against the polished, marble floor. On the wall was a painting of sea lavender in blossom, with a calm ocean in the distance. A clock ticked. Marie led us into the parlour, a room with overstuffed velvet chairs and a grey couch that looked like an elephant resting on its side.

Marie was the daughter of my father's eldest brother, a wine merchant. He and his wife had died in an accident when Marie was twenty-five and I was seven. Theirs was the first funeral that I had attended. I remembered the coffins being lifted onto the back of a black wagon pulled by two black horses.

'How is your father?' Marie asked.

'I haven't heard from him in a long time. When the German planes arrived overhead, I was in the park. I ran home, then Hava came to my house and we went out looking for her family. They said they'd be at the synagogue, but they weren't there. No one was there, except the rabbi, who told us everyone had gone. We don't know where they are. We never found them.' I glanced at Hava, whose eyes were brimming with tears.

Marie stroked her powdered cheek with her left hand when I said the word 'synagogue'.

'The planes kept coming, shooting at us! Bombs were dropped. Buildings burned. We ran to the train station and took the first train that was leaving the city.'

Hava sat motionless beside me. She didn't speak. Her knees were together, her hands folded on her lap.

'The train couldn't continue as the tracks had been damaged. Then the planes caught up with us and the bombing started again. The train caught fire, so we ran into the woods. The planes kept shooting at us, but we were protected by the trees. The conductor said that we weren't far from Roeselare and I remembered that you lived here. A woodcutter let us spend the night in his home, then gave us directions here.'

There was an awkward silence. My cousin stood up from her chair. I heard the ticking from a large clock embedded in the belly of a bronze Greek warrior that sat triumphantly on the mantelpiece of the empty fireplace.

'I have my profession to think of,' Marie said as she looked at Hava. 'I have a delicate position in my bank, Simone.'

Marie looked at me and then back at Hava.

'Money is built on trust. The people in my community trust me to follow orders … The Germans will be here soon, and we've been instructed to comply with their instructions. I'm not in a position to disrupt the traditions of my bank or jeopardize my future.' She stared at Hava, and then she turned to me.

'I can give you some food and money, but I'm sorry, you can't stay here. It's business, Simone. I'm sure you understand. The bank … I … we have a reputation to maintain.'

I thought about the sea lavender at that moment, how pretty the flowers were in the painting and how smooth and beautiful the marble floors were in Marie's house. 'It's alright,' Hava said in a near-whisper as she stood up from the couch. 'We won't disturb you. Let's go, Simone.'

I was not going to stand up and I was not going to say it was alright.

'But Marie,' I protested, 'Hava is my friend.' I felt like kicking the couch and chasing Marie across her marble floors and into the streets.

'Misguided associations can jeopardize your future too, Simone.'

I stood up then and moved next to Hava. 'We won't disturb your *delicate* position, Marie. We'll not stain your velvet chairs or scratch your polished floors. But have you really forgotten that the Germans, in the First War, invaded France and marched through Belgium first? And what did we do? We blew up the train tracks and delayed the German advance. Remember? The Germans were so angry that they slaughtered over 6,000 Belgian people who weren't even soldiers! They *murdered* over 6,000 innocent people!'

'Times have changed,' Marie said. 'There are other solutions these days.' She looked at Hava again as she rubbed her powdered cheek.

'Changed?' I almost shouted. 'Changed? The Nazis are invading Belgium! My father was nearly killed trying to protect the people of Belgium the last time, and it's happening again! The Nazis are in Brussels. People are flying their flags, they're *shooting* at us from aeroplanes, and you're worried about the bank?'

'The bank,' Marie replied calmly, 'is built on the trust of the people and I cannot be seen to have the wrong associations. As I said, there will be other solutions. My manager said the Germans will be here at any time, perhaps even today. There have been planes, yes. And there will be tanks. I cannot take the risk. She – *you* – must leave. I'm sorry.'

'Come on, Simone,' Hava urged. 'We'll make our way. Let's go.' She took my hand. I was numb. She tugged a bit. We walked past the elephant couch, past the velvet chairs, past my cousin, who stood in the centre of the room like a bronze statue in the park.

Marie walked to a chest of drawers, took out an envelope, counted out a number of bank notes and extended them towards me in her delicate hand. 'This is all I can do.'

I refused the money.

As Hava and I walked back down Rue St Germaine, Hava said, 'I'm sorry that I'm the cause of so much trouble.'

I looked at my friend and I said, 'Hava, I'm sorry my cousin was so horrible in there. I can't believe I'm related to her. But we don't need her. We'll put our feet together, lift our heels, and reach for the moon. No one can touch us if we reach the moon.'

'I feel like a trespasser, Simone. Perhaps I belong on the moon.'

Hava and I walked aimlessly. The people in the streets shuffled in and out of the shops. The trams in the small city clicked along with the familiar sound of iron wheels on iron tracks. Smoke rose from every chimney on that cool May morning.

'I don't really know my cousin,' I said after a while. 'I thought because she was my family that she would help us.'

'I think she only believes in the *idea* of family. My father says that we're all one family, one soul.' Hava squeezed my hand.

'Marie is afraid for her job.'

'Your cousin is afraid of *me*, Simone. She's afraid of Jews. If you ask my father who he is, what does he say? Something like, he's a soul that was chosen by God to be a Jew; to be one who prays and lives by the rules of an ancient book.

'Your father is a great general. People know what a general is, and what a general does, but people don't know the job of a prayerful man, or a Jew. People are afraid of what they don't understand.'

Moments later we heard a train whistle. I didn't know Roeselare had a train station, but I did know we had to leave. In the distance, we heard a low, thumping sound, the sound of a giant moving forward, stomping his heavy feet through the countryside, coming closer and closer. The German army was pushing west, pushing French soldiers and British soldiers west, squeezing them closer and closer to the English Channel.

A dog ran down the cobbled street, a black dog with short hair.

Bombs dropped far in the distance and I recognized the muffled sound of man-made thunder.

A man approached us and said kindly, 'It's time to get off the streets. The Germans are coming. It's on the wireless, they're coming.'

There was another sequence of bombing in the distance, and then a black plane drifted overhead, banking to the left and right in what appeared to be a victory salute to the pilot's success.

Hava looked at the man and said, 'Would you like to go to Tahiti? The artist Gauguin lived in Tahiti.' The man stared at us and said, 'Are you girls mad? The Germans are here!' Then hurried down the street.

CHAPTER 38

When Adolf Hitler ordered the invasion of France, German tanks had crossed the River Meuse and had opened up a gap in the Allied front. The Luftwaffe was given the green light to fly low and shoot refugees in the roads to slow down the French and British troop movements.

A train was preparing to leave. The station was deserted, except for a man in a grey suit struggling with three bags of luggage as he stepped up to one of the carriages. A conductor in a blue suit with gold buttons and an official hat helped the man onto the train.

'Hava, why aren't there any people?'

She seemed to be in a trance, unaware of the silence, the empty platforms, the solitary train with few passengers.

Once the man with the luggage stepped into the train, the conductor waved vigorously to us. 'Hurry! You'll miss the train. It's leaving now. Hurry.'

I always liked sitting next to a window at the rear of the train and when the train curved to the right, I could see the engine guiding the train between the trees or into a tunnel.

On my first train holiday with my father, we went to the Zwin, a small part of the coast on the North Sea. Holland and Belgium share the Zwin, and their beautiful fields of sea lavender. I arranged the flowers in my hair saying to my father, 'Look at me! I'm Greta Garbo!'

My father was very angry when I said this. 'How do you know who Greta Garbo is?'

'At school, Mary Noel had a magazine about Hollywood. She showed me a picture of Greta Garbo. She had flowers in her hair like this.' I tried to turn my head as Garbo did in the magazine picture.

'She's nothing but a silly German actress. Don't copy her.'

And my father pulled the sea lavender from my hair and told me to go and swim with a group of girls who were already in the water. *She isn't even German!* I had wanted to argue.

That was the first time I heard my father's disdain for Germany. I was eleven years old, and I had yet to know that my father's arm had been destroyed in the First World War by a German bullet. I was just annoyed that he didn't think I looked like Greta Garbo.

For the second time, Hava and I were on a train without knowing its destination.

When the conductor walked by, I asked him where we were heading.

'Dunkirk, mademoiselle.'

'Is it far?'

'No, mademoiselle.'

'Perhaps we should have taken a later train. My friend and I are so hungry and tired.'

The conductor looked over at Hava. 'But, mademoiselle, this is the last train. Didn't you know? The Germans will be here in a day or two. The British and French troops are being pushed into the sea by the tanks and planes. This will be the last train out of the station.'

I thanked the conductor as he continued down the aisle.

Turning to Hava, I said, 'We'll be okay. The Germans are quick, but we are quicker. We're still ahead of them. They can't catch us. We're Belgian.' I took Hava's hand.

Hava looked out of the window and whispered, 'Simone! They're already here!'

Through the window, with each passing moment, with every inch we travelled west, the fields grew thicker and thicker with soldiers; thousands of soldiers in green uniforms carrying packs and rifles.

Hava's shoulders slumped. 'They're already here. We're lost.'

'No,' I said after a few minutes of scanning the fields. 'No, they're not German soldiers. Look at their helmets. They're British and French helmets. My father has a collection of helmets like those in his study at home, and he'd never own a German helmet. They're French and British soldiers.'

We passed roads lined with hundreds of army trucks carrying men and pulling heavy artillery. As our train curved to the left, we saw the sea, the shoreline, and thousands of soldiers. Hitler was pushing from the east. The British and French troops were trapped.

'Mademoiselle?'

I turned from the window.

'*Ici*. For you and for your friend.'

The conductor handed me a small bag. 'It's all I have. You'll find food in Dunkirk but this will help you for now.'

I opened the bag, and before I could look up and say 'thank you', the conductor had disappeared into the next carriage.

Inside the bag was a thick piece of bread and a pork sausage. I broke the bread and gave half to Hava.

'No, you eat it all, Simone. I'm stronger than you are.'

'No, you're not,' I said. 'I'm just as much a Belgian as you are. We're like sisters, and sisters split everything down the middle.'

Hava and I ate our bread in silence as we continued to stare out of the train window. Soldiers stood near the tracks, and as we slowly made our way some waved. We waved back. One man blew us a kiss. Hava returned the kiss and waved. I thought about Sergeant De Waden.

When I offered Hava the sausage, she whispered, 'It's forbidden. You eat. Be my strong gentile, Simone.' I felt so guilty because I could have given Hava all the bread and I could have eaten just the sausage. After that day, I never ate pork again.

Suddenly, the train squealed to a stop. The passengers were silent. The sunlight danced on the floor in little squares. The train's engine idled in a slow rhythm. 'Why have we stopped?'

Hava stood up, pulled down the window, and stuck her head outside. 'Why have we stopped?' she asked a group of soldiers walking along the side of the tracks.

'To marry me!' a redheaded soldier called out in a British accent.

'Why has the train stopped?' Hava insisted.

The redheaded soldier pointed towards the front of the train. 'No more track. It's been blown away; it's twisted and bent. But my marriage proposal is still on the table!'

'Maybe at the next war,' Hava said as she sat back down beside me.

'We can't stay here,' I said.

'Everybody off. End of the line,' the conductor announced confidently as if announcing the train had just arrived in Paris. 'End of the line.'

'Let the others off first,' Hava suggested. 'We may as well sit for as long as we can.'

We remained in our seat and watched children being led down the aisles holding the hands of their parents. An old woman steadied herself with the backs of each seat as she made her way to the exit. Two women in elegant furs and stockings stood up with startled expressions on their faces. One of the women turned to the other two. 'How can we walk in these shoes?'

When the carriage was empty, the conductor stepped in. 'Mademoiselles, you have to leave. The train has stopped, and we can go no further. Dunkirk is just four more miles. You'll have to walk, I'm sorry. There is nothing we can do.'

As Hava and I headed towards the exit, I asked the conductor 'And you?'

'Ah, mademoiselle, I will stay with my train. It's my duty. Duty still counts.'

'But the Germans are coming.'

'If not the Germans, then old age will catch up with me.' The conductor shrugged.

Just before we stepped off the train, I turned to the conductor. '*Vive la Belgique.*'

He looked at me, and smiled. '*Vive l'amour.*'

When the train had been moving it seemed that all else was still. When the train stopped, and Hava and I stepped onto the ground, everything else moved: horses, trucks, columns of soldiers, refugees moving forward in massive turbulence and disorder. Even the spring blossoms seemed to move forward, leaning away from the advancing wind.

In a distant field, soldiers were shooting a herd of cows, their guns a terrifying companion to the cow's horrible lowing.

'Simone, why are they shooting the cows?'

A man behind us said, 'Because they're in pain. They haven't been milked. No one can milk them. They're suffering.' It was the redheaded soldier.

'But I can milk them,' Hava said. 'I know how.'

'Sure. You can milk all the cows in France, but there's no time. The Germans are hot on our tail. We must keep moving, ladies. Keep moving.'

And then, as if a curtain had been drawn back, Hava and I looked ahead. Cannons, trucks, tanks had been abandoned. A dying horse kicked its legs in a ditch. A sea of humanity walked towards a tall plume of black smoke. The landscape was charred, farm houses were in flames. Their skeletal frames trembled, collapsing into piles of ashes.

'That's Dunkirk,' the redheaded soldier said as he pointed forward. 'The Germans have dropped a few calling cards there already. At least we know where we're going now. The smoke is a good marker.' He seemed almost nonchalant, like he couldn't smell the terrifying stench of rot and decay.

'What should we do?' I asked the soldier.

'Do? Why, my little lady, it's every man for himself. This is a retreat. The Panzer divisions have already crashed through Brussels. We were supposed to retreat to the west. The word is out that Dunkirk is our last stand. There's nowhere else to go. The sea is to the west and the Nazis are to the east.'

Hava and I walked with the redheaded soldier between us. 'We tried to stop them,' he continued, pulling out a crumpled pack of cigarettes. 'Want one?'

We both declined.

'We were even told to blow up your bridges to slow them down.' The soldier lit a cigarette, inhaled with vigour, and blew smoke out of his mouth. 'Didn't help. They're organized: first the planes, then the tanks, then foot soldiers and trucks swept right through. We lost thousands of troops. We've already lost the war. Start learning German, girls.' He inhaled on his cigarette once again, coughed, and repeated, 'Start learning German.'

I hadn't expected a plane. I hadn't expected the sudden panic and shouting. From over the tops of the thick trees to our left a German Stuka appeared, banking right, flying low over the stream of people staggering along the narrow country road. Then the machine guns began, one under each wing. Helpless, desperate people dropped to the ground, hands covering their heads hoping to hide from the onslaught. The bullets spat from the plane with a quick, cracking sound.

More people began to drop as the plane flew closer. Our redheaded companion yelled, 'Get down!' and pushed Hava and me as if we were two rag dolls on either side of him. I fell hard to the ground and rolled into the ditch. Hava and the soldier disappeared into the sea of people. The plane droned relentlessly overhead with speed and horror. I could not hear much over the noise, but I could hear screaming.

Lying there on the cold ground, hugging my arms and trying to pretend that I was anywhere else, I heard the plane finally return to wherever it had come from. The ear-splitting whirring of the engines became a distant hum, giving me enough courage to sit up. Crying, shaking, terrified, I look around and tried to work out how long it had been. Seconds? Minutes? Hours? I looked down and saw blood on my dress. I stood up on my wobbly legs and climbed out of the ditch back onto the road. A few others stood up around me. The road was covered with blood and bodies, some moving an arm or a leg, but most not moving at all. Children wailed, and the black smoke of Dunkirk continued to plume into the horizon.

'Hava!' I croaked, my voice hoarse with desperation, 'Hava!' And there she was in the middle of the road like Michelangelo's *Pietà*, cradling the dead redheaded soldier in her lap, looking into his face. She didn't look sad. She didn't look shocked. She held him as his blood trickled onto her arms and legs. And then she looked up at me and said as she stroked his hair, 'I would have married him if we had met in Tahiti.'

Another plane appeared over the trees.

'Hava!'

Gently she laid the British soldier onto the ground and kissed his cheek. I reached out for her hand. The plane flew lower. I pulled her to her feet and we both ran for the ditch just as more bullets began cutting once again into the people who were running and diving for cover.

The pilot pulled up the nose of the plane, rose quickly into the clouds, and disappeared.

CHAPTER 39

The Dutch defenders fell back westward, and by noon on
12 May, German tanks were on the outskirts of Rotterdam.
Queen Wilhelmina and her government fled the country for England
on 13 May, and the next day the Dutch army surrendered to the
Germans. France was next.

We arrived in Dunkirk that night hungry, our clothes stained with blood.

We stopped beside a broken lamp-post. I whispered to Hava, 'Would you like to seduce the lamp-post?' She looked at me with a weak smile.

Soldiers walked around us as if we were ghosts, intangible and invisible. Across the square men stood beside a fire, their silhouettes moving like shadow puppets: arms thrust outward, heads bobbing to the inflections of their voices that carried words of distress and sorrow. I heard soldiers talking.

'The planes are coming again.'

'We're trapped.'

'I saw a train on fire.'

'I haven't heard from my son in three weeks. He's missing.'

Hava covered her ears with her two hands. 'I can't listen anymore. There's no explanation!' Then she grabbed my shoulders and began to shake me. 'There's no explanation! Where's my family?'

'Hava!'

'My father!' Hava let go of my shoulders. 'My mother! Benjamin! Have you seen Benjamin, Simone? He was right here!'

Hava stood before me, her hands on her hips.

Every café was filled with people. There were no street vendors. I told Hava that we must get something to eat, but she insisted that we had to stay beside the streetlamp. 'Benjamin will come back and recognize the light, Simone. Look how beautiful the light is. It's like a star, a yellow star. Look how pretty the star looks at the top of the pole.'

It was no use telling Hava that there was no light, that the streetlight was broken.

'I want that star, Simone. Reach up for it and pin it on my chest.' Hava leaned back and stretched out her arms upward as if trying to detach the star in her imagination from the top of the streetlamp. 'Benjamin will see the star and he will recognize me.'

'Hava, we must find a place to eat. We need food.'

Hava lowered her arms. 'I need my star. It's my shield, Simone. My father will recognize me. Benjamin will find me. He'll be impressed that I look like an angel with my shield.' Then she knelt on the cobblestones and wept.

I bent down beside her and as I looked into the eyes of my friend, I saw terror. Her pupils were black and wide. Her hair fell on either side of her face like a veil. She dropped her thin arms and whispered, 'I'm so hungry, Simone.'

It seemed as if no one could distinguish us from the quilt of humanity stitched together in grey grief and fear. *We may as well be stones or dirt on the street*, I thought, so I was startled when a young man leaned over me and asked, 'May I help you?' He was a soldier, another British soldier in a brown army uniform, wearing a helmet that looked like a turtle shell, and carrying a rifle.

Hava looked up. 'Have you found Benjamin?'

'Benjamin?'

'It's her brother. He's missing.'

'Here?' the soldier asked.

'No, at home.'

'Where's home?'

'Brussels.'

'You two girls are far from home.' The soldier leaned his gun against the lamp-post and offered me his hand. I took it as he helped me stand up.

'Can you help me with my friend?'

'What's your name?'

'Simone Lyon.'

'Hello, Simone Lyon. I'm Bill Lacey, Private Lacey, from Portsmouth.'

'England?'

'Yes.'

'You're far from home too.'

'Just over the water there.'

The soldier waved his arm in the direction of the English Channel. I turned to look where he pointed, but all I saw was smoke, rubble in the street, and a burned-out post office.

'Oh, it's there, miss, believe me.' As he helped me pull Hava up onto her feet, he said that the Nazis were only a day away, and we couldn't stay in Dunkirk. 'You'll have to leave tomorrow. Hitler is on the way. We have nowhere to go. The Germans have pushed us with their tanks right across Belgium and France to this little place. I hear there are over 400,000 troops, French too, and your folks and your soldiers, in and around the city, all waiting to be evacuated. We don't know what to do. We're trapped here at Dunkirk. We're still fighting. The guys left behind are probably giving us a day or so extra to escape. My regiment was pulled back and here I am. You girls had better get out of here fast.'

'I'm fine. I can stand now,' Hava said. 'I'm sorry, Simone. I don't feel well.'

'Hava, you need something to eat.' I looked at the soldier.

Private Lacey of the British army looked at me. 'Right. Food.' He picked up his rifle. 'Stay here.' He stepped to his left and disappeared into the crowd.

'I really thought there was a star at the top of the lamp-post, Simone.'

'Maybe the star fell down and turned into a British soldier.'

CHAPTER 40

We have before us an ordeal of the most grievous kind. We have
before us many, many long months of struggle and of suffering. You
ask, what is our policy? I will say: it is to wage war, by sea, land and
air, with all our might and with all the strength that God can give us;
to wage war against a monstrous tyranny, never surpassed in the dark
and lamentable catalogue of human crime.
Winston Churchill's first speech as Prime Minister of Britain
to the House of Commons, 13 May 1940

It began to rain. People rushed past us. I tried to pretend that
everyone was in a hurry so as not to get wet, instead of running
from tanks and bombs and the end of something. Hava and I stood
like statues, the rain wetting our hair. French rain. May rain. Rain
from the clouds in the sky – clouds that were free to float away. I
wanted to float away with Hava across the English Channel, across
England; to keep floating across the Atlantic Ocean, to Hollywood.
To find Clark Gable and tell him that Hava and I were hungry,
ask if he had warm clothes. Then I thought about my father and I
wanted to go home.

We remained there with nowhere to go. No food. In the rain.

'Right, what's this!'

I looked up and there was Bill Lacey, Private Bill Lacey of the Royal British army. He didn't have his rifle. Instead he had two blankets. He draped one first over Hava, and then the other over me. The blankets were warm and dry.

'Come with me, my Belgian girls.'

He walked ahead of us, holding out his arms, making a path for us between the soldiers and refugees. For some reason people stopped and let us through. We followed the soldier to the front of a little café. The door was wide and made of dark wood. On both sides of the door were generous windows, giving the appearance that the whole front of the café was made of glass.

The café was crowded. Glasses clinked. Talk was a loud, mixed murmur. Chairs scraped the floor. When we stepped inside, it was as though someone had given a signal and everything paused: the talking, the movement of the forks and knives. Silence extended to the waitress who was opening one of the windows, but stopped midway. And in the right-hand corner of the room were a small, empty table and two chairs.

Private Lacey turned to me. 'Right, there you go, ladies. All set.'

'But there are hundreds of people here and so many waiting outside. How did you arrange this?'

Private Lacey leaned over and whispered, 'I told the owner that you're the daughter of General Joseph Lyon.'

Hava leaned over and whispered in my other ear. 'Your father has spies everywhere.'

'Yes,' I said to the soldier, 'but how did you know?'

'Well, I didn't until right this second when you just confirmed my suspicion. Back in England, in boot camp, we had to read up on France and Belgium. We were told that we had to have a feeling for the place, care about the places we'd be trying to protect. We read all about the history of Belgium and the First World War; how your father was a part of the White Lady and how he grabbed that shovel and began to dig a trench under fire. I laughed at first when I read that – a general as a white lady. But I didn't laugh when I read how he inspired the other soldiers to dig that trench. The book said he became a general, lived in Brussels, and had a daughter named Simone. It all got stuck in my head: a general with a shovel who was a white lady, who had a daughter named Simone. And here you are and here I am, just a bloke from Portsmouth delivering mail.'

'But there must be hundreds of girls named Simone Lyon.'

'What difference does it make? I convinced the owner of the café that you were the general's daughter and everyone knows of General Lyon. Even if he hadn't been your father, it got you a table and a free meal. We Brits are resourceful, you know.'

'But there are only two chairs.'

'Oh, I can't stay. I've got a boat to catch. Strict orders. Dockside at 08.30. I've got a war to go to.'

A man in an apron and red shirt walked up to our little group. He looked at Hava and said 'Mademoiselle Lyon?'

Hava smiled and pointed to me.

'Oh, excuse me. Are you sisters? You look like sisters.'

Hava and I looked at each other. Our blankets were wrapped around our shoulders, our hair was wet and clinging to both sides of our faces.

'This is Marie Armel, my cousin.'

I looked at Private Lacey and said, 'Belgian girls are resourceful too.'

'Mesdemoiselles, follow me. I have a table waiting for you.'

Private Lacey stepped aside and reached behind a counter for his rifle. I noticed how lithe he was, how confident in the way that he picked up the rifle and slung it over his shoulder. I would always remember the colour of his brown hair, his helmet hanging on his back. I thought of the Tin Man in *The Wizard of Oz* and how sad Dorothy was when she had to say goodbye.

'Well, ladies, I'm off.' He extended his hand to Hava first.

She shook it gratefully and said one word: '*Merci*.'

'And Mademoiselle la General, look me up if you're ever in Portsmouth. You can't miss it. It's in the southern part of England. We're the only island city in the country. We like being special; an island unto ourselves. Right, I'm off. Enjoy your meal, and remember, you must leave tomorrow morning.'

'Thank you.'

'Cheerio.'

I watched as he turned, saluted, and stepped out of the café, back into the chaos that filled the streets of Dunkirk, France, in May 1940.

The man in the red shirt escorted us to the little table, and when we sat down, the forks and knives rattled again, the talk and murmur resumed, the waitress finished opening the window, and a basket of bread and a bottle of wine appeared on our table.

We hadn't eaten anything since the train, and that had been very little.

'We have no menu, mesdemoiselles. There is not much left, but the sea always provides. We have salmon. That is our menu. The bread is the last as well. There is nothing left. The Germans have cut off the supplies to the city. No flour. No vegetables. The strawberries were just coming in from the farms, but now even the strawberries are gone.'

'But we don't want to take away what little is left,' Hava said.

'Ah, no. You know the saying, mademoiselle. Eat, drink and be merry, for tomorrow we die.'

'I won't die.'

I looked at Hava and said to the man in the red shirt, 'You're very kind. Salmon will be very good.'

He nodded and, pulling out a small box of matches from under his apron, he lit the single stump of a candle; a little candle that had seen happier nights. The flame from the match illuminated Hava's face. She looked angelic.

We sat in silence for a moment. The voices of the other patrons carried throughout the café in a collection of disjointed sounds. The walls had pictures of Paris: the Eiffel Tower, Notre Dame, a boy feeding a swan at the Tuileries Garden. I took the bottle of wine and poured some into Hava's glass, and some into my own.

'Tell me something happy, Simone. I want you to tell me something happy.' Hava placed her arms on the table and propped her head in her hands.

I placed the bottle back onto the table as the man in the red shirt brought our salmon.

I thanked him repeatedly, but he just waved his hands above his head. 'Eat, drink, for tomorrow the Nazis will be here.'

Before she ate, Hava said, 'I don't know anything happy, Simone, but prayer helps when one isn't happy,' and she recited a simple Jewish prayer: 'Blessed are You, Lord our God, King of the Universe, by Whose word all things came to be.'

As we raised our wine and tipped together the edge of each glass, Hava said, 'L'Chayim'.

CHAPTER 41

*We shall not flag or fail. We shall go on to the end. We shall fight
in France, we shall fight on the seas and oceans, we shall fight with
growing confidence and growing strength in the air, we shall defend
our island, whatever the cost may be, we shall fight on the beaches, we
shall fight on the landing grounds, we shall fight in the fields and in
the streets, we shall fight in the hills; we shall never surrender.*
Winston Churchill's words delivered to the House of
Commons, 4 June, 1940

An old man sitting at the next table suddenly spoke up. 'What
brings you girls to the coast? On holiday?'

I was about to say something sarcastic like, 'Oh yes, Hitler gave
us an all-expenses-paid trip to this beach town for the summer.'
Instead, I smiled and almost laughed. It was good to smile again.

'Forgive me for intruding. I just heard your prayer. It's the
prayer my mother said before each meal. You reminded me of
my mother.'

'That's disappointing. So, in your eyes, I'm like an old Jewish
mother?' Hava chuckled.

'No, mademoiselle, in my eyes you are memory, and all that is present.'

Talking to this man so suddenly was, for me, like talking to the funny Mad Hatter in *Alice in Wonderland*. He seemed to speak in riddles.

'What do you dream of? Clouds or mountains?' the man asked us.

I was confused, but Hava answered right away, 'Why, I dream of mountains. How do you know to ask?'

'I always asked my students about their dreams. My name is Ira Alberg. I was a teacher once; Shakespeare, Dante, Dickens. I like to know people's dreams.'

'My name is Hava Daniels. This is my friend Simone Lyon.'

'Ah, yes, I heard the rumours that we might be in the presence of General Lyon's daughter. And what do you dream of, Simone? Clouds or mountains?'

I wanted to tell this man that I didn't dream of either clouds or mountains, so I just picked one. 'I dream of mountains, like Hava. We're like sisters.'

'Yes, you two act like sisters. I thought you were sisters when you entered the restaurant. Why do you dream of mountains?'

'I want to be important,' I said.

'The rocks are important. They make the mountains. Are you a rock, daughter of the general?' He paused, 'And, Hava Daniels, what is your father?'

'He is also a great man, a printer. He is respected in the synagogue.'

'Where is he?'

Hava's facial features changed quickly from her dream face to her war face: stoic, hard, not the face of Hava the opera lover. 'I don't know. My mother and brother, they all disappeared. The rabbi said they had gone.'

'We shall all return someday, Mademoiselle Daniels.' We sat in silence for a moment. We heard the distant shelling of the coast by German artillery.

Everyone in the restaurant stopped talking and we sat in silence as one explosion after another echoed in the background. An air-raid siren sounded. The night sky outside the restaurant suddenly radiated a yellow aura. Then, the shelling and the siren stopped.

'There was a great Jewish soldier, Mademoiselle Hava. He was never a general like Simone's father. Have you heard of William Shemin?'

The people in the restaurant began talking again.

'In the First World War, German machine guns cut across a field. Many Americans were killed. Shemin ran across the field and dragged many of his comrades to safety. Then he did the unthinkable. He ran back three more times, and each time the machine guns fired at him and at everyone else on the field. A bullet passed through his helmet and lodged inside his skull, just behind his ear. He had lied about his age and said he was 18 when he joined the army, but he was only 16. After the war he owned a plant nursery and sold flowers and shrubs in New York City. Now, *he* is a general of a man. He saved his friends and he sold flowers in New York City.'

Hava and I finished our meal. The restaurant owner stepped up and said that there was no charge. The British soldier had paid for our meal. We were about to get up to leave when our dinner companion asked, 'Where are you girls sleeping tonight?' I explained that the soldier had told us we had to leave in the morning, so we had decided to walk through the night and escape.

'The Germans don't travel at night. You are safe for one more night here.'

'Yes, our soldier friend said the same thing, but there are no rooms left anywhere.'

'I have a room, right next door in the Hotel du Beffroi. It's already paid for. I will give you my room. You both need to sleep, daughter of the printer, daughter of the general – mountain-dreamers.'

The old man stood up. 'But first, you must grant me a favour.'

As the three of us walked out of the restaurant, Monsieur Alberg said, 'I'd like you to escort me to the hotel, so I can pick up my things.' Monsieur Alberg extended his left arm to Hava, and she hooked her arm into his. He extended his right arm to me, and I hooked my arm into his, and the three of us walked along the cobblestones in Dunkirk, France, on that night in May 1940.

The sky lit up again as bombs exploded further down the street. 'You see,' Monsieur Alberg said, 'an old Jew with two princesses, one on his left and one on his right, will never be touched by bombs.'

As we entered the little lobby of the hotel, Monsieur Alberg said, 'Wait here a moment while I get my things.'

'Hava, why is he giving us his room?'

She shrugged and smiled. 'Perhaps he dreams of clouds.'

Hava and I sat on a pink marble bench, where on each corner was carved a small, plump angel. I rubbed the belly of an angel for luck, the marble cold against the tips of my fingers. There was no heat in the hotel, no electricity, just candlelight. The concierge sat at her desk folding towels. I thought it was funny that she was folding towels. The next day the Nazis would enter the city with their guns, and tanks, yet the concierge was folding towels peacefully, as if she were expecting an eager weekend crowd.

Monsieur Alberg reappeared in the lobby with a suitcase in one hand and a birdcage in another, in which sat a plump canary.

'I take my little bird, Firoo, with me wherever I go. She sings to me at night before I switch off the lights – a gift from my niece.'

Monsieur Alberg placed the cage before Hava and me as we sat on the marble bench. 'Look closely. She is my soul.' The bird jumped from the little wooden perch to the bottom of the cage, then back onto the perch. Back and forth the bird jumped. The seeds in a small glass cup scattered out between the bars of the cage each time the canary made her sudden dash to the bottom of the cage and back up to the perch.

'Would you like Firoo?' Monsieur Alberg asked Hava. I didn't think she wanted the soul of an old man. She looked at the bird in silence. Monsieur Alberg shrugged and then said to Hava, 'Ah well. I have a favour before I give you the key to my room. I hope you might indulge an old man's wish.' He hesitated, then looked at Hava sadly.' I wonder if you might let me touch your hair .'

I gave Hava a secret pinch to her thigh.

Hava told me later, as we prepared for bed, that no one had ever touched her hair except Joff the woodcutter's son, and her little neighbour who liked to visit Hava's home to sing songs with her family.

Hava said that the girl always liked brushing her hair. 'This little gentile girl would come to our door about once a month and say, "Mademoiselle Hava, I have come to brush your beautiful golden hair today."' Hava told me that she'd invite the little girl into the house. 'I would sit in the front room and she would stand behind me and brush my hair with long, gentle strokes. Sometimes she and I sang "Sur le Pont d'Avignon"; other times she would ask me to tell her a story. Her favourites were the Baba Yaga stories about the famous Russian witch who lived in a house on chicken legs.'

'When it was time for her to go home, I'd send her along with a sugar biscuit, and each time, before leaving, she'd say, "Mademoiselle Hava, thank you for letting me touch your hair. It's very beautiful."'

I didn't think that Hava would let old Monsieur Alberg touch her hair with his crooked, arthritic hands.

But after I pinched Hava's thigh again, she looked at me and then at the old man with the sad eyes, and said, 'Of course you can touch my hair.'

The old man placed his single bag beside the bird cage and stood before Hava. Then he reached out slowly with his right hand and stroked her hair gently, letting the strands filter through his fingers. I had never seen a man touch a woman with such gentleness and majesty – such grief.

'You have beautiful hair, Mademoiselle Hava. It reminds me of my daughter's.' Then he reached into his pocket, took out a brass key, and placed it into Hava's soft, thin hand.

'I will now take Firoo and go.'

'But where will you stay? There are no rooms.'

'Ah, a canary and an old man can always find a place to sleep.' He smiled.

When Hava thanked him for the room, he looked at her and said, 'You know the Jewish proverb, "*When you have no choice, mobilize the spirit of courage*"?' She nodded as understanding passed wordlessly between them. Then, picking up his bird cage, and tipping his head in farewell, he said to me, 'Your father is a brave man.'

As Monsieur Alberg walked out of the hotel, he stepped quickly among the moving mass of people. Hava and I followed him out, then watched as he negotiated the crowd, his arms going up and down, before he disappeared into the night.

CHAPTER 42

At the end of the Second World War, at least 11 million people had been displaced from their home countries

'I wonder where Mr Alberg's daughter is now,' Hava said as she reached into her pocket and pulled out the key. 'I hope touching my hair brought her back to him briefly.' She looked down at the key in her hand. 'I'm tired. Let's go inside.' And she walked back into the hotel.

The concierge explained that our room was up a flight of stairs and to the left. She gave us a small kerosene lamp.

The stair rail was made of black iron with filigree spiralling under the rail like bits of liquorice. Hava climbed ahead of me, her footsteps echoing on the wooden stairs. The heels of her shoes were hard. The soles of her shoes rubbed against the steps.

'Are you coming, Simone? Just a few more steps.'

I was so tired that my legs felt ready to fall off.

We were barely women, and had stepped out of the pink shells of adolescence expecting Clark Gable, but instead we had found Hitler greeting us with his fast-approaching invasion and with bullets that could penetrate through us, into us, without regard for our names, our well-being, or our performance of scenes from *Romeo and Juliet*.

In the room there was a single bed and a large chair covered with overstuffed pillows.

'Hava, you take the bed. I sleep in a chair at home often enough.'

She didn't argue, but unlaced her shoes, placed them side by side near the door and then slipped into the bed. Before I settled into the chair, I blew out the flame in the lamp, and Hava and I were in the dark. We were silent. I was sure she had fallen asleep when she asked in a low, quiet voice, 'What did you learn at your Catholic school?'

I sat in my chair and looked out the window. I could see that the sky glowed orange to the east where exploding bombs encroached towards the city.

'One summer,' I told Hava, 'we were on holiday and I was walking past the empty school. The front door opened, and Sister Bernadette stepped out, shaking a rug. When she saw me, she called out, "Good afternoon, Mademoiselle Lyon." I waved back and said, "Good afternoon Sister Bernadette."

'She asked me how my father was, and about my summer. I told her that I was reading *The Good Earth*, a novel about China. Then she asked me if I could help her for a few moments.

'Soon enough I found myself in the convent, in the laundry with Sister Bernadette. She showed me how to use an iron, and how to iron a nun's handkerchief. I pressed it flat on the board, sprinkled a bit of water onto the handkerchief, and when the iron touched the cloth, a puff of steam rose, and a small hissing sound sighed from the hot iron. That's what I learned at Catholic school: how to iron a handkerchief.'

There was silence again, and I thought Hava was asleep when

she said, 'Jewish girls are like myrtle: we have a sweet smell and a bitter taste – like Esther. She listened well and fought against the wicked Haman. My father said that Jewish girls must be proud of their heritage.' I looked out of the window once again to the orange night, and then we slept.

Once, Hava had come to meet me after school. She wanted to see if anyone would notice her horns as she waited outside my Catholic school.

'Don't you know, Simone? *All* Jews have horns?'

That's ridiculous,' I said.

'Oh no, it's true. Even artists of the Middle Ages depicted Jews with horns on their heads.'

'That's ridiculous,' I said again.

But Hava took my hand and said, 'Rub my head.'

'I will *not* rub your head.'

'Go on, Simone, rub my head and feel my horns.'

'Hava, that's a horrible thing to say, and I will not rub your head.'

Hava grinned mischievously as she grabbed my hand. 'Even the great artist Michelangelo knew about this. One of his famous sculptures in a church in Rome is a statue of Moses, and he has two horns sticking out of his head.'

She giggled and forced my hand onto the top of her head, dragging it back and forth across her scalp. I was shocked to feel two little horns sticking up beneath her thick, blonde hair.

Then Hava laughed, reached up into her hair, and pulled out two little combs in the shape of the Eiffel Tower.

In class Sister Bernadette had taught us, 'Our human body is so beautiful and so precious that God in all his power could never invent anything better.'

Recalling this, I muttered to Hava, 'And he certainly didn't give the human body horns.'

At the end of school that day, we were all nervous about a big test the next day. Before the bell went and I rushed off to meet Hava, Sister Bernadette had looked at the thirty girls sitting before her and said, 'If you all come to the exam room tomorrow with a flower in your hair, I will give you all 100 for your exam.'

After school, as Hava and I walked back to my house through a small park filled with lilac bushes, she said, 'Well?'

'Well what?'

'Are you going to wear a flower in your hair tomorrow for the exam?'

'I'm sure Sister Bernadette was joking, Hava.'

'Do you know,' Hava said, 'that pollen from brightly coloured wildflowers was discovered in the grave of a man buried 60,000 years ago in a cave in Iraq? They used to bury people on beds of hyacinths.'

'What does that have to do with Sister Bernadette?'

'Nothing, but it means that thousands of years ago, Neanderthal man liked flowers, Simone, just like us.' Hava stopped walking. 'Maybe Sister Bernadette thinks that flowers are far more important than exams.' Then Hava leaned over a low fence, snapped two sprigs of lilac from a large bush, and pushed them into both sides of my hair. 'See? Now you have two purple horns on *your* head.'

The next day, one by one, thirty girls entered Sister Bernadette's classroom each with a fresh, spring flower in their hair: daffodils, lilacs, columbine, clipped flowers from an azalea. We all received 100 for our exam, and I wore my purple horns.

CHAPTER 43

On 14 May 1940, when Winston Churchill asked the French
General, Maurice Gamelin, 'How many reserve troops do you have?'
the general turned to the new Prime Minister of Great Britain and said
'Aucune [None].' Churchill was dumbfounded. It never occurred to him
that any commander would be so unprepared.

When I woke the next morning, I was startled to see that Hava was not in bed. She was not even in the room. Her shoes were gone. The sun was up. There was no bombing. All was silent.

I walked down the stairs and asked the concierge if she had seen Hava.

'Yes, she left early, just after sunrise. She said to tell you she went out to look for some food and that she'll be back shortly.'

Relieved, I returned to the room and stood at the window that looked out onto the street, hoping to see Hava. The entire world seemed to be spread out on the street that May morning. There was a slow awakening. Already hundreds of soldiers were on the move towards the sea. It was as though I was witnessing the final act of a play: everyone was prepared for the climax, but no one knew what the end would bring.

It was the end of something, the shuttering of the city, the advance of the Nazi troops. Word was that many French and British soldiers were hoping to be rescued from the shore, as England might send boats across the Channel.

All I wanted to see was Hava making her way back to the hotel. And then, there she was, in the distance, among the soldiers and refugees, walking towards the hotel among children, farmers, nuns, all moving in a circle of confusion, trying to decide the direction in which to turn, trying to decide the direction of their fate.

Then their moment of calm indecision came abruptly to an end, as over the horizon German planes materialized once again with their bombs and machine guns. When the first plane flew overhead like a deranged crow, it dropped a bomb directly into the middle of the street, as if there had been a target painted on the cobblestone square. Muffled cries rose from below. The hotel shook so violently that I had to grab the windowsill to stay on my feet. The window panes rattled loudly. A vase shattered onto the trembling floorboards. I looked out of the window and watched the building to my left catch fire.

People ran into the side streets, dodging broken glass and scattered debris. Chairs outside the restaurants were jumbled like broken cobwebs. And thousands of British and French soldiers walked, almost aimlessly, between the buildings, making their way through the chaos.

Two soldiers bent down and gently moved a motionless, blood-soaked body from the middle of the road. Another soldier helped a dishevelled and panic-stricken woman to her feet. When I opened the window, smoke and fumes swirled around me like devils trying to blind me. I rubbed my eyes, coughed, and quickly slammed the window shut. I covered my ears, trying to block out the cacophony of aeroplanes, shouting, terror.

From the hotel lobby a radio announcement blared up the stairs:

This is an urgent message from M. Reynaud, Prime Minister of France: France will soon be unable to count on the help from the Belgian army. There are fears that it must capitulate to the Nazis under the orders of its King and that the roads to Dunkirk will be open to the German dictator. Holland has already fallen and Hitler is advancing quickly through the Netherlands, a barrier we thought would hold.

In the south, the French divisions are trying to hold a new front which follows the Somme and the Alps with the hopes of joining the Maginot Line.

Dunkirk is a critical supply port for the Allies, and we are making every effort to defend this sector. However, it has been reported that our soldiers and the British soldiers are being pushed quickly from Belgium into the northern corner of France. We are doing all we can to defend our borders, but we must be prepared for the inevitable. We will keep you informed, and there may be a time in the near future when all citizens need to evacuate Dunkirk.

I raced down the stairs of the hotel; my shoes untied, my hair a mess. I had difficulty breathing. I was halfway down the steps when I nearly crashed into Hava, who was running halfway up.

'Hava! Thank goodness! I just heard on the radio, the Belgian army is struggling. The roads to Dunkirk will be open soon to Hitler!'

'Yes, I've come for you, Simone. We've got to get out of here.'

She had a long piece of bread in her hand. 'Here, eat this. We need to hurry.'

She took my free hand as we both ran down the stairs together. Girls our age ought to have been running down a flight of stairs into the arms of our boyfriends. But Hava and I ran for our lives.

'I found the bus station. There's a bus – the last bus. It's leaving in twenty minutes.'

It is odd how, during war, a bus schedule is still maintained. That morning Hava, in her search for food, had also looked for a way out of the city. Everyone was trying to escape. Everyone knew the Germans were advancing.

We had escaped Brussels, run from a burning train, made it through the woods and found our way to Dunkirk, and still the bullets of the Nazi guns were upon us.

'If there's a bus, Simone, maybe there's still a chance we can escape!'

As odd as it may sound, it was an exhilarating moment, running with Hava as if being chased by a bull, the devil, or death. Our legs were strong. We were young, bold in our tattered, bloodstained dresses. We ran past women laden with suitcases, past shops that were shuttered, churches that were silent, and schools that were closed.

'We can make it, Simone.' Hava kept up my courage as we ran and ran. 'There's the bus station. Just a little more, Simone!'

When Hava and I reached the end of the next street, we turned right and there, surrounded by hundreds of people, was a single bus, its engine running, the driver at the wheel, the ticket agent standing at the door waving his hat in the air, trying to create order from chaos.

Hundreds and hundreds of people had had the same idea: *We can leave Dunkirk by bus. The Germans are coming; the bus will take us away.*

'Hold my hand tightly, Simone!' Hava ordered, as she began pushing her way through the throng of wild people. She didn't stop. When she said, 'Excuse me', people moved aside. When she yelled, people moved aside. When she pushed with her hand in front of her, people moved aside. She just kept dragging me behind her until we were at the front of the mob trying to board the bus.

We were standing near the middle of the bus when the ticket agent called for calm: 'There are only fifty seats! Only fifty seats! If you don't move back, I will tell the driver to leave you *all* behind!'

When people heard that they would be left behind, there was a sudden roar – a combination of fear and desperation.

Then all at once, the ticket agent stepped off the bus and waved his hat at the driver. The driver closed the door to the empty bus and it began to creep forward slowly. When the crowd realized that the bus was moving, devoid of passengers, leaving them behind, there was a sudden surge forward, like a giant wave rolling towards the shore.

Hava and I found ourselves trapped between the bus and the crowd behind us. We tried to stand our ground, to keep our balance, to maintain our place at the front in the hope that the bus would not leave. But the bus advanced slowly, trying to force its way through the people, as the mob continued to shove, pushing, pressing, and propelling itself forwards.

Then, with a sudden wild yell from behind, the mob thrust itself forward once more, and I lost my footing as I was shoved from behind and fell under the bus. The front wheels rolled forward. The rear wheels moved towards me. I was on my back. I turned my head and saw the large black tyre rolling towards my arms.

That is when I heard, as if from the depth of the universe, a scream, a pleading cry: 'Stop the bus! Stop the bus!' It was Hava. She broke through the mob, pushed aside the ticket agent, and pounded on the door. 'Stop the bus! Please! My sister is under the bus! Stop the bus! You'll crush her!'

The bus stopped. The driver opened the door, stepped out, and remonstrated with Hava. 'How dare you interfere with the bus system! How dare you try and stop my bus!'

'Please! My sister is under the bus. You're going to crush her!'

The driver looked at Hava, then bent down, and there he found me. I couldn't move. The rear wheel of the bus had rolled onto my dress. That is how close I had come to being killed. One more rotation of the wheel and I would have been crushed to death. The driver rushed back onto the bus and returned with a small pocket knife. He had to cut the side of my dress so that I could slip out.

He pulled me out from under the bus. I was shaking, my knees were bleeding. Word spread quickly that a girl had nearly been killed under the bus. Hava knelt down beside me and started stroking my hair. 'Are you okay? Are you hurt, Simone? Are you okay?' Then she began to cry.

'Hava, I'm fine. Yes, look, I still have both my arms.' And with my arms I embraced Hava and held her, then I too began to cry.

'Because you've had such a shock,' the bus driver said to me, 'you and your sister may enter the bus first.'

The bus driver helped me onto my feet, and as he led Hava and me to the bus door, the crowd stepped aside. The pushing had stopped. Panic had ceased. After we entered the bus, we walked down the aisle in a daze and took two seats to the left. Then, forty-eight other people entered calmly. Once the bus was full, the driver closed the door and began to drive away as if we were on a normal route, on a normal day. I gazed through the window. Those left behind all had the same look of despair on their faces.

Jean-Paul Sartre wrote that 'freedom is what you do with what has been done to you'. As Hava and I sat in the bus, as the war vanished behind us with each mile, I felt more and more triumphant and free.

Hava broke off a piece of bread and offered it to me. No one spoke. The groan of the engine was enough for our nerves. We had heard enough engines, planes, bombs, and screams. The steady hum of the bus soothed us, so much so that within minutes Hava and I were asleep.

CHAPTER 44

The best political weapon is the weapon of terror. Cruelty commands
respect. Men may hate us. But we don't ask for their love; only for their fear.
SS Commander Heinrich Himmler, quoted in "Visions of
Reality – A Study of Abnormal Perception and Behavior" by
Alberto Rivas, *Psychology*, 2007

The sound of the bombs and planes reverberated through my
dreams as I slept, intermingled with random images: the
colour of the eiderdown in our room in Dunkirk; the face of our
redheaded soldier; the large white Belgian clouds in July against
an azure-blue sky. Then suddenly a German word – '*Papiere!*' –
roused me from my slumber.

'*Papiere!! Los, auf geht's!*'

I had never seen an SS officer before.

'*Papiere!! Los, auf geht's!*'

I opened my eyes. A soldier stood in the aisle of the bus, dressed
in a black uniform with a red swastika sown on an armband. His
hat was peaked, his boots black. I didn't even realize the bus had
stopped. I was groggy. Behind him a regular German soldier held a

machine gun. Next to the bus there were three trucks, a tank, and a number of German soldiers sitting on a wall smoking cigarettes.

Hava leaned against me and without warning yanked my chain with the gold Star of David roughly from my neck.

'Why'd you do that?' I was startled.

'Don't say a word, Simone. I think they're here looking for Jews.'

People in the bus immediately pulled out documents. The SS officer walked down the aisle, checking each paper. He asked no questions until he came to Hava and me.

'*Papiere!!*'

Hava shrugged and offered the man some bread. He slapped it out of her hand.

'*Papiere. Ich habe Ihnen einen Auftrag gegeben.*'

Identification papers. I gave you an order.

I didn't speak German, and it was clear that he didn't speak French. I nodded. 'Yes.'

'*Papiere. Sind Sie Jüdin?*' Are you a Jew? I glared at him blankly. Obviously annoyed that we did not understand, he turned back to the soldier with the machine gun and spoke a few words. The soldier stepped off the bus and quickly returned with another haggard-looking soldier.

'I speak French,' the new soldier said to us. 'I'm a translator, Joseph Becker. My commanding officer asked you for identification, and wants to know if you're Jewish.'

I didn't have any form of identification, no passport, or baptism certificate, but I did have something. I reached into my pocket and pulled out a folded paper that I waved in the soldier's face. I glanced at Hava's clenched fist, then said, 'This is all I have. And, yes, I am Jewish.'

The man in the black uniform grabbed the paper from my hand, unfolded it, and laughed.

'*Juden tragen kein Kreuz.*' And he waved Benjamin's drawing of God in the air. I didn't smile. Still laughing, he repeated, '*Juden tragen kein Kreuz*,' and handed Benjamin's drawing to the translator.

'What did he say, Monsieur Becker?' I asked.

'He said, Jews don't carry a cross,' and he pointed to the two crosses above God's head in Benjamin's drawing.

'They're not crosses. They're kites,' I protested.

The translator looked at me doubtfully and asked, 'If you are Jewish, tell me ... what are the Five Books of Moses?

'Tell me. What are the Five Books of Moses?' he repeated.

I froze. He repeated the question. I shrugged.

The translator looked at the Nazi officer and said, 'Not a Jew.'

The SS Nazi officer looked at Hava and asked, '*Jüdin?*'

She was about to speak when I said, '*Nein*' – the only German I knew. 'She is Marie Armel. She is a banker. This is Marie Armel, my cousin, and a very important banker.'

Joseph Becker, the translator, laughed and then turned to the man in the black uniform and spoke some words in German. They both laughed.

The translator turned to me and said, 'Marie Armel is my banker. I've lived in Roeselare all my life. I am a language teacher, but I heard they needed translators in France, and they pay well. France has a new order and it's your lucky day. It's not clever to lie to an SS officer, but my commander is a compassionate man, and just wants to know if your friend is Jewish.'

I was about to protest again when Hava looked into my eyes and said to the translator at the same time, 'Yes. I am a Jew. My name is Hava Daniels. Bereishit, Shemot, Vayikra, Bamidbar, Devarim … these are the Five Books of Moses, and I am proud of being a Jew.' Then she opened her hand and showed the translator the gold chain and the beautiful five-pointed Star of David. 'I wear this all the time. I tried to hide it when you stepped inside the bus.'

The SS officer flatly stated an order. '*Stehen Sie auf.*'

The translator said, 'Stand up!'

Hava rose to her feet.

'*Es ist eine Schande, daß sie so hübsch ist. Die Jüdin kommt mit uns.*' It's a shame she's pretty. The Jewish girl is coming with us.

The soldier gripped Hava's arm, and tore the gold necklace from her hand. She didn't resist, but I did. I stood and pushed the soldier away from Hava. The SS officer grabbed my wrist to pull me back.

'Simone, stop,' Hava said. 'Stop! I'll be alright. Don't worry. Let me go.'

I looked at the translator and asked, 'Where are you taking her?'

'To a relocation centre,' he replied flatly.

The SS officer let go of my wrist. I had one more chance to save Hava. 'My name is Simone Lyon. My father is Major General Joseph Lyon.'

Joseph Becker translated my statement and then the SS commander said, '*Ja, und mein Vater ist Winston Churchill.*'

The two soldiers began to laugh. The SS officer joined in. The translator looked at me still laughing. 'My commander says, sure and his father is Winston Churchill.'

The soldier with the machine gun yanked Hava's arm to lead her off the bus. Hava turned back and said to me, 'I dream of clouds.' Then we embraced.

'I promise I'll find you,' I whispered as I kissed her cheek.

'*Los, auf geht's! Los, auf geht's!*'

'Remember me, Simone,' Hava said as she was wrenched from me and dragged down the aisle.

The SS officer glared once more at everyone in the bus. Then he stepped up to me, smiled and spoke, as Joseph Becker translated:

'Open your hand.' He slapped Hava's Star of David and chain into my palm. 'Stuff this filth in your father's coffin.' Then he turned and marched off the bus, the translator following quickly behind. My fist tightened.

I watched helplessly from the bus as the SS commander grabbed Hava by her golden hair, so hard that she could barely walk upright, until she reached the back of one of the trucks.

I saw the Nazi officer grab Hava by her neck and force her to her knees in supplication. Then the translator lifted Hava and shoved her into the back of the truck, where she disappeared behind a green tarpaulin that flapped back into place. The truck drove off, leaving behind a shroud of dust.

I opened my closed fist. Hava's star was tangled in the gold chain. And I remembered Mr Alberg's proverb: *When you have no choice, mobilize the spirit of courage.*

Later I discovered that the SS officers routinely told Jews, *If you can name the Five Books of Moses, you will be spared.* In their desperation to survive, people had unwittingly identified themselves as Jews and thus sealed their fate. But Hava had not been tricked. She had made a conscious decision.

I had promised Hava that I would find her. Hava Daniels; my Esther. Hava Daniels; my friend. Hava Daniels has a name: Hava … Hava Daniels.

As I looked at the crumpled chain in my hand, I wondered

about the relocation centre. I had made a promise. I would follow her trail and I would find her. I would be a brave Belgian, the daughter of Joseph Lyon. Brave like Hava, for she had not been afraid to admit to the SS that she was a Jew.

Chapter 45

*Jews were ordered to hand over fur coats. Jews were not allowed
to receive eggs or milk. Jews were forbidden to use public telephones,
forbidden to keep cats, dogs, or birds. Jews were banned from parks,
restaurants, and swimming pools. Jews were evicted from their homes
without reason or notice. All schools closed to Jewish children. Jews were
forbidden to use the German greeting, 'Heil Hitler'.*

The bus driver's veins bulged over the top of his hand, blue veins,
as he reached for the lever that closed the door to the bus.

As a child I did not know that the colour of the blood in my
veins was dark red; I thought it was blue.

When my father told me that my blood contained iron, I
felt like a magician with great powers. I knew about iron: the
gate to the garden behind our house was always described as
'the iron gate'.

'Make sure the iron gate is closed, Simone,' my father said one
late afternoon, as we sat in the garden on little iron chairs reading
our books. I was reading *Black Beauty*, and when my father asked
me what it was about, I told him, 'Beauty, the horse, is always

brave. Beauty runs fast because he knows someone is dying, and Beauty saves the woman's life.'

In my mind Black Beauty was like my father's horse, Charlotte. He leaned over, held my book in his hand and quickly thumbed through the pages until he stopped and pointed to this passage: 'There is no religion without love, and people may talk as much as they like about their religion, but if it does not teach them to be good and kind to man and beast, it is all a sham.'

When the bus driver closed the door to the bus, I thought about the iron gate in our garden and my father's hand reaching for my book. I looked again at the bus driver's blue veins.

Hava was not with me. In that moment, I wanted to ride Black Beauty and save her. Instead the gears of the bus groaned and growled and I, not in the saddle with Black Beauty, wept.

CHAPTER 46

We have no flag, and we need one. If we desire to lead many men,
we must raise a symbol above their heads. I would suggest a white flag,
with seven golden stars. The white field symbolizes our pure new life;
the stars are the seven golden hours of our working day. For we shall
march into the Promised Land carrying the badge of honour.
Theodor Herzl, Jewish Austro-Hungarian writer, from his
book *The Jewish State* (1896)

'Mademoiselle, why are you crying?'
I turned to my right, not realizing that I was now
sitting beside a little girl. The bus rocked back and forth. The smell
of petrol was overwhelming.

'Did you hurt your arm? I fell on the pavement this morning
and hurt my arm. Look.' The girl showed me a long, purple bruise.

'*Non, ma petite*, I'm sad.'

'Why are you sad?'

The angry bus strained up a hill.

'I had to say goodbye to a friend.'

'Does your friend like fire engines? My friend, Eli, likes fire engines. He lives next door. His mother is a baker and she always invited me into their kitchen. I love her apple pie. Do you like apple pie, mademoiselle?'

I looked down at the child who sat on the bus as if she was on her way to church. 'Yes, I like apple pie very much.'

'Well,' said the girl, 'when I asked Eli if *he* liked apple pie, he shrugged and said that he likes fire engines and that someday he's going to be a fireman like his father.'

The voice of the child replaced the sounds of the grinding, shaking, rusting old bus, as she continued. 'One day Eli was sad too, not because he said goodbye to a friend, but because he couldn't be a fireman. We were eating apple pie in the kitchen and he said that he couldn't be a fireman. When I asked him why not, he walked out of the room, and came back with his outside coat.'

The girl looked up at me and asked. 'Mademoiselle, do you have an outside coat?'

I realized that the child must have been curious about my dishevelled appearance. My dress was dirty, my face was dirty. All I had was my torn dress, my shoes, and my journal.

'Yes, *petite*, I left my coat at home. It's being washed.'

'Well, Eli came back into the kitchen with his outside coat and he showed me his yellow star. He called it *David's yellow star*. His mother said that he had to wear it, and that she had sewed the star onto his coat. She said that Eli will be like a cowboy sheriff in America. Eli said that he didn't want to be a sheriff; he wanted to be a fireman. He had tried to rip the yellow star off his outside coat, but his mother had forbidden him from doing it, Eli said. Then he and I ate our apple pie.'

The little girl's legs dangled over the seat and didn't reach the floor of the bus. Then she said quietly, 'After that day I never saw

Eli or his family again. Do you think he will be a cowboy sheriff in America?'

CHAPTER 47

The Battle at Hannut in Belgium took place 12–14 May between Belgian and Nazi tanks. It was the largest clash of armoured warfare in history.

The bus driver took us to Calais, and from Calais I took a train to Biarritz in southern France, as far from the Nazi invasion as I could go.

When I stepped off the train that morning, I felt a sudden surge of peace. The engine was silent. There were no refugees, and squawking gulls replaced the throb of Nazi planes. All I had was my journal in my hand, Hava's necklace, and Benjamin's drawing in my pocket.

I had nearly forgotten it was spring. The warm sea air almost made me forget the way Hava had been thrown brutally into the truck. The lapis lazuli sky almost blotted out the Nazis' red and black flags. I had heard about Biarritz, the famous coastal resort town on the south-western coast of France.

Quickly though, reality returned to my aching body. My dress was stained, my face smeared with dirt and tears, my hair tangled. As I walked out of the train station and into the open streets of the town, people looked at me as if I was an urchin, something to be avoided, or looked through as if I were invisible.

I was alone. My father had disappeared. My aunt was in Luxemburg. Hava was on her way to a relocation centre of some sort. Brussels was over 1,000 kilometres away. It was there, at that moment, that I thought about my mother.

My steps were slow. I nearly staggered from fatigue and hunger. With each step I asked myself a question. 'Had my mother been happy that I was about to be born? Why did she name me Simone? How did her laugh sound? Did she know that she was going to die in childbirth?' I had never asked my father these questions, but he did tell me once that my mother had loved the idea of me very much.

I didn't know that I was walking towards the ocean until I heard the distant waves curling on the beach.

Did my mother like daffodils? Had she read *Romeo and Juliet*? I felt faint with sorrow. I pulled each step from the last amounts of energy that I possessed. The sound of the waves increased just beyond the dunes. Was my mother waiting for me there, stretched on the sand like a film star?

I climbed the dunes, stumbling again and again. Sand slipped into my shoes, mingled with my matted hair. I heard Hava's voice in my delirium: *'The Nazis will not find a filthy Belgian girl, Simone.'*

When I reached the top of the dunes, the Atlantic Ocean spread out like a painting, all foam and blue water, all sky and eternity. It was the end of my journey. I could not run any further from the Nazis. I looked to my left and saw the Hotel du Palais. When I looked to my right, I began to sway. My heart raced. In the distance I saw a woman on the rocks, a woman dressed in white. I touched my cheek. The woman in white stood tall and aloof. *'Maman?'* I asked aloud, as the surging waves drowned my voice, and then I fainted.

I do not know for how long I had been unconscious, but I awoke with the feeling of a hand behind my head and water touching my lips. As I drank slowly, I opened my eyes.

'You had me worried, mademoiselle.'

I closed my eyes again for a moment, not remembering where I was.

'What is your name, mademoiselle?'

I opened my eyes and saw an old woman with the bluest eyes peering back at me. Her wrinkled face offered a small, reassuring smile. 'Simone. I am Simone Lyon.'

The woman sat beside me and helped me sit up. She offered me more water from a small canteen, which I accepted immediately and drank and drank.

'Are you the woman?' I asked in a daze.

'Woman?'

'I saw you, dressed in white, on the rocks. You were standing there so confidently.'

The old woman took the canteen, replaced the cap, and pointed towards the ocean. 'There, mademoiselle Simone. There is your woman in white.'

On the tip of a large outcrop of rocks stood a statue of Mary, visible from a great distance.

'It's the Rocher de la Vierge, the Virgin Rock, Simone. She is holding the Christ child in her arms.'

I wish the virgin on the rock would hold me, I thought.

'It's a great tourist attraction. But, mademoiselle, you are not a tourist. Where do you come from?'

I looked up at the statue again, thought about my mother, looked at the curling foam of the waves and whispered, 'Brussels.

I'm from Brussels. The Nazis …Where am I?' When I tried to stand up, I stumbled onto the sand again.

'You don't want to be like a shell, mademoiselle, and be swept up by the ocean. You will come home with me. Don't be frightened. Stand up, but let me help you this time.'

I was in such a daze that I complied easily. As I leaned against the woman and as she looped my arm around her waist, she said, 'My name is Madame Bisset. I've lived here in Biarritz for over forty years.'

As she spoke, we made our way slowly back to the other side of the dunes and towards the streets.

'Each morning I come to the sea and look for shells. I collect them.'

Madame Bisset's strength surprised me.

She stopped for a moment so that she could get a better balance. 'This morning, I looked across the dunes and saw you. At first I thought you were just a clump of seaweed, but then you moved a bit.'

'Thank you,' I whispered.

'Save your strength. Just walk with me. We don't have far to go.'

With each step, and with each breath of the fresh, salted, air, I began to revive a bit.

'You said something about the Nazis?' Madame Bisset asked after a few moments.

'We tried to run away. We kept ahead of them. My friend Hava and I … we tried our best.'

'Who is this friend of yours? Where is she?'

'Hava Daniels. We were almost free. Then they took her away in a truck. I have to find her.'

Madame Bisset guided me down a wide street and when we both stood before a grand, stone house with a blue door and blue shutters, she said, 'Tell me about your friend later. For now, you need food, fresh clothes, and rest.'

She produced a key from her pocket, inserted it in the large blue door, and looked at my puzzled face. 'This is my house. I live alone now, but my husband and I bought this place together as a summer home, many years ago. We liked the view. I still do.' She turned me around and there stretched before us was Biarritz: its grand hotels, its squares, the ocean, and the beach.

'Come inside, Simone.'

The interior of the house was made of stone, polished wood, and mirrors. Tapestries hung from the walls. Portraits of society women and officers in uniform hung in a large room to the right.

In the front room was a glass shelf filled with shells: white shells, orange shells, shells that looked like swirls of fresh cream. I picked up the one I liked best: a soft pink shell.

Madame Bisset smiled. 'That is a French scallop. I found it on the beach after a violent storm. It's one of my favourites too. I call it the *Fan of a Japanese Empress*.'

I held the shell in my hand and looked around the room filled with books, silver goblets, and an ivory statue of St George and the Dragon.

'People think that I live in a museum.'

As I stood in the room, I began to shiver.

'What am I doing? You're cold, of course! Let me help you, mademoiselle.'

That first evening, Madame Bisset offered me a warm bath, a room, and a wardrobe of clothes to choose from; and later as I sat at her dining-room table with a plate of chicken, green beans, and even a scone, I asked, 'Why did you help me? I'm a stranger. No one wanted to help me. I must have looked like a savage.'

Madame Bisset stirred a hot cup of tea. 'My husband and I moved here after the First World War. We are German.'

I stiffened visibly.

'No, no, not those Germans, Mademoiselle Lyon. You'd be surprised how many German people are good, decent people, but also just victims of fear. My husband was an engineer in the car industry in Germany, and in the 1930s, when Hitler became head of the Nazi Party, my husband was hired to work on a project. Hitler wanted to strengthen his appeal to the people and provide inexpensive cars for everyone, so he developed a car company.

'When my husband refused to work for Hitler, he was shot, and his body buried in an unmarked grave somewhere north of Berlin.

'So, like you I, too, ran away from Hitler. I'm a refugee of the First World War, and when I saw you, I knew you were like me – escaping. I didn't know from what, but now I know that, ironically, you are running from the same Hitler, from the same hate. You are lucky. You made it.'

Madame Bisset sipped her tea.

I began to cry.

'What is it, Simone?'

And I told Madame Bisset about Hava, and how unlucky she was. 'They dragged her by her hair,' I wept.

Madame Bisset stood up from her chair and wrapped her arms around my shoulders. I wept as she comforted me. 'The woman in white that you saw, Simone, the Rock of the Virgin ... All who live here know the story about the fishermen from Biarritz who were caught in a terrible storm when hunting for whales. When they finally returned battered and exhausted, they spoke about a divine light that had guided them back. Those men were so grateful that they built a statue to Mary in gratitude. We must believe in divine light, Simone.'

I stayed with Madame Bisset for two months, until 10 July 1940. She fed me, let me take long baths, and gave me a soft bed. She provided me with a candle for my room, and with the warmth I had been so desperate for. I spent my time regaining my strength, walking along the shore collecting shells, and plotting how I would find Hava.

One night, when I was nearly asleep, there was a sudden brightness outside. I said to myself as I yawned and rubbed my eyes, 'The divine light.'

I pushed back the blanket from my body, and walked to the window. The radiant light dissipated, danced around the cobblestone square, and melted into the headlights of three army transport trucks flying the Nazi flag.

My thoughts drifted to Hava, to the day we met at the Red Cross, the fun we had at her house during Benjamin's play. I thought about the way Hava had given Joff his medicine. Hava Daniels, my friend. *Where was she beyond the dark sky outside my window?* I thought.

After those short restful months, Nazi troops bled into that coastal town as well, marching past Madame Bisset's house in their frightening goose steps. All of France had been taken over, conquered, and occupied. It was no use. My journey of escape was over, and there was nowhere else to run.

CHAPTER 48

The French army soon succumbed to the Blitzkrieg. Following, the Armistice of 22 June 1940 established a German military administration in occupied France, including Biarritz and all of the French Basque Country region.

The next morning, at breakfast, Madame Bisset made a suggestion. 'They say there are trains for refugees, to take them back home. You can return to Belgium, Simone, to look for your family. I packed a suitcase for you.'

Madame Bisset led me to the front room, where she had set up a suitcase on the couch. She pointed out the different things she had packed for me. 'Here, the dress you wore that first day you were with me; cheese; a small blanket in case you are cold on the train; and this.' She reached under the blanket and handed me the Fan of a Japanese Empress.

'But it's your favourite shell,' I protested.

'It's for you. It will remind you of a time when Biarritz was free, and it will remind you of me. We all liked to be remembered.'

That afternoon, at the front door, Madame Bisset embraced me.

'Bon voyage, Simone.'

'Thank you, Madame Bisset. Thank you for saving me.'

'If we save one, we save all.'

As I walked down the steps and into the street, I saw the red and black Nazi flag with the crooked black cross mocking the colour of the blue sky. I turned to wave goodbye to Madame Bisset, but her door was already closed and she was gone.

As I made my way slowly back to Belgium, on 19 July Adolf Hitler addressed the German nation from the Reichstag in Berlin, boasting of victory.

> *The German Reich, in particular with regard to Poland, has shown restraint. In the days of 6 May and 7 May, telephone conversations between London and Paris took place, of which we gained intelligence and which reinforced suspicions that an invasion of the Netherlands and Belgium by the so-called Allies had to be expected at any moment. Thus, on the following day, 8 May, I ordered an immediate attack for 10 May, 5:35 in the morning. The international Jewish poison of the peoples began to agitate against and to corrode healthy minds. No other statesman could have afforded to propose a solution to the German nation in the way I did. Paris fell.*

All of France had been taken over, conquered, and occupied. It became known that if you were not Jewish, you could return safely to Belgium. I was going home. I had lost my chance to escape the Nazi occupation, but at least I was going home.

I took a train from Biarritz back to Brussels. When I arrived home, I placed my pink shell on my nightstand, and my life in

Brussels under Nazi rule began.

So much of those four years is a blur as loneliness, confusion, and fear monopolized my thoughts about my father, my country, and about Hava.

When I first returned home, I found the house unchanged, except for a thick layer of dust that took up residence in my absence. Somehow, my house had survived the chaos, the bombs, and the madness. I wished my father had been there too, but he was still far away. I was frantic to find him, but all the Belgian offices were filled with Nazi bureaucrats who were no help, and simply ordered me to go home.

After one exhausting day of searching, I entered my house and found a note someone had slipped under my door. *Your father is safe. He escaped over the Pyrenees and into Spain.* I didn't know where it came from, but I chose to believe it was true. I chose to believe he was safe, and I let myself feel relieved.

During those first few months I made it my mission to find Hava. She was young; she was strong. I knew that she would be okay wherever she was. I just needed to find her. I thought my father's medal and reputation might give me some clout with whoever was in charge of locating and releasing prisoners. If they knew Hava and her family were good friends of the general, surely they'd let them go.

I spent weeks visiting offices, spent hours scrutinizing lists of names. There were so many people named Daniels, but they were never the right ones. No Hava. No Benjamin. No Yaakov. No Avital. I hoped that one clue, just one clue, might lead me to Hava, but the answers were always the same: the Polish and Jewish people who had been taken away by the Nazis couldn't be found, couldn't be brought home.

When I went to Hava's synagogue, there was only rubble. When I asked in the neighbourhood about Rabbi Menke, or about the Daniels family, all I received was silence. It was as if there had been no Jews in Brussels; as if the Nazi Pied Piper of Hamelin had swooped into Belgium and lured away not rats and children, but all the Jewish people.

So many nights I cried myself to sleep. I prayed for my father, for Hava, and for her family. I prayed for the war to end. And that prayer became my mantra during those lonely days. I would tell myself, 'When the war is over, I will find Hava. When the war is over, everything will go back to the way things used to be. When the war is over … When the war is over.'

But the war dragged on month after month. I felt like a prisoner in my own home as the Nazis marched in our streets, attended our opera, ran our government and used most of our city's resources for their soldiers.

There was a nightly curfew, food was scarce because of rationing, and the neighbourhood tried to survive in as normal a manner as possible on the little that was available to us. It took so much energy just to endure, just to keep going, that living itself started to feel like a monotonous chore – a dreary cycle of waking and sleeping. I did find moments of solace in books, and I was grateful for my father's library, but those moments never lasted long as I'd always find my mind wandering back to Hava.

CHAPTER 49

February 1945. Allied leaders Franklin D. Roosevelt, Winston Churchill, and Joseph Stalin meet at Yalta, on the Crimean Peninsula, to plan the final phase of the war. That month, Belgium was declared fully liberated.

M any years later I learned that after my father had joined the Belgian Resistance, he had received word that the Nazis' SS elite had discovered his activities, so he'd fled Belgium with two of his comrades. They walked through France under the cover of night, hiding in barns during the day, avoiding German trucks and troops, dodging Nazi soldiers on motorcycles and in planes. They walked and walked, until they reached the foot of the Pyrenees. There, they hired a guide who took them over the mountain and into Spain, where they were ultimately captured and imprisoned.

Six months later, Spain, then an ally of Nazi Germany, was in desperate need of fuel, so the Government made a deal with England: oil for prisoners. And so my father was released and sent to England with over 7,000 other Belgian and French refugees.

There had been no way for him to contact me, but one evening during the third year of the war, as I was listening to Radio Belgium, to a broadcast transmitted to Nazi-occupied Belgium from London, I was startled to hear my father's voice: 'The time for courage is upon you. It is known throughout the world of your struggles. Salvation is at hand. The Allies will not be thwarted. Roosevelt and Churchill will prevail. *Vive la Belgique.*'

During his four years in London, my father was able to broadcast such encouraging words to his country as part of the Resistance campaign, and during his time there, he helped thousands of European refugees who had escaped across the English Channel. Towards the end of the war, he had become a significant player in the reconstruction of Europe, having received personal awards from American General Dwight Eisenhower and British General Bernard Montgomery.

The war ended for me when, one day, there was a robust knock at my door. When I opened it, there standing before me was Major General Joseph Lyon, in full dress uniform and white gloves. My father.

'Papa!' I cried. I fell into his safe arms and wept.

'Simone.' I felt his strong arms around me. I felt tears on my cheek.

I looked up into his face and said 'Wait, Papa. Wait.'

I reached into my pocket, fumbled for the Croix de Guerre, and pinned it onto my father's chest. I stepped back, saluted and then once again fell into his open arms.

CHAPTER 50

In these three decades love and loyalty to my people have guided all my thoughts, actions and my life ... It is untrue that I or anyone else in Germany wanted war in 1939. It was wanted and provoked solely by international statesmen, either of Jewish origin or working for Jewish interests ... Above all, I charge the leadership of the nation and their followers with strict observation of racial laws and with the merciless resistance against the universal poisoners of all people, international Jewry.
Adolf Hitler's Last Will and Testament, 29 April 1945

After my father and I were reunited, I was able to focus once again on my concerns for Hava. The war was nearly over. I didn't know where to begin my search, but then I thought to start at the beginning: Hava's home.

I had walked past her house many times during the Nazi occupation and each time, I saw that it was empty: no lights, boarded-up windows, and someone had painted the word 'Jew' in bold black letters across the front door.

When my father returned home, I was filled with new hope. 'Papa, it's such a beautiful day, I think I will go for a walk.' He was sitting once again in his chair, with his newspaper on his lap, just where he belonged. He looked up at me and smiled. 'Yes, Simone. The Brussels air is fresh once again.'

When I opened the door, I almost expected to find Nicole with a carrot in her hand, but she was not there. I thought about Sergeant De Waden and the beautiful white horse. As I walked through the park I looked up into the sky and was happy to see pigeons instead of low-flying aeroplanes.

I walked by the convent. It was closed. I walked aimlessly through the streets, happy to see fresh gingerbread and *speculaas* biscuits once again in the baker's window.

I bought a small bag of chestnuts from a vendor under a green and white striped umbrella and savoured the taste. As I was peeling the last one, I looked up and realized that I was standing in front of Hava's house. There were lights inside and blinds on the windows. The door was freshly painted green. 'They're back!' I laughed out loud and tossed the last chestnut shells up into the air like confetti.

I ran to the green door and knocked, and knocked, and knocked. 'Monsieur Daniels! Madame Daniels!' I knocked again. 'Benjamin!'

When the door opened there stood a tall, young man. 'May I help you?'

I looked at the man's face, and into his eyes, and then I knew.

'May I help you?' he asked again.

My shoulders slumped; my voice subdued. 'My name is Simone Lyon. Do you know the Daniels? They live here. They're my friends. I haven't seen them since the beginning of the war.'

A young woman appeared at the door and asked, 'Roger, is everything alright?'

'Yes, yes. This is Mademoiselle Lyon. She is looking for the

Daniels family.'

The man turned to me and kindly said 'Come in, mademoiselle. This is my wife Claudine. I am Roger Peeters. Come in, please.'

I hesitated to step into the memories that had been carried away by the war. The rooms were a different colour, the furniture unrecognizable. We sat in the parlour where Benjamin had stepped out from behind the curtain and announced, *Good evening, ladies and gentleman.* At least the curtains were still there.

When I clasped my hands together, Monsieur Peeters stood up. 'I'll be right back. Claudine, perhaps we can offer the mademoiselle some tea?'

'No, no thank you. I don't want to disturb you. I was just hoping to find my friends. I don't know what happened to them.'

Madame Peeters looked at me as her husband left the room. 'Roger is an architect. He was a corporal in the war. When Belgium fell in those first eighteen days, Roger was taken prisoner with the other thousands of Belgian soldiers. He was lucky; he was not sent to the factories in Germany. The Nazis had too many prisoners and just let some go home.'

I looked around the room.

'We were fortunate,' Madame Peeters continued as she placed her hand gently on her abdomen. 'We're expecting our first child. We were looking for a home to begin our new life. When we went to the bank for financial help, we were told that many abandoned homes were available, but in disrepair. We loved this house right away, and because of my husband's profession, he was able to redesign and repair the damage. It's a beautiful place.'

'Yes, yes,' I said as I closed my eyes for a moment. 'It is beautiful.'

'Mademoiselle Lyon, I have something to share with you,'

Monsieur Peeters said as he returned from the back room.

'When we first moved here, a postal clerk came to the door, happy to see that his postal route was being re-established. After he introduced himself, he explained that at the beginning of the war, this packet had been sent to this address. He said that he had known the Daniels well, but that he couldn't deliver this, for no one was ever home. And then the widows were boarded up, the building condemned, so he kept this at his home, thinking perhaps the Daniels would someday return.'

'I remember how the house was closed during the war,' I said, anxious to know what was in the packet.

'These letters,' Monsieur Peeters said, holding up a thin bundle of papers tied together with a red string, 'they were written by the Daniels family. Your name is mentioned ... When you said your name just now, I recognized it.'

Monsieur Peeters handed me the small packet of letters.

His wife looked at her husband, and turned to me. 'We'd like you to have them. We hoped that perhaps someday you would come.'

When I held the letters, I could almost feel Hava's hand in mine. 'Thank you, thank you, monsieur and madame.'

At the door, before I left, I said, 'I promised my friend that I would remember her and find her.'

'I hope you do. Good luck, Mademoiselle Lyon,' Monsieur Peeter said.

'*Bon chance,*' his wife said warmly.

'Good luck with your baby,' I replied.

As I walked down the street, the warm sun caressed my cheeks. A man and a woman walked past me arm in arm and smiled. A child carrying a small wooden sailing boat said to the old man walking beside him, 'The swans like to chase my boat on the pond.'

When I saw an empty bench up ahead, I had to restrain myself not to run, so I walked up to it casually, sat down as if it was just an ordinary day at the park, and held the letters tenderly in my hands, then started reading.

Hava, my daughter,

Your mother, and I, and Benjamin are okay. We waited for you when you went off to get Simone, but at the synagogue we received word that Jews were going to be beaten and their families slaughtered. We met some friends – you remember the Bergmanns? They had a car. I believed that since you were with Simone, a gentile and daughter of General Lyon, that you were safe. Still, we asked the Bergmanns to drive us back home, in case you had returned. Before we got there, we were stopped and taken to Germany.

Now, we are told that we will be going to some sort of camp. They tell us we will be going by train to the industrial town of Oświęcim in southern Poland. We will be asked to work. We can work. When we get home we will once again pray together. Be brave, my Hava. We love you.

Papa

I sat on the bench, closed my eyes and heard Yaakov Daniels telling Hava, 'Remember what we say: *God Blessed are You, O Lord, who consoles all men and women and builds every home, for we shall all be restored.*'

In the distance I heard children laughing and the music from the carousel playing once again. I took a deep breath and continued.

My dear Hava,

Your father is his usual grumpy self, and Benjamin can't sit still. We miss you and hope the house is warm enough. As your father said, we had to leave. We were not given a choice, but Germany is beautiful, though we have been told we won't be staying here very long. There was an issue about a transfer at a train station. We were told that we will be taken to a comfortable town in Poland where we will be safe during the war and fed and even given a shower. Plumbing! Can you imagine how nice it will be to take a warm shower?

Take care of the house. Stick close to Simone. She is a lovely girl. We all need friends. I love you my darling. Don't worry about us. Benjamin is pestering me for the pencil so I will let him write. We love you.

Mama

'Mademoiselle Lyon?'

I looked up from Avital's letter.

'Mademoiselle Lyon, is it you?'

'Nicole?' I reached out, hugged the girl and wept softly into her shoulder.

'Mademoiselle?' Nicole whispered after a few moments. 'I saw you from the carousel. Are you okay?' She wriggled slightly loose from my embrace and looked into my eyes. 'I am thirteen now.

My mother and I, we moved to a new house. Does your father still have his beautiful horse?'

I let go of the child, wiped away my tears, and slipped Avital's letter under the first one. I took a deep breath.

'I'm okay, Nicole. You are all grown up! No, the horse is gone. I think she must have fought very bravely for Sergeant De Waden.'

Nicole stepped back and sat next to me. 'I remember the carrots. I was so frightened at first to feed the horse. I was afraid Charlotte was going to bite my hand if I placed the carrot too close to her mouth.'

'You were a brave little girl. It's important to be brave.'

'I like listening to American music. I heard a song called "My Dreams are getting better". Doris Day sang it. I like Doris Day. Someday I'm going to be just like her.'

'It's good to have dreams, Nicole. Do you dream about clouds or mountains?'

Nicole smiled and said, 'That's a funny question, mademoiselle. I dream about Hollywood.'

I inhaled the fresh Belgian air. Once Hava and I had had the same dreams.

'I have to go. My mother said that after the park, she'd take me to the Grand Place for lunch.' She hugged me, stood up and said, 'My mother will be happy that I found you. It's good to be found, isn't it, mademoiselle?'

'Yes, Nicole. It's a good to be found. Please say hello to your mother.'

'*Bonjour*, mademoiselle.'

'Goodbye, *ma petite amie.*'

As I watched Nicole run down cobblestones, I tapped my hand against the last letter.

Hi Hava,

Mama said I should write a letter. She didn't give me the pencil. I'm hot. Are you coming? I'm also thirsty, but Papa said not to tell you anything bad so I will tell you something else. We are going to take a train, in a cattle car! That should be fun. I hope the cows don't smell too much. Okay. I wrote you a letter. Now you have to write me back.

Benjamin

'It's good to be found,' I said to myself as I walked home.

CHAPTER 51

With the backing of the approaching Allied armies commanded by Generals Eisenhower and Bradley, and with the French people and their triumphant fighting of the Nazis in Paris, Charles de Gaulle announced triumphantly, 'Paris! Paris humiliated! Paris broken! Paris martyred! But now Paris liberated! Liberated by herself, by her own people with the help of the armies of France, with the support and aid of France as a whole, of fighting France, of the only France, of the true France, of eternal France.'

A few weeks later, with the war nearly over, I found myself in the filthy attic with my father. For once, the loud explosions outside were not from bombs, but from a powerful thunderstorm. The storm split open the night; the most ferocious storm I had ever experienced.

During the night, the rain leaked into the attic, saturated the floor, and poured into the bedrooms, causing great havoc for my father and me. The next morning, we climbed into the attic where we found a thick layer of sludge. The attic had accumulated layers of dust over the many years, and because the storm had been so powerful, the rain had washed away part of the roof and soaked into the dried dirt.

My father and I had buckets, rags, and sponges, and we began wiping, scrubbing, and gathering the muck. At one point, my father looked up at me. His face was smeared with dirt. Because I felt sorry for him, I said that I would clean up the rest. But in response, his eyes wide and determined, my father spoke of how much he had suffered in the Spanish prison. 'Cleaning this attic is a joy and great fun.' He flicked muck into my face and we laughed. Then I threw muck into his face, and he *didn't* laugh ... at first.

I grimaced, realizing that I had just retaliated against a general, but then he wiped his face with a rag, saluted me, and smiled.

We endure. We bend like the trees in an angry wind. We learn fortitude. We fling muck back at the sorrows of our lives and laugh. We are sometimes happy and sometimes not. But in between there is victory, solace, and contentment.

As we continued to mop up the mud and dust in the attic, my father said, 'I'll be going to Paris for a few weeks. The war will be over soon and there will be delegations of business people and military personnel from each country to organize the rebuilding of Europe.'

At that point, I knew that I had a fugitive's spirit. Hava and I had tried once to escape the horrors of indignity and failed. Now that the war was almost over, I felt within me again that urge to break free from the war, from the fear, and from the internal oppression I felt. I wanted to go to Paris with my father.

During the war I found it desperately hard being alone without Hava, and without my father. Belgium was still in the grip of sorrow and hate, and I felt the instability of my soul at the war's end.

'We need to begin rebuilding,' my father said as we climbed down from the attic. 'You are safe in Brussels, Simone. The war is coming to an end. Can you manage here alone for a few weeks?'

'But, Papa,' I said, nearly pleading. 'I've been confined to this house for four years. I'm 22 years old and I have barely been out of Brussels. Can I come to Paris with you?'

'No. I will be on a military train, and it's February. It'll be very cold. There's no heat, no fuel, and very little food. No. It's out of the question.' As we made our way down to the kitchen to clean our hands, I continued to argue. 'But I won't get in the way, and I'll be able to continue my search for Hava!'

'Simone, it's a military train. No civilians will be allowed.'

I stepped away and walked back upstairs, to my father's bedroom. There I unhooked one of his early uniforms from his closet, a corporal's uniform, which I carried back into the kitchen. I placed his old green corporal's uniform against my body and said, 'I can wear this.'

My father looked at me with a slight grin. 'You know, Simone, there are no women in the Belgian army.'

'But you're a general. I'll be your military attaché. No one will stop us.'

And no one did stop us, as my father and I stepped onto the train to Paris filled with officers in their serious uniforms. No one stopped us as we ate at the American military canteen, where I had white bread for the first time in four years.

In the excitement of Paris and the reparations, I was slowly putting the war behind me, and forgetting about planes, and bombs – but I could not forget Hava.

CHAPTER 52

Noble Belgium, o mother dear, to whom we stretch our hearts and arms.
Words on the wall of the Belgian Embassy in Paris

What does a 22-year-old Belgian girl do in Paris when her father is attending government meetings all day long? First, I tried to find information about Hava. I tried to go to the French Council's office, but it was closed. Next I tried the Belgian Embassy. I was surprised to see the building was brightly lit from the inside and a new Belgian flag hung over the main door.

I entered the building sheepishly, my footsteps echoing on the hard marble floor. I didn't know where to begin. On the wide wall were words carved in stone, a few words from the Belgian national anthem: *Noble Belgium, o mother dear, to whom we stretch our hearts and arms.*

I wanted to stretch my heart and arms around Hava. I looked to my left and there, sitting at a small, single desk was a man in a Belgian military uniform. When I approached, he looked up and asked kindly, 'May I help you?'

'I don't know. I don't know if I'm allowed to be here.'

'What can I do for you?"

'I'm Belgian. I had a friend during the war. We were separated and I promised that I would find her.'

'You have come to the right place. My name is Sergeant de Monge. I will take you to the proper office. We might be able to help you.'

I wanted to ask the sergeant if he'd ever ridden a horse in the Royal Park in Brussels, but instead I just said, 'Thank you. That would be very kind.'

As we walked down a long corridor with windows on either side, the sergeant told me that he was from Ghent, and that he had been in the military all his life. When I told him who I was he looked at me and said, 'Daughter of the Shovel Hero? Your father is a great man.'

'He is here in Paris to help with the reconstruction. So I came along to look for my friend.'

'Right. Come with me, Mademoiselle Lyon.'

As we continued to walk down the hall, the sun bathed me in light and warmth, the most heat I encountered in my entire stay in Paris.

When we reached a door with the words *Robert Vizard: Archives* painted on the frosted window, the sergeant stopped and said, 'Good luck. Your friend is lucky to have you. Oh, and please tell your father that there's a soldier in the embassy who's grateful for what he did for Belgium.'

I stood before the frosted window and knocked gently.

'Yes? Come in.'

'Monsieur Vizard?'

'Yes, I am Robert Vizard. How may I help you?'

'My name is Simone Lyon. I'm from Brussels. I had a friend at the beginning of the war and we were separated ... I was hoping that you might be able to give me some advice on how to find her.'

Robert Vizard was a short man with little hair. He wore a well-fitting blue suit and a matching tie, and he sniffled. On his desk were large, neat piles of red folders and a small pile of yellow folders. To his left, spread out on a work table, I saw many more thick red folders.

'Forgive my cold. There is so little heat.' Monsieur Vizard reached for the handkerchief in his pocket and wiped his nose. 'Sit down, sit down, Mademoiselle ... ?'

'Simone Lyon.'

'Yes, Mademoiselle Lyon. I am not sure I can help you. See those red folders? In each one there are over a thousand names of missing people.'

'And the yellow folders?'

Monsieur Vizard blew his nose. 'Found. There are perhaps twenty names in each folder of people who were reconnected to their families or friends. It is not a large number. I keep trying, making phone calls, searching through documents. Each time I can find someone's husband or son – or in your case, a friend – each time I feel that in my small way I am putting the world back together again.' Monsieur Vizard sneezed.

'You will help me?'

'Yes, of course. What is your friend's name?'

'Hava. Hava Daniels.'

Monsieur Vizard sighed. 'Jewish?'

I was about to stand up immediately and leave the room, when he wiped his nose again and said, 'So many lost. So many lost. It's unthinkable. Where was God? How can we find so many when so many have been lost? Let's see.'

I relaxed a bit and spoke in a sudden rush of hope. 'She's from Brussels! She worked for the Red Cross! Her father is Yaakov, Yaakov Yosef Daniels and his wife Avital, and she has a brother Benjamin!'

'Mademoiselle, not so fast. Let me write this down.' I watched Monsieur Vizard place a small pad of paper before him. He uncapped a green fountain pen, and I watched him write in elegant script *Yaakov Daniels. Avital Daniels. Benjamin Daniels.*

'In 1935, the Nazis took away the right to citizenship and the nationalities from millions of Jews. They had no papers, no passports, no official names, no country. This makes it hard to find people. Do you know from where your friend was taken?'

'Yes!' I was excited that I was able to give Monsieur Vizard some concrete information. 'Dunkirk, she was taken at Dunkirk, at the beginning of the war.'

Monsieur Vizard wrote, *Dunkirk.*

'Today people are struggling to stay alive, mademoiselle, and searching for relatives. You said your friend worked for the Red Cross. Have you contacted them? Have you asked them about your friend?'

'She and I were volunteers just for a day. That's where we met.'

'There's also the chance that your friend went to Palestine. There is much talk about a new Jewish state. Perhaps she's there?'

'She was taken away by the SS in a truck. They said something about a relocation centre.'

Monsieur Vizard looked up from his desk and into my eyes.

'Have you ever heard of the *Kindertransport*, mademoiselle?'

I slowly shook my head.

'The *Kindertransport* was a rescue plan. Jewish children were taken over to England by steamship. Many were smuggled from convents and hospitals.'

I thought about Sister Bernadette and the children with soup. 'I will check my lists.'

Monsieur opened one filing cabinet after another, pulling out files, notes, lists. 'There are many people with the last name Daniels, but I cannot seem to find your friend or her family. I'm sorry to disappoint you. Leave me a number where I can reach you, and I will contact you if I come across anything useful.'

When I left the office, I walked slowly down the long hall of windows. Clouds hid the sun. The corridor was bleak and empty. When I reached the lobby, the sergeant at the desk was gone.

I stepped out of the embassy and onto the grey streets of Paris. I buttoned my coat. The cold air slapped against my cheeks. I walked to the cathedral of Notre Dame, which sat bathed in the grey light.

I entered the building and immediately inhaled the scents of burning candles and incense. The church was nearly empty. A man in a heavy brown coat knelt in the last pew, his head down, his prayer a whisper. Three women in fur coats walked slowly down the main aisle towards the altar. I too began my walk down the aisle, but felt suddenly faint, unexpectedly weak. I leaned against one of the great columns, and then I wept.

'Mademoiselle?' Someone touched my right arm. 'Are you okay?'

It was the man in the brown coat. 'Forgive me. I couldn't help but notice you.'

I wiped my tears away with the palm of my hand. 'No, it is nothing. I'm fine.'

'To cry in Notre Dame is something, mademoiselle.'

'The war, it's taken everything. I was just 18, just a girl. I'm not a girl any longer.' I looked at this stranger and felt compelled to tell him about the death of my mother. For no reason I told him about my father's shattered arm, about Sergeant De Waden's kiss, about the soldier who died in Hava's arms. I told him about Hava. 'She's my friend. I promised I would find her. I've tried, but I can't find her. I don't know where she went. I promised that I'd find her.'

'A promise is answered in many unknown ways,' the man said as he reached into his pocket and placed a coin in my hand. 'Go and light a candle for your friend and think of her as a single flame of light.'

I felt the coin in my fist. I looked down at my hand and opened my palm. When I looked up to thank the man, he had already walked away, but in the distance, I saw tall candles with a flame dancing on each tip. I approached the rack of candles and dropped the coin into the small slot marked *Donations*, then I picked up a new candle, held the tip to a flame, and watched the wick jump alive with its own flame.

I placed the candle into a vacant holder and watched the wick burn steadily. I stared at the yellow and white flame. In my mind's eye, I could see the Virgin of the Rock. I felt that I could see my mother. I could see Hava dancing with the lamp-post. Hava – a single flame of light.

CHAPTER 53

*Marlene Dietrich entertained Allied troops at the Stage Door
Canteen in Paris, 10 March 1945, and sang 'No Love, No Nothin"*

During my days in Paris I walked just to stay warm. When I
wasn't visiting the Belgian Embassy hoping for news of Hava
or her family, I found little other distraction from my loneliness.
My father was busy at meetings most days, and I ached for a friend
or companion. I visited museums, where there was no heat. I
visited cathedrals, where there was no heat. Everything in Paris
was gloomy and cold. I was miserable.

My father, recognizing that it had been a mistake to bring his
daughter to Paris, asked a business associate if he knew someone
who could entertain me. 'Yes,' he told my father, 'I will send you
my assistant.'

One day soon afterwards, in the lobby of my hotel, a man
approached me and said, 'I am Pierre St de Coinick. Your father
sent me to escort you into the city today.'

'I am Simone Lyon. I'm cold and tired.'

The assistant was a 32-year-old man, who lived like the Great

Gatsby, waltzed every weekend, enjoyed pheasant-hunting, and wanted nothing to do with entertaining the daughter of a Belgian officer. But his boss had insisted, so this disgruntled man, who had practically lived in a dinner suit for the first thirty years of his life, trudged to my hotel through the cold winter air.

When we met, he did not say that he was a Belgian baron. He did not tell me about the size of his summer and winter estates. He didn't speak about his chauffeurs, gardeners, washerwomen, cooks, and private tutors. All he did was invite me to walk along the River Seine which, to this day, still flows in and out of my imagination.

'You look exhausted,' Pierre said as we walked along the river. That is when I told him about Hava, about how I'd made a promise to find her, and how I hadn't succeeded. 'It was so many years ago when I saw her last … when I made that promise.'

'Yes, many years ago. A lifetime ago.'

Nothing more was said until the general's daughter and the baron discovered the famous bouquinistes: the used-book stalls that had existed for over 400 years and still do to this day. People refer to the Seine as the only river in the world that runs between two bookshelves.

Pierre and I quickly discovered that we had the same interests in books and authors.

'Look at this poetry collection,' Pierre said. 'Yeats.' He picked up the book and turned quickly to a poem, then he read aloud: '*How many loved your moments of glad grace, / And loved your beauty with love false or true, / But one man loved the pilgrim soul in you.*' It was the way that he read those last words that made me fall in love with him then and there.

'I love his poetry,' I said simply.

As we walked to the next bookstall, I found a used copy of *Madame Bovary*. 'I've always wanted to read this,' I said.

Pierre said, 'I love the line in that book that says, "It was the fault of destiny."' I thought about my first meeting Hava at the Red Cross so many years before.

At the third bookstall Pierre and I reached for the same book at the same time, a book about the fourteenth-century Italian writer and mystic, Angela of Foligno. We both wanted to buy the book and Pierre said, 'Well, if we both want it, the only thing to do is to buy it together and get married.'

In three days, Pierre St de Coinick and I were engaged, and three months later we were married.

PART V: LIBERATION

CHAPTER 54

1945

15 April: The liberation of Nazi Concentration Camps begins
25 April: German forces leave Finland
29 April: German forces in Italy surrender
30 April: Adolf Hitler commits suicide
2 May: German forces in Berlin surrender
4 May: German forces in North-West Germany, Denmark, and the
Netherlands surrender

At the end of the war Pierre and I listened to the BBC radio as King George VI of England addressed his nation and all of Europe:

> *Today we give thanks to Almighty God for a great deliverance. The Nazi tyranny that drove all Europe into war has been finally overcome. At this hour, when the dreadful shadow of war has passed far from our hearths and homes, we may at last make one pause for thanksgiving and then turn our thoughts to the tasks all over the world which peace in Europe brings with it.*
>
> *Let us remember those who will not come back: their constancy*

and courage in battle, their sacrifice and endurance in the face of a merciless enemy.

Let us think what it was that has upheld us through nearly six years of suffering and peril. The knowledge that everything was at stake: our freedom, our independence, our very existence as a people; but the knowledge also that in defending ourselves we were defending the liberties of the whole world.

The war was over. My father continued his work with the Government, representing the military in the reconstruction of the Belgian infrastructure, and was in charge of the repatriation of Belgian refugees. His career advanced at the end of the war with the position of Inspector General of Engineering and Signals for the entire Belgian army and, in 1946, he was appointed Aide de Camp to King Leopold III of Belgium.

Pierre and I returned to Belgium, and Brussels came alive again, resurrected from the death of war. Restaurants stayed open late, the streetlights were lit, the fruit markets spilled out onto each square, and the trams ran on time taking people to work. My husband and I liked to walk in the park on Sundays after church, when it seemed as if all of Brussels had decided that Sunday afternoons were, once again, for walking. I even saw balloons for sale for the first time in four years. The carousel spun with renewed confidence.

I was dazzled when Pierre took me to his summer house: a large chateau with gardens, horses, and a tennis court. I was embarrassed the first time I sat on the veranda with Pierre and a butler stepped outside with two silver cups on a tray. Each cup was filled with thick tomato juice.

I had worn sombre dresses and coats for four years, but with Pierre at my side, I bought a summer suit with a short-sleeved jacket and a flowered skirt. Pierre bought a new tailored, doubled-breasted suit. I was becoming a woman of the world with a husband, money, and a gilded future.

Pierre and I decided a year later that we would move to America. By that time, I had forgotten the war. I had forgotten Hava, the burning train, the hunger. I was too busy deciding what to take to America, packing large leather suitcases with clothes and books, while Pierre arranged accounts in New York. I felt that I had abandoned childish thoughts and had evolved into a confident society woman.

I had a new life. We wanted children. We bought a dog, an Airedale, and named her Pamela. Pierre booked us passage on the *Queen Elizabeth* bound for New York and we were scheduled to leave in September 1946.

'Darling, you know it might not be easy at first when we arrive in the States,' Pierre said one evening, as we settled into the parlour of our city home. The chairs were comfortable, and the evening breeze caressed our cheeks with warmth and pleasure. I glanced down at the atlas on the coffee table, remembering how much I had liked the sounds of the different states: Connecticut, Florida, Alabama.

'Any new adventure is a bit difficult at first, but I'm sure we'll manage,' I said as I shifted in my chair, Pamela at my side, and a glass of wine in my hand.

Each week, it had become our habit to tune into the Sunday night concert on the BBC. Pierre leaned over the radio, switched it on, and sat in an opposite chair with a glass of wine in his hand.

We were content, lulled by the fresh air, and the complacency of wealth and comfort.

The radio crackled a bit as its tubes warmed up, and then the voice of the BBC resounded: '... *and if you are just tuning in, we have a special broadcast for you tonight. Here is John Charles Tillman, the famous baritone, singing "I'll Always Remember".*'

Pamela stretched on the floor. Pierre leaned back in his chair and took a sip of wine. I held my glass in my hand.

The music swelled, as the lyrics soared into the air, enveloping me, removing me from my immediate surroundings, taking me back to another time, another life ... to another person.

> *I'll always remember your laughter, dear,*
> *The sound of your voice from year to year.*
> *Each day was a splendid melody,*
> *The days of adventure not tragedies.*
> *I'll always remember the dance and applause,*
> *Your light the night's success the true cause.*
> *Each moment today does not easily compare,*
> *To the days we were together my dear, my dear.*
> *I'll always remember we were a duet,*
> *I'll never forget you; I'll never forget.*

At the end of the song, I stood up, stared at the radio, looked at Pierre – then I fainted.

When I woke up I was in my bed. Pierre was at my side as he gently placed a cold compress on my forehead. 'Simone?'

'I promised,' I kept repeating as I revived slowly. 'I promised.'

'What, darling?'

'I said I would find her. I said I would remember. I promised, Pierre, I promised.' Then I cried in his arms.

'Simone, what's this all about?'

'She loves John Charles Tillman. She loves his voice. I promised that I would find her. That was John Charles Tillman on the radio, singing "I'll Always Remember". I heard those words, but I forgot my promise, Pierre. I forgot about Hava.'

I had only told Pierre about Hava once. Perhaps I had wanted to forget her. Perhaps I had wanted to eat white bread, buy beautiful clothes, and sit on a cushioned chair with a glass of wine in my hand. Perhaps I had wanted to believe in water lilies again and forget that I had ever been 18.

'Who's Hava, Simone?'

'Hava Daniels, remember? I told you about her when we first met. She was my friend. She was taken away in the war. The last thing I said to her was that I would find her; that I'd never forget her. I must find her, Pierre.'

I sat up in bed and began pulling the sheet and blanket away. I tried to stand. 'I'm going to find her. I'm going to find my friend.' I felt dizzy.

'Not tonight, Simone. You need to sleep. We can talk about this tomorrow.'

I protested, and then I slept.

CHAPTER 55

I marvel at the resilience of the Jewish people. Their best characteristic is their desire to remember. No other people has such an obsession with memory.
Elie Wiesel, Romanian-born American writer, Nobel laureate, Holocaust survivor

That BBC programme had reminded me of who I truly was. I had forgotten about my journal, about Sister Bernadette, and the flowers Hava had picked for me. I had forgotten that I had promised Hava that I would find her.

'I'm leaving for France today,' I said to Pierre over breakfast the next morning.

'France? Why France, Simone?'

'I must go to Dunkirk. That's the last place I saw Hava.'

'But Simone, that was six years ago. You'll never be able to find her.'

'I must try. I promised.'

'I'll go with you. I can postpone my meetings at work. We can go together. I'll help you if it means that much to you.'

'No, Pierre, I must go alone. It's my journey, my pilgrimage. I'll be back soon.'

'Our ship leaves for America in three and a half weeks.'

'I'll be back. I need this time. I need to go alone.'

Two hours later I was on a train – the same train line that Hava and I had taken when we'd escaped Brussels six years earlier.

I didn't go to Dunkirk after all. On the way, I realized I might have a better chance at finding Hava if I started with my cousin back in her town of Roeselare, because, as names and faces started flooding back to me, I remembered the German translator. He was one of the last people who had seen Hava on the day she was taken, and he'd said he'd lived in Roeselare. My cousin had been his banker. Joseph Becker. Maybe this time my cousin would help me.

The train was comfortable. The trees had grown taller in six years. The cows on the distant hills were healthy. The sky was filled with crows and clouds under the blue light of the horizon. When the train's whistle suddenly screeched, I shook for a moment, remembering the piercing cry of a woman weeping over her dead daughter: 'Julie. Julie.'

When the train stopped at Roeselare station, I hesitated to step off. I touched the seat and remembered the odour of the burning train. I touched the glass in the window and remembered the red-headed soldier's marriage proposal.

'Mademoiselle,' the conductor said, 'your ticket is for Roeselare. We have arrived. This is your stop, the end of your journey.' That is what I feared.

I stepped down from the train and pretended that Hava was there waiting for me. I walked from the station to my cousin's office, pretending I was a grand major-general liberating Roeselare. When I stood before my cousin's bank, I stopped and became, once again, a lost 18-year-old girl.

As I sat in Marie's office, I asked her if she knew a man named Joseph Becker. 'He said you were his banker.'

'Why do you want to know this, Simone? You know private information about a bank's client is privileged and not for publication.'

'I'm looking for a friend.'

'That Jewish girl you were with at the beginning of the war?'

'Yes, *that* Jewish girl.'

'I had to protect the bank's reputation, Simone. The Germans were taking over and we were told in advance to freeze all Jewish accounts. We were told to gather a list of all the Jewish patrons we knew. I had to do what I was told – I was following orders. I couldn't help you or that Jewish girl.'

'She has a name.'

'That's no concern of mine, Simone. The past is past. I was just following orders.'

'Her name is Hava Daniels. She loves the opera and liquorice. She knows the entire play of *Romeo and Juliet* by heart. And she is missing and I promised that I would find her.'

'She's just another missing Jew, Simone. What difference does it make?'

I looked at my cousin and once again couldn't believe that we shared the same genes.

'If one person is missing, Marie, the world is lost.'

'Forget the past, Simone. You can't change the past, and you can't blame me. I was just doing what I was told. The law is the law, and I was following orders.'

'Do you know a man named Joseph Becker?'

'Why that man?'

'He was the last person I saw with Hava. He was from here, a

Belgian, a schoolteacher who found work in France as a translator for the SS. He told me his name when he came to translate for the Germans: Joseph Becker. He said he lived here, right in Roeselare, and that you were his banker. Perhaps he knows where they took my friend. Perhaps he knows where they took my *Jewish* friend, Hava. Hava Daniels.'

My cousin adjusted her hair awkwardly with her right hand. 'We still have rules, Simone.'

'I made a promise that I would find her. Joseph Becker is the only link I have. She has a mother, a father, and a brother, Benjamin. I made a promise.'

Marie sighed as she stood up from her desk, walked to a filing cabinet, shuffled through some papers, and pulled out a folder.

'This is not only highly unusual, but it's against the law. I could lose my job.' She opened the folder and returned to her desk, grabbing a pencil and pad. 'You're foolish to do this, Simone. Millions of people are missing because of the war. One Jewish girl isn't worth the risk. What difference does one Jewish girl make?'

She pushed the paper towards me. 'Here. Make good on your promise. Find your *Jewish* friend. Now go.'

Just before I stepped out of her office, I looked back and said 'She's in love with John Charles Tillman.'

My cousin's face softened then, just a bit, as she said, 'They threatened my family, Simone. I was afraid.'

I looked into her eyes. 'I understand, Marie. I do understand.' War was not black and white.

After I walked out of the office, and out of the bank, I stood in the sunlight and unfolded the paper and there, written in a neat script, was the address: *Joseph Becker, Vlamingstraat 8800 R.*

CHAPTER 56

You can cut all the flowers but you cannot keep spring from coming.
Pablo Neruda, Chilean poet, Nobel laureate

It was easy to find the street and the house. What was not easy was knocking on the door. When I did, I did not expect anyone to answer so quickly.

From inside the house I heard someone call, 'Yes?'

'I'm looking for Joseph Becker.'

Silence.

'My name is Simone Lyon. I'm from Brussels, and I'm looking for Joseph Becker.'

The door opened slowly, and I was startled to see a young woman about my age.

'Yes?' she repeated.

'Is this the home of Joseph Becker?'

'Yes. That's my father. He's out in the back garden. Follow me.'

The young woman led me through the house. The floors were covered in wool rugs. The walls were blue. At each window there was a small shelf, and on each shelf were pots of African violets:

blue flowers, white flowers, all pruned and healthy.

As we stepped outside, I saw a man kneeling at the edge of a small garden pulling weeds.

'Papa, there's someone here to see you.'

The man looked up, and squinted in the sun that fell onto his wrinkled face. 'Yes?'

'Papa, she's from Brussels.'

The man stood up with difficulty, wiped his hands on his overall and shuffled slowly towards me.

The girl turned to me and said, 'Would you like some tea? I've just made a pot.'

'Yes, that would be nice,' I said as I looked at the man. I did not recognize him. The girl stepped back into the house.

'Yes? How can I help you?' the man asked as he extended his gnarled hand. I could not bring myself to shake it.

'Are you Joseph Becker?'

'What is this about?'

'My name is Simone Lyon. I'm looking for a friend of mine and I think perhaps you can help me.'

'I don't know you, mademoiselle. How can I help?'

'Were you ever a translator?'

The second the word 'translator' left my lips, the man lifted his hand and rubbed the back of his neck.

'Did you ever work for the SS?'

The girl with the pot of tea stepped back out into the garden.

'Anne, take the pot into the kitchen and wait there, please. I have some business to discuss with Mademoiselle Lyon.'

'Yes, Papa.'

When the girl left, the man said, 'Come with me,' and the two of us walked across the grass and sat on two metal chairs beside a rose trellis.

'Yes, I am Joseph Becker. Yes. I was a translator. It was a difficult time.'

'I'm not here to cause you trouble, Monsieur Becker.'

'It was a difficult time. I had no choice. The Vichy Government took over everything. Food was scarce. Everything seemed to stop, except the war and the German occupation. They offered good jobs to anyone who could speak German. They gave me a uniform, a good salary. I was assigned to various SS commanders during the war.'

'I'm looking for a friend of mine. You were there as a translator.'

'But I can't help you. I was a translator for four years. I translated for the SS commanders hundreds and hundreds of times. I don't see how I can help you with one case.'

'We were on a bus outside Dunkirk. The German army was coming. Hava and I – that's my friend, her name is Hava – she and I escaped on the last bus from Dunkirk. We thought we were free.'

'Dunkirk? That was at the very beginning of the war.'

'Yes, the planes were bombing Brussels. Hava and I were looking for her family. The Nazis were coming. We escaped Brussels in May 1940.'

'I had just begun my work for the Germans.'

'We were in a bus, miles from Dunkirk. Hava and I fell asleep and suddenly we were awoken by a man in a black uniform, who was demanding identification. He didn't speak French. You must remember, Monsieur Becker. There was a soldier with a machine gun and he couldn't speak French either. The SS officer ordered the soldier with the gun to fetch the translator. *You* were the translator. Don't you remember? Hava had blonde hair. You must remember. You're the only link to her I have. Do you remember? Do you know where they took her?'

Joseph Becker looked at me and again he rubbed the back of his neck with his hand. 'The reason I do remember, Mademoiselle Lyon, is because of her hair. There weren't many blonde Jewish girls. And also because that was my very first assignment. What was her name?'

'Hava Daniels. Do you know where she was taken?'

He paused, then mumbled, 'Auschwitz.'

CHAPTER 57

The German phrase 'Arbeit macht frei' [Work sets you free]
was embedded into the entrance gate at Auschwitz and other Nazi
concentration camps.

Mr Becker, the translator, said, 'I can tell you about your friend, but you won't want to know everything. I was forced to stay with those SS troops all the way to the camp. The people in the cattle cars couldn't move their arms and legs.'

'Please, tell me everything. I need to know everything. I need to know what happened.'

Mr Becker stood up, paced back and forth, stopped, and looked at me. 'When the train arrived at Auschwitz, SS soldiers in black uniforms were waiting. As the people stepped off the train and walked in lines, the SS officer in charge pointed at each Jew who walked in front of him, and directed them to the left or right: left to the gas chamber; right, forced labour. I had to translate for the officer who sat at the desk.

'When your friend stood before the officer, he looked at me and said "*Ziemlich blond. Schade, dass sie so krank aussieht.*"'

I asked the translator what that meant.

'What a pretty blonde. It's a pity she looks so sickly.' The officer turned from me, looked at your friend again and pointed to the left.'

In my mind's eye, I recalled Hava's father reading aloud. 'For you, O Lord, did consume her with fire and with fire you will restore her.'

'What was your friend's name again?'

'Hava Daniels,' I said. 'I need to know. I need to find her. Tell me, Mr Becker.'

'Yes, your Hava walked to the left, following the people ahead of her. They were told that they were going to take a shower. As they stood outside a bunker, they were ordered to strip off all their clothes.'

I closed my eyes and thought about Hava pretending that she was Romeo's Juliet dying in the damp air of my father's cellar.

Mr Becker continued. 'The SS officer told them, "You will be disinfected and you will bathe." Then the people were escorted to the black doors of the huge chamber.'

I opened my eyes.

'I can't go on, Mademoiselle Lyon,' the translator said as he paused, overcome with grief.

'You must. I need to know.'

Mr Becker sat down, bowed his head and said, 'I saw them – your friend and 600 others – enter the chamber and the doors were locked behind them.'

I closed my eyes again and remembered the empty pews in the synagogue and the old rabbi telling Hava and me, 'They are all gone.'

I opened my eyes. Mr Becker looked at me, his expression blank, reliving the horror of that day. 'The doors to the shower building were shut and bolted. They were screwed shut before the

SS poured gas through shafts in the ceiling.'

I breathed slowly as Mr Becker lowered his voice and whispered, 'Should I continue?'

'Yes, Mr Becker. Please. I need to know.'

'I am told that death in the gas chamber occurred after a few minutes.'

I heard Hava's voice: 'I spend my time dreaming, Simone. What do you dream of? Clouds or mountains?'

The translator looked into my eyes. 'Afterwards, I was ordered to help remove the bodies from the chamber. I remember your friend because of her hair. Her body was dragged out of the gas chamber and her hair was cut off.'

I closed my eyes and thought about Joff, and Monsieur Alberg, and how they had touched Hava's hair with such tenderness.

'Once your friend's hair had been cut, I was ordered to put her body on a wooden cart headed for the oven.' He stopped, unable to continue.

'I need to know every detail.' I told him, as I looked into his eyes.

I remembered Hava telling me about the time she and her father had stood tall and straight together as they lifted their heels and recited the prayer to the moon.

Mr Becker said, 'I didn't want to, but I was told what to do. I shovelled your friend's ashes, and those of all the others, out from the bottom of the oven and dumped them in a pond on the outskirts of the camp. All those ashes … so many ashes.'

I closed my eyes and wept.

PART VI: IN MEMORIAM

CHAPTER 58

I am an old woman now. I live in a small town in America. I was able to tell this story because I carried it with me in my journal, all the way from Belgium into my future. People remember Anne Frank. Perhaps they will also remember Hava Daniels.

Each 4 July I go to bed early, but I do not sleep right away. As the sun sets, after I've read a bit, I lie on my pillow and wait for the fireworks. The first explosion is the hardest. It always makes me think of that first bomb in Belgium, the black planes overhead, and I think of Hava and me climbing a silo to reach for the stars.

I sometimes think of that carousel in the park, and the children riding the painted horses, and how my father rode Charlotte sitting high in his uniform and white gloves.

I lie back on my pillow and my room is illuminated with a fountain of light from the fireworks. I think of Hava pretending that she is Juliet, dead on the table in my father's cellar; how we laughed after my father took us upstairs and she and I had our tea and biscuits. I remember how the steam of the hot tea curled up towards Hava's lovely face as she smiled at me across the table. I remember the lipstick we made and the lilacs we placed in our hair.

Each time a firework explodes, another image of Hava seems to appear in the flash of the red and blue lights that illuminate my room: Hava dancing with the lamp-post; Hava riding the bronze horse in the city square; Hava holding the dead soldier in her arms.

I rest my head on my pillow and still hear the screams and echoes of people calling out, pointing at the sky, watching the approaching planes. I remember a man sitting on the cobblestone as the bombs dropped, his knees pulled up to his chest as he rocked forwards and backwards. What was moving? The earth or the man?

With each new explosion of the fireworks I close my eyes and see myself at the Holocaust Memorial Museum, scanning a list of those who perished at Auschwitz: Jews, Poles, Gypsies, intellectuals … Sister Bernadette, Joff, Yaakov Yosef Daniels, Avital Daniels, Benjamin Daniels, Hava Daniels.

CHAPTER 59

When my father retired from the army, he'd come to America every two years to visit me here in my little town. He loved flowers and tending to the garden, and I always looked forward to his visits.

My father didn't speak often about the war, and I didn't like pressing him too much about it. But I remember one afternoon, during one of his visits, that I found the courage to ask him about those years long ago. I was in my early thirties and my husband had just taken our eight-year-old daughter to a small carnival for her birthday.

'Papa? Can you tell me about the war?'

The afternoon was hot. As I was sipping my cup of tea, I watched my father from the kitchen window. He wore a white shirt, loose khaki pants, and braces. He was stooped; his useless arm dangled at his side; his good hand worked the pruning secateurs. As I watched the limp, dying roses fall to the ground, I thought about the death of my friend Hava. I thought about the bombs I had heard dropping from Nazi planes. I thought about Sergeant De Waden trying to kiss me.

I placed my tea cup on the counter, opened the back door, and stepped down from the porch onto the fresh grass.

My father had commanded thousands of men, had earned

the Croix de Guerre twice, and had been a powerful man in the ranks and heroics of his country, yet there he was, gently pruning flowers. I noticed a shovel by his side, and I smiled.

'Papa?'

He turned slowly from his private waltz with the rose bush, squinted, and said, 'Yes, Simone?'

'Papa, can we talk?'

He turned for a moment to look at the abandoned rose bush, turned again, and pulled out a white handkerchief from his pocket. I smiled, thinking that the general was waving a surrender flag. He wiped the small beads of perspiration from his brow.

'What is it, Simone? What's the trouble?'

'No, Papa. No trouble. I just want to ask you a question.'

My father slipped the secateurs into his pocket, the same way I had seen him slip his revolver into his holster before he left the house for the day. Generals wore uniforms and revolvers strapped to their sides ... and now secateurs.

'What is it, Simone?'

'Papa. Can you tell me about the war? About when you went away?'

My father looked back at the rose bush, then said, 'Let's sit on the grass.' He extended his good, right hand. As we walked a few steps, I felt the stiff bones in his fingers intertwined with mine.

'Here,' he said as he leaned down, then carefully sat in the middle of the lawn.

'We were afraid,' I said. 'The Nazis were approaching Brussels. You grabbed your briefcase, Papa, then you kissed me and suddenly you were gone. Hava and I were so afraid we took a train, trying to escape the Nazi invasion. You were gone for four years. You never told me much about those four years.'

'Perhaps, Simone, some memories are like dead flowers. It's better to dead-head them from memory.'

As my father and I sat on the grass in the sun on that summer afternoon, I remembered the flower that had been my best friend Hava. I remembered the dangerous journey we had shared on a train to Dunkirk; the SS officer dragging Hava by the hair to a waiting truck. I had spoken about Hava Daniels often during the rest of my life, and yet my father rarely spoke of the war, the prison camp he endured in Spain, the beatings he endured, the starvation he experienced.

'It was a time of survival, Simone. War is a curse, a wound in the history of our souls. When I looked at the blood oozing from my arm, when I heard the thunder of grenades and the agony of others, I made a promise to God: if I was spared, I would fight ugliness in silence for the rest of my life. You ask about the war, Simone. Listen to the peace here in this garden. That is victory enough for me.'

'Hi, Mom! Hi, Grandpa. Hey, Mom! We're back!' I turned to see my daughter running towards us.

'Daddy said he's getting the mail and will be right back. The carnival was great; the best birthday present. I loved the big wheel and I had cotton candy.'

My daughter sat down between my father and me, like a new rose in the garden. 'Grandpa, you look sad.'

'No, no, my sweet. Just getting ready to get back to work.' He stood up, pulled out his secateurs, made two quick snip, snip sounds with the tool in his good hand and walked back to the edge of the garden.

'And Daddy and I both had funnel cake.'

'I'm so glad, my darling, that you had a good time with your father. I'm so glad.' I reached into my pocket. 'Here, darling, a small birthday gift for you. Open your hand.'

My daughter opened her little hand and I placed a necklace in her palm, right where it belonged. A gold necklace.

'It's so pretty. Such a pretty star. Can I wear it now?'

I nodded and fastened my long-ago friend's gold chain around my daughter's neck and watched as the Star of David hung gently on her chest.

'Thank you, Mommy. I love it.'

'You're welcome, Hava. I love you too.'

CHAPTER 60

When I received a call on a Saturday morning from my aunt to tell me that my father had died in his sleep, I spent much of that day in the house. Pierre was in the city attending a meeting with his company. I remember reading *The New Yorker* magazine, trying to laugh at the cartoons. I flipped through some travel books about pyramids in Egypt and mountains in Peru.

That evening as I prepared dinner, I felt an urge to go out into the garden and see if I could find any late summer flowers for our dining-room table. I grabbed my father's small pair of pruning secateurs and stepped outside. There wasn't much left. My father had been away for two years already. The apple tree had fallen a week after he'd flown back to Brussels. The raspberry bushes had withered the following year. The day lilies had succumbed to the cold September air. There were no more irises, but there, clinging to what was left of the rose bush, was one white rose. I thought of the white gloves on my father's hands as he rode Charlotte in the Royal Park when I was a girl.

I looked at that single flower: white petals overlapping like folds in the ocean tide, the stem with its strong grip onto the flower. I thought about how my father had planted that rose bush so many years earlier. Hava would have said it was beautiful.

CHAPTER 61

I only have one piece of physical evidence that Hava Daniels lived: a photograph.

On the day that Hava and I made our way to the opera for the first time, we came upon a self-photo booth inside a small grocery shop. Hava thought it would be fun if we had our picture taken.

'Let's do it,' I answered. 'Then we can send it to a Hollywood agent and be discovered.'

I pushed the curtain aside, bowed, and invited Hava to step in first. She bowed, giggled, and the two of us entered the little booth. We were both wearing blue shirts. In the background was a trellis and what looked like pink roses.

I inserted a coin, there was a little click, and in a few minutes our picture dropped down into a small slot.

I still have the photograph. I like how Hava's golden hair curls on each side, and I like her small white hair clip.

We both look happy.

I asked Hava once to make of list of things that she liked. This is what she wrote:

Sounds I like:
Sap crackling in a log fire;

Brittle leaves crunching as I walk in autumn;
The spine of a new book breaking;
The ball rolling down the chute of a pinball machine;
The symphony of crickets during a summer night.

Smells I like:
The musty delight of old books;
The romance of honeysuckle;
The nostalgia of baked bread.

Things I like to touch:
The tops of freshly cut bushes;
Flowing water;
Fine sand;
Cats.

Things I like to taste:
Chocolate ice cream;
Ice cream made from chocolate.

Things I like to see:
Dancers;
The light green during the first days of spring;
Yellow daffodils.

Whenever I see daffodils, I think of poetry and of Hava. I think of walking through the field of daffodils with her on our picnic.

The poet Percy Bysshe Shelly wrote, 'Poetry lifts the veil from the hidden beauty of the world, and makes familiar objects be as if they were not familiar.' Hava taught me to look at an ordinary lamp-post and see how it could be transformed into John Charles Tillman waltzing with her in the streets of Brussels.

She taught me that what may have seemed familiar to my neighbours, what appeared to be an ordinary back garden, was filled with beauty, worthy of attention. Hava lifted the veil of hidden loveliness each moment I was with her.

Once she said, 'Simone, listen to the sound of your back door when it opens. Do you hear a gentle *swooshing* sound as the rubber weather strip brushes against the tiled kitchen floor?' And then Hava said, 'A tiled kitchen floor! Over one billion people in the world live on dirt floors. You live like a queen as you walk on your tiled floor.'

The deck behind my house is made of pressurized wood, with spindles in its railing like sturdy soldiers in a row protecting the planks and stairs to the garden. Hava would have said that she wanted to dance with all the spindle soldiers.

I like walking along my deck, looking down at the wide expanse of my small garden, saying hello to a passing neighbour, and I like listening to the chimes from the nearby Dutch Reform Church tolling out the hour in a beautiful tone of mixed joy and sorrow.

I endured four years of Nazi occupation in Brussels during the Second World War. During the war the church bells were silent, but at the end of the war, on the first day of liberation, all the church bells in Brussels rang, and rang, and rang – in joy and victory. Bells in the world's cathedrals, or the bell in my local church, all have the same effect, all cause the same piercing thump in my chest.

I wish I could have said to Hava, 'Walk with me down the steps of my deck. Step onto the grass. Look at the grass. Look at each blade, the green colour, the sharp, soft edges. Look at the green carpet as beautiful as any Persian rug, as lush as any floor of malachite in any palace.'

I wish I could have shown Hava the daffodils in my back garden. They look like happy trumpets in the orchestra of the flowerbeds. I wish I could have asked, 'Hava, remember the daffodils in the woods when we were running from the Nazis and the planes? Remember, Hava?'

China, Japan, France all bulge with daffodils – the same daffodils. A Chinese daffodil is the same as the daffodil in my little garden. A Jewish daffodil is the same as a Christian daffodil.

A Jewish girl is the same as a Christian girl.

Different soil; different garden – the same girls.

I wish Hava were here with me today. I would tell her, 'Take one of my ordinary daffodils, fix it in your hair, and earn a final mark of 100 for Sister Bernadette's exam.'

Hava taught me that we are not ordinary human beings. We all need to make a choice. She taught me to choose life and live with gratitude – to gather daffodils.

Wordsworth saw a thousand daffodils 'tossing their heads in sprightly dance'.

I saw one daffodil, one flower – one young woman who represented six million human beings. Six million flowers that were not allowed to bloom.

My garden is my paradise; a single flower, my Eden – Hava, my Eve.

I often think of my return trip to Brussels, after my visit with Monsieur Becker. I was drowning with the final truth about Hava's death. I had difficulty breathing, difficulty looking to the future, but then I remembered Sister Bernadette telling me once about how much she liked the English burial service, after I told her that I had never known my mother.

'Simone, remember the words of hope: "Ashes to ashes, dust to dust; in sure and certain hope of the Resurrection to eternal life ..."'

To find my way to eternal life, I had to resurrect Hava back into my life of inner peace, and two weeks later, I was ready to say goodbye to Europe, as Pierre and I sailed to America on the *Queen Elizabeth*.

As the ship slowly entered New York harbour, I looked for a young woman hooked on the arm of John Charles Tillman, and standing on a yacht moored beneath the Statue of Liberty.

I closed my eyes, and there she was.

ACKNOWLEDGEMENTS

A writer does not write in isolation. From books and experiences, he culls a vision into words, hoping his narrative will express universal truths and sympathies. From there, a book does not become a reality without people who hope to duplicate this vision for others to share.

I am deeply grateful to Elissa Greenwald and Melene Kubat, the first readers of *Ashes*, and the first to encourage me to continue refining the text.

My agent Peter Rubie has been with me for over nine years, offering guidance, kindness, and encouragement, and always speaking about my work with his professional conviction that I am a writer.

Even though my twelve previous books have been published, when Rose Sandy, editor and publisher at HarperCollins Inspire, accepted *Ashes*, I was startled with delight and humility more than ever before because of her wide experience in publishing, and because of her belief that this book could whisper words of hope in a world that seems, at the moment, so hopeless. I am forever grateful to Rose.

Bengono Bessala of HarperCollins Inspire took on this book with her marketing skills, extraordinary enthusiasm, and joy. She is among the best professionals I have worked with in my 35-year career as a writer, and I thank her with a flare of gratitude.

Finally, I need to thank my daughter Karen Mock. Karen must have read the manuscript at least five times, spending days editing the work, making suggestions, and following Rose Sandy's editorial suggestions. Karen and I laughed often when I wanted to retain a word or sentence, and she insisted with humour and conviction that 'Dad, you have to make this line sound better'. Karen is not only my daughter, but a terrific editor, who pulled me out of numerous slumps when I was discouraged over the progress of the book.

So, alongside editors, agents, friends, and daughters it is my ambition that *Ashes* will capture the hearts and imagination of those who read about Hava Daniels and her friend Simone.

I hope this little book will help us all remember that, among the sorrows of the world, we all can rise up from the ashes and discover, once again, what it means to be people of compassion, dignity, and love.